CRITICS RAVE ABOUT NINA BANGS!

THE PLEASURE MASTER

"Enter Nina Bangs's world of humor, sensuality, and memorable characters. You won't want to leave."

—Bestselling author Christina Dodd

AN ORIGINAL SIN

"Ms. Bangs has written a fun comedy of people out of time. It is a romp and should be enjoyed in large gulps."

—*CompuServe Romance Reviews*

"If you're looking for a funny, heart-wrenching and truly lovely romance to read, try this one. You won't be disappointed."

—*All About Romance*

"Nina Bangs has come up with a completely new and unique twist on the time-travel theme and has delivered a story that is both humorous and captivating."

—*Romantic Times*

AN IMPORTANT LESSON

"Heed me, Kathy of Hair. A woman's need and fulfillment start *here.*" He placed only his index finger against her forehead, yet she felt the connection all the way to her toes.

"Not here." He ran his finger down the side of her jaw, her neck, then stopped as he touched the tip of her nipple.

Could've fooled me. She sucked in her breath at the sizzle of sensation that spread like honey on a hot day. Why couldn't she move away, break the connection? Why didn't she *want* to?

"Nor here." He drew his finger between her breasts, down over her stomach, then laid his palm flat against her skirt, and her thighs clenched as though no material separated his flesh from hers, as though she could hold his touch warm between her legs.

"No!" With her last ragged shred of willpower, she rolled away from him.

He let her go.

"Pleasure Master, my foot. You're just like my ex. You're nothing but a womanizer with a fancy title. I bet you never met a woman you didn't love."

He leaned back and stared at her. He seemed truly puzzled. "'Tis not about love, lass. 'Tis about joining with another for pleasure. I teach women how to take a man's body and enjoy the taking."

THE PLEASURE MASTER

NINA BANGS

LOVE SPELL   NEW YORK CITY

A LOVE SPELL BOOK®

June 2001

Published by

Dorchester Publishing Co., Inc.
276 Fifth Avenue
New York, NY 10001

ISBN 0-505-52445-7

Visit us on the web at www.dorchesterpub.com.

*To my parents, who instilled in me
a lifelong love of reading.
Thanks.*

THE
PLEASURE
MASTER

Prologue

Men. Cars. Great form, no function, and they both overheated at the wrong time. Who needed them?

Kathy Bartlett glanced in her rearview mirror hoping to spot her hero of the moment, Rod's Reliable Tow Service. Nothing.

Okay, so she'd lied. She needed her car, but she needed it *functional.*

"Speaking of function . . ." She glanced at the shiny hourglass-shaped toy perched on the seat beside her. "What the heck do you do?" She picked up the toy, turned it over, tapped the amber lights on top of its head, then plunked it back onto the seat.

"The strong silent type, huh? Hate to break this to you, but young America likes toys that *do* something. Loudly. That's why you were left on the

11

shelf, kiddo." She stared out her sleet-blurred windshield at the passing New York traffic. Great Christmas Eve. "You know, you sort of remind me of my ex-husband, Peter Matthew Stone. Looks hot, does squat. A major PMS moment in my life. Mind if I call you Peter?"

The toy was cool with that.

"What did I do to deserve this, Peter? I'm an okay person. I make women's hair safe for America. When Alice asked me to pick up some toys for the shelter, I said sure. I didn't hire a hit man to knock off old PMS because he's suing me for mental anguish. And I never once laughed when he called a certain body part his love gun. So why is this happening to *me?*"

Peter hadn't a clue.

"This is all your fault, Peter."

Peter didn't think so.

"I get out of work late, then run to a few stores looking for toys. You know what's left on Christmas Eve? Rejects. No offense."

Peter handled it.

"Now I'm stuck on the side of the road with a sack of slightly weird toys in my trunk and one beside me. Fine. So I'm a pushover. I bought you because you were just sitting on the shelf. Admit it, though, you were feeling kind of lonely all by yourself. Hey, I understand what it's like on the shelf. Besides, no one should be alone on Christmas."

Kathy cast another look in her mirror, then sighed with relief when she saw the tow truck edging toward her out of the darkness on the shoulder of the highway.

She took a deep breath and opened the door. Sleet and frigid air hit her in the face. Yech. Shoving her cell phone into her purse, she grabbed her backpack full of hair supplies, climbed out, then went to retrieve her bag of toys from the trunk. Maybe she could convince the driver to swing past the shelter. She'd hate to think of kids without toys on Christmas morning.

Darn, she'd forgotten Peter. She'd just shove him into the sack with the other toys. Pulling open the passenger door, she watched blankly as he tumbled out of the car and landed on his face. At least she guessed it was his face. Sort of hard to tell.

Amazed, she stared at him. "Gee, look what shook loose. You're now the proud owner of three sturdy legs." Sighing, she picked him up and set him next to her. "You'll make someone a great bedside table, pal, but you won't fit in the bag with those legs sticking out."

Staring into the darkness, she hunched her shoulders and tried to stop shivering. Damn, damn, and double damn.

"I *hate* this. I need a vacation, Peter. Somewhere warm, peaceful, with every modern convenience at my fingertips, and no stress. And I may as well throw in a man. Yeah, a man who'll do everything I want, never argue, and won't *ever* tell me to relax and enjoy it."

A gust of wind blew sleet into her face.

"That's it, Peter. I want warmth, peace, conveniences, and a subservient man. How's that sound?"

Peter must've thought it sounded pretty good because his amber lights flashed, and he rose to his full height, which wasn't too spectacular.

A sudden wave of dizziness drove away all thoughts of Peter. A kaleidoscope of whirling colors made her slightly nauseated. She knew she couldn't be freezing to death because she could still feel her toes.

Please, don't let me pass out. She couldn't let Mrs. Tierney down tomorrow. The ninety-year-old woman would be waiting for her monthly cut, knock-em-dead blond coloring, and the latest issue of *Cosmo.* Mrs. Tierney's cheapskate nephew had stopped paying Kathy years ago, but that didn't matter. Mrs. Tierney called Kathy her hair princess. It felt good to be someone's princess.

Kathy blinked, trying to clear her vision. Kick her if she skipped any more lunches trying to squeeze in frantic clients.

The whirling colors had become a long tunnel with Peter's flashing amber lights at its end. A near-death experience?

She sank to her knees still clutching her purse, backpack, and bag of toys. If the tow truck driver discovered her cold stiff body, she hoped he'd find Peter a good home.

And as the whirling colors took her, Peter spoke. *"Hasta la vista,* baby!"

Chapter One

Arnold Schwarzenegger? Big bad voice for cute little toy? Poor marketing decision. No wonder good old Peter was left warming the shelf. What parents would want their kid to have a two-foot-high tin Terminator?

"Ye must prove yer worthiness, Ian. 'Tis the only fair way. What say ye, Neil?"

Kathy winced. Talking about big bad voices . . . The tow truck driver? She knelt on the ground, still clutching her things.

"Aye. Ye're the eldest, Ian, but that doesna mean ye're the best. Neil Ross has satisfied many a lass."

Well, cheers for Neil Ross. At least satisfied customers meant he knew which end of her car to hook up to.

Letting everything slide from her grasp, Kathy

held her head. Maybe if it would stop spinning she'd make a stab at opening her eyes.

"Ye must let us choose, Ian, if 'tis to be a true test. Do ye agree, Colin?"

What? What test? All they had to do was hook up her car and tow it to Mel's, where for the nominal fee of her firstborn child, she could get it back in running order.

"Aye. We will find one wi' a heart that canna be touched."

Yep, that was Mel. Cash or credit card. No personal checks. Against her better judgment, she opened her eyes. She blinked.

Uh-oh. No busy highway, no sexy car. No *city*. Only stark green hills and the morning mist rising from a small stream. Morning? What had happened to the night? And *silence*. A silence so intense it terrified her.

Had she passed out? No, she'd fainted once when old PMS had decided that aromatherapy would loosen her up. He'd said the scent was discovered in an ancient Egyptian tomb. She believed him. It smelled like Essense of Mummy. Anyway, she didn't remember having any strange hallucinations then. She pulled her wool coat tightly around her, warding off the chill, an unspeakable fear tapping on her shoulder.

"I dinna know where we might find such a cold creature, Colin."

Here. Here. She'd never felt so cold in her life, and the brisk wind numbing her ears had nothing to do with it. Still on her knees, she turned toward

16

the welcome human voice. "Please, you've got to . . ." She stared.

Two male behinds stared back at her. *Bare* behinds. A *Playgirl* chorus line. She resisted the urge to rub her eyes. Two guys mooning her wouldn't be that strange in New York. . . . New York? Where in New York?

"Mayhap we will find one in England, Neil. English lasses can freeze a man's . . ."

England? Suddenly, she realized what they were wearing. The wool thingees, belted at the waist, didn't quite reach their knees, and from what she could see, the question of boxers or briefs would never be a burning issue with these guys.

Kilts? She had to be dreaming. Nothing else made sense. Okay, dreams were symbolic, so she'd just figure this baby out. The empty landscape probably meant she needed some inner peace and tranquility, an escape from the frenzy her life had become. The bare buns? Easy. She thought of her ex as a butthead on a daily basis, so here he was in duplicate.

The rocks she knelt on dug into her knees through her long skirt, and she shifted uncomfortably. Funny, but she couldn't remember feeling anything physical in dreams before.

"Aye, Colin. But even though an English lass may have a cold nature, it matters not to a Ross. 'Tis hot enough she'll be in bed wi' . . ."

She shivered as the chilly wind whipped around her and lifted the kilts of the leaning men. . . . Wait a minute. There was another man sitting on the ground, his back braced against a large boulder.

"Ye have reason to fear us, Ian. We will beat ye and take what we want."

Beat? Ohmigod, a mugging. At last, something familiar. She couldn't see enough of the man on the ground to know how badly he was injured, but she knew she had to do something to save him and probably herself because any second now the muggers were bound to notice her.

Her logical self reminded her this was a dream, so she didn't have to do anything.

Her logical self could take a hike. She needed a weapon.

Reaching inside her purse, she fumbled around for something she could use. Nothing. No handy little gun, no pepper spray. Rats.

Her can of mousse? Right. That would certainly scare the pants off . . . Okay, no pants to worry about. Maybe if she wrapped both hands around the can she could bluff them into believing she had a can of Mace. She drew a deep breath. She had to go for it.

Pulling the mousse from her purse, she shook it, then climbed shakily to her feet. Her whole world seemed out of kilter, but she could only focus on one thing right now: saving the man on the ground.

She tried to clear her throat, but her voice still came out in a wavery croak. "Get lost, scumbags, before I Mace you. The cops are on their way."

As one, the two men straightened, then swung to face her. She gulped. *Large.* Very large. And hairy.

With dry split ends that would challenge even her expertise.

"A lass." Translation: yum-yum.

Her heart pounded madly. The Three Little Pigs would've been laying bricks like crazy at the sound of that voice.

They moved toward her. Forget trying to hit them in the eyes. They were too tall. While she was jumping into the air trying to get one in the eyes, the other would tear her apart. She needed a lower target.

The wind whipped and swirled, lifting their kilts high enough to offer a more accessible body part. Without hesitation, she moussed each of their love guns with a defiant squirt. Hey, one patch of voluminous and shiny body hair was better than none.

Staring down in horror at the fluffy globs of mousse sticking to them, the men stumbled away from her.

Strange. Against all reason, Kathy had the feeling neither of them knew the mousse was harmless. Well, she recognized an advantage when she saw one. "Hmm. I wonder if they'll fall off now or later."

With wild bellows, the kilted giants turned and fled.

She watched them disappear as she let the mousse slip from her fingers.

The man on the ground. But by the time she turned back to him, the mist had closed in. A flowing sea of gray created shifting shapes of fear, twining like skeletal fingers around the dark silhouettes of trees and shrubs. Kathy could almost believe the mist was alive—feel it breathing, waiting.

She swallowed past throat muscles that refused to work, fighting the terror of *knowing* she was the only person on earth.

"Come to me."

His voice. She could taste it. Hot chocolate, smooth brandy, and sex. She recognized it. All the forbidden things Mom had warned her against—going out in public without panties, talking to strangers who tempted you with pictures you'd never forget, touching yourself in the darkness of your room while you imagined unimaginable acts.

Crazy thoughts. Whatever this was, it was affecting her mental balance.

"Are you okay?" Her words echoed in the cold gray void, while her mind warned *she'd* never be okay again. She stumbled in the general direction of his voice.

Just as she was losing her battle with hysteria, she saw him.

He sat relaxed against the boulder, one leg bent at the knee, his head turned from her as if watching something only he could see.

Then, he looked at her. And as much as she wanted to forget the rest of the dream, *this* moment she'd remember. Always.

"Ye must need me badly, lass." His husky murmur warmed the damp chill of the mist, made her remember needs she'd vowed not to think of again.

His face was harsh beauty and raw sensuality. Half hidden by a wild tangle of dark wind-blown hair, his eyes held secrets, his smile pure sin.

"Yer heart is cold and alone. Ye must think of all things warm, all that would make yer heart pound, all the feelings and scents that have brought ye pleasure. Live them now to bring ye peace."

"No." She rubbed her eyes with a shaking hand. *Come to me.* The image. A hot summer night. This man and her. Their naked bodies, sweat-sheened skin, and stark white cotton sheets tangled at the foot of a brass bed. Her bed. And the scent of honeysuckle drifting in the open window, moving the sheer curtains in a lazy rhythm. She could see the heat, touch the scent, taste the passion.

"I . . . I have to get back to my car." She'd never been so frightened in her life. Where had the image come from? The last time she'd smelled honeysuckle had been on Grandpa's farm when she'd been about sixteen. And . . . the other things. They weren't connected to her life with Peter and his love gun. And they'd felt . . . real. Too real.

Wake up. "I don't understand. Where . . . ? How . . . ?" Her trembling legs couldn't support her as she sank to her knees in front of him. "Why honeysuckle, the brass bed?"

"Whate'er yer thoughts, they brought ye pleasure for the moment. Hold them tightly to ye." Effortlessly, he reached out and pulled her onto his lap. "Let me warm ye."

"Have you seen New York around here anywhere? I . . ." She was ice flung into his flame. The

21

helpless melting, the absorption, the sizzle and spark, the steam as the two met. She *felt* him, through her heavy coat, through the rough wool of his clothing. Sinew, muscle. His sharp exhalation hot against the side of her neck, his heat touching her everywhere.

"This isn't a dream, is it?" The intensity of a dream like this would have brought her to sweating, shaking, heart-pounding-awareness. Then what *was* happening? "Are you familiar with out-of-body experiences?"

"Out of body?" He wiped a tear from her cheek with his finger.

Crying? When had she started crying? She sniffed. She wouldn't resort to tears. Old PMS had taught her that criers were losers.

" 'Twould be passing strange to want to be out of yer body when ye're wi' a bonny lass. 'Tis the body that makes it so wondrous."

What about the heart? What about love? "Sure. Stupid comment." Who was she to dis the senses when they seemed to be the only things working right now?

Reaching down, she braced herself against his hip, fixed her attention on the checked pattern of the cloth. Her legs were wedged between his thighs, but she had no strength to move, could barely concentrate. . . . "All of you are wearing kilts. Just what New York needs, another street gang. Guess you don't need guns and knives. You just moon anyone you don't like. I bet grossed-out enemies keel over by the hundreds at the fanny display put on by those two I chased away."

She felt his deep exhalation. " 'Tis the cold making you blather so."

"Right." She didn't even make sense to herself. Not a dream? Then *what?*

When she finally managed to lift her gaze, she looked into eyes as gray as the mist surrounding them. A midnight tangle of hair framed a face meant for a dark god or fallen angel. And something so explosive it took her breath away passed between them.

She'd imagined it. Nothing explosive had *ever* passed between a man and her. After her failed marriage, that's the way she liked it, that's the way she meant to keep it.

"Are ye feeling a wee bit better?"

"No." Too much. Her confused mind could make no sense of what she saw, felt. And so she focused on just one thing. His hair. She reached out with fingers as icy as the dread building in her soul, then slid her hand the length of his hair, past his shoulders to where dark strands spread across his chest.

Fascinated, she watched the rapid rise and fall of his broad chest, a rise and fall matching the beat of her heart.

With all her questions fighting for supremacy, she could only force one comment through her lips. "You have virgin hair."

"I dinna think so. I havena had any virgin parts for a verra long time."

She felt his deep chuckle shudder through her and raised her gaze once again to his face. The white flash of his wicked smile fixed her attention on his lips. It was a full lower lip, sensual, but somehow it did not soften the hard angles of his jaw and cheekbone.

His gaze slid the length of her body, and the caress was as real as though he'd touched her with his fingers, his mouth.

A dangerous man. Perhaps the two she'd chased away were the ones who'd needed saving.

His smile turned wolfish. "Ye wouldna enjoy a man who hadna lain wi' a lass."

Panic clattered around in her mind, frantically trying to get her attention. It finally succeeded. She tried to push away from him, but he simply closed his thighs on her legs. She might as well have been shackled in iron.

Even as she raised her fists to pound whatever part of him became available first, she sensed the uselessness of her effort. He wrapped his arms around her and held her still.

"Dinna be so quick to run." His breath fanned against her cheek, heating her senses, her anger. "Ye must have been fair desperate to gain my advice. I've ne'er seen Colin and Neil bested before. But ye took unfair advantage of their fear for their manhoods. 'Twasn't needed. I would have asked my brothers to speak wi' me later." He drew his finger along the line of her clenched jaw.

"Your *brothers?*" Jerking her head from his touch, she looked frantically around for help. She'd kill for the sight of a golden arch or even a New York cabby offering her a friendly finger signal because she'd cut him off. "Those two are your brothers?"

"Aye. We were born together. Still we dinna resemble each other overmuch."

"Born together . . . ? Oh, triplets." Hard to believe. The other two were lumbering bears, while this man . . . this man was a dark jungle predator.

Where *was* she? Had she taken a wrong turn in Central Park and landed in Oz?

"Even though we were born together, I came first. They dinna want to accept me as the eldest."

"Hey, I feel for them. Who came out first is important." Horse pooky. She had *really* important things to worry about.

She drew in a deep breath to hold her panic in check. He hadn't hurt her, and already his faded red plaid was growing sort of familiar. *No.* She couldn't let anything in this nowhere land get familiar.

She shivered as the mist's damp fingers touched her with an unspoken promise that nothing in her life would ever be the same again.

Some women might still think they were dreaming. Not her. She recognized dreams. She'd certainly had enough nightmares after the collapse of her marriage. This wasn't a dream.

Then *what?* Amnesia? Could she have lost her memory, wandered to a different place?

Stop shaking. You're New York tough. New Yorkers are survivors. This time when she pushed

25

at him, he let her go. Scrambling away from the man on the ground, she reached her purse and yanked out her cell phone.

Breathlessly, she pushed 911, then waited until a male voice answered.

"Please, I need help." Her teeth chattered. With cold or fear? Probably both. "My name is Kathy Bartlett and I—"

The voice interrupted.

"No, I'm not hurt. I don't know about the imminent danger part. I'm—"

Interruption.

"Where am I? Somewhere in *Braveheart*, I think."

The voice wasn't amused.

"Okay, okay, I'm . . ." She turned to the man, who still sat leaning against the rock. "Where am I?"

He wasn't smiling. A frown creased his forehead as he stared at her phone. "Ye're betwixt Cromarty and Dornoch Firths."

"*Firth?* What the heck is a firth? Firth doesn't sound like a New York name." He didn't sound like a New York man. She fought to control the nauseous fear trembling in the pit of her stomach and faithfully repeated what he'd said.

"What do you mean there're no streets with those names? Sure there are. I bet you could find dozens of Cromarty and Dornoch streets. I bet there're two named after Dominic Cromarty and Christine Dornoch."

The voice had no sense of humor.

"Fine, so I'm not hurt, so I'm not in *imminent* danger, but . . . Why do I have to call my local authorities?" She glared at the man on the ground, then glared at her cell phone.

"Emergencies? You think this isn't an *emergency*? You'd better . . ." Damn! He'd hung up. Carefully, she returned the phone to her purse, afraid she'd drop it from her shaking fingers. *Save the power until you figure out the right person to call.*

She was in deep doo-doo, but she'd calmly and logically reason things out. Hah! She was so scared that any minute the fright fairy would swoop down and crown her Queen of Queasy Stomachs.

She turned back to the man, then gasped when she found he now stood beside her. Sitting, he'd looked formidable. Standing, he was downright intimidating. Towering above her with shoulders broad enough to block out the sun, if there'd been a sun, and dressed in clothing that looked way too authentic for Kathy's taste, he practically oozed raw primitive power.

She wanted to step back. Step back, turn, and run for her life. But where? And she didn't doubt he'd catch her before she'd taken five steps. Clenching her shaking hands into fists, she glared at him. "Don't touch me or I'll—"

"Or ye'll what, lass?" He smiled. "Cover my manhood wi' a potion that will deny the pleasure of a woman's body to me forever?" He walked over

27

and picked up her can of mousse. Handling it carefully, he returned it to her.

Without comment, she put it in her purse.

"Be ye a witch?" He didn't smile when he asked.

An incredible *explanation* was jumping up and down just outside the door to her thoughts, shouting to get her attention. She couldn't make it go away, but she didn't have to answer the door.

Just stick with the facts. Two hulking giants run screaming from mousse attack. General landscape in no way resembles Times Square on Christmas Eve. Conclusion. Primitive area inhabited by big scary primitive men. Hmm.

Think. If she was in a primitive area, then she'd better squash this witch thing. Being burned at the stake was *not* on her list of fun things to do on a Saturday night. No, she definitely couldn't be a witch. "I'm . . . I'm a princess. That's right, I'm a princess, and I'm lost."

"A princess?" He looked puzzled.

She relaxed slightly. He didn't seem so threatening when he was puzzled. "Yes. I'm . . . the hair princess."

"Hare?" A smile once again tugged at the corner of his mouth. "Ye rule a kingdom of rabbits?"

If she hadn't been so confused, so *terrified,* she might have laughed, but who could laugh with her teeth chattering and her mind racing for an explanation. Any explanation. "No, hair." She reached up and fingered a strand of his incredible hair, then jerked her hand back at the instant connection between them. "I'm Kathy, the Princess of Hair." A coma? Did people hallucinate when they were in a coma? "And I need to get back to New York."

He frowned. "I've ne'er heard of this New York."

Oh, God, please. "The United States?"

He shook his head, and her gaze involuntarily followed the way his hair shifted like heavy silk across his shoulders. "I dinna know these places. Who is the king of yer land?"

The *explanation*, so fantastic, so impossible, was now pounding on the door, tapping at the windows. "Uh . . . Clairol. My father, King Clairol, rules our kingdom."

He exhaled sharply, and his breath misted against her cheek—warm, compelling. "Yer father would do well to keep his daughter safe beside him. 'Tis a dangerous land ye've come to."

New York or wherever, men's attitudes didn't change. She took a mini-break from mental handwringing to strike a blow for women everywhere. "Women can take care of themselves. *I* can take care of myself." Right.

His gaze turned thoughtful, assessing. "Aye. I've seen proof of that. Henry would find ye amusing."

"Henry?" She glanced around her again. Hills, grass, a small grove of trees, the smell of the sea. No, she'd never been here before.

"Surely even in yer kingdom ye've heard of King Henry."

The *explanation* gave up on polite knocking and tapping. With a roar of frustration, it kicked down her door, then stood with hands on hips, confronting her with its horrific magnitude, its *realness*.

"What . . . year is it?" Strange, but her lips felt frozen, unwilling to form the question.

"The year of our Lord, fifteen hundred forty-two." His answer seemed distracted, his gaze suddenly fixed on something behind her.

She squeezed her eyes shut, as if that would keep her mind, her soul, from shattering into a million shards of panic. *No!* How? Why? No, she wouldn't accept his words. Time travel was impossible.

Please let her open her eyes and find herself back on the side of I-95, smelling the wonderful smells of home—exhaust fumes and pollution. She'd never, never, never complain again about overbooking, clients who wanted green hair like the Grinch, or sexy cars that broke down.

She opened her eyes. Nothing had changed. Feeling suddenly disconnected from the strangeness around her—probably a defense mechanism of her mind—she turned to see what her companion found so interesting.

A large cat sat watching them. Mostly white, it had red on its head and tail. Auburn. Denise Lane, third Thursday of every month. Kathy had told her all women deserved to be redheads at least once in their lives.

The man moved up beside her, and they watched silently as the cat stood, then hobbled toward them.

"That cat only has three legs." She was switching into automatic poor-kitty mode when the man put his hand on her arm. She drew in her breath at the contact.

" 'Tis Malin. Ye must pretend ye dinna notice.

30

He willna accept yer pity." He bent down and ran his hand the length of the cat's back. The cat sat down regally at the man's side, disdaining to glance her way.

"Malin?"

"Aye. The name means wee strong warrior. 'Tis a fitting name."

Kathy lifted her gaze to the man's face. There was dark intensity in his stare and an unnamed emotion that seemed to ripple between them, pulling her into its undertow even as she fought it.

Nope, she wouldn't get sidetracked because she had really important issues to think about, like . . . *Even though I really, really don't believe in time travel, well, if I have time traveled—and, of course, I don't believe I have—please, someone send me home.*

"Run this King Henry and 1542 stuff past me again. Slowly." She wet her lips nervously as he watched her with unwavering gray eyes. "Oh, and have you spoken with your shrink lately, maybe missed your medication?"

If only it were that simple. But what about the two kilted brothers she'd terrified with a can of mousse? What about their Scottish burr, and what about the primitive untouched land around her? *What about if you have a screaming fit of hysterics?*

It was as though she hadn't spoken. Without comment, he grabbed her hand, scooped up her bag of toys, purse, and backpack, then started dragging her away.

Bag of toys, purse, backpack. Something important. Remember. "Whoa. You can't just pull me along behind you. That's . . . kidnapping, a criminal offense. Besides, I don't go off with strange men." She jerked ineffectually at his grasp.

Pausing, he looked back at her. "If ye're truly lost, then all men would be strange to ye."

True. "Yeah, but some men are stranger than others."

He finally seemed to relax. The beginning of a smile crinkled the corners of his eyes and turned up the corners of that incredible mouth. "Ye dinna understand, lass. Ye have no choice in the matter. Ye're coming wi' me." He shrugged, and despite the plaid thrown across his shoulders, she could see the ripple of muscles. "Besides, where else would ye go?"

Stark raving mad? No, she thought she'd already taken that trip.

He must have taken her silence for assent, because he resumed dragging her away.

"Wait. You forgot Malin. Aren't you going to carry him?" She glanced at the cat, who stared malevolently back at her. Definitely *not* carry-on luggage.

"Malin is a warrior. Ye dinna carry a warrior. He would be insulted." The man continued walking.

God forbid she insult Malin. "Peter. We can't leave Peter here."

Peter. Now she realized what had bothered her when he'd picked up her other things. She'd been holding the bag, backpack, and purse when *it* happened. She hadn't been holding Peter. So why was Peter here? Why not her sexy red car with the balloon payment due in two months? Two months. Which reminded her, if she didn't show up in court on February 14, her slimy, cheating ex-husband would win his stupid mental anguish case.

Once again the man paused. He cast her a long-suffering look. "Peter?"

"He's one of my toys. I have to get him." She pointed.

He narrowed his gaze on the shiny metal hourglass waiting placidly beside a large bush. " 'Tis passing strange."

Inexplicably, she felt the need to defend Peter. "You have no room to talk, buster."

He led her back to the toy, and when he would have picked Peter up, she rushed to grab her toy first. Clutching the shiny body, she smoothed her fingers over his two amber lights. She felt a rush of affection for the metal misfit and, yes, a sense of comfort in holding him. He was one of her last contacts with a life that seemed to be fading even as she stood clasping him.

Fear drove her into speech. As long as she could talk, she might stave off the bout of tears gathering at the back of her throat. "Who . . . who are you, and how did you do that thing with the honeysuckle and the brass bed?"

"Ian Ross." He started walking again, obviously assuming she'd follow him. "And I did naught but urge ye to find the things ye treasured so ye might weave them into yer desire."

He assumed wrong. "That wasn't my desire."

She sensed his smile. "Ye dinna *wish* it to be yer desire."

"Okay, forget the desire thing. Who are you *really?*"

For what she sensed was the last time, he paused and turned toward her. Moving close, he invaded her space, and Kathy felt like she'd wandered into a sensual magnetic field. He slid his fingers along her jaw, down the side of her neck, then, lowering his head, he brushed her lips with his.

Searing heat and a need so strong it made every inch of her body clench held her rooted to the spot even as her mind screamed for her to run. *Close.* So close his eyes seemed silver rather than gray, his lashes dark smudges against his beard-shadowed skin. So close she inhaled the scent of mist, hot male, and danger.

She stumbled away from him. There was something about his closeness that—

"If Ian Ross be not enough for ye, mayhap ye need to know what others call me." He followed her retreat until she was backed against a large boulder.

His size, pure maleness, and her unexplained re-action to him left her breathing hard, her breaths emerging as white puffs into the cold mist.

Grasping her chin, he gently raised her head till she was forced to meet his dark gaze. "Know me,

Kathy, Princess of Hair." His smile ignited a flame that burned away her chill, that sent liquid fire through every vein.

"I am the Pleasure Master."

Chapter Two

Ian stepped back, knowing his effect on her as he knew his effect on all women. But that was not why he moved away. He enjoyed being close to women—watching their breathing quicken, the soft unfocused glow of their eyes, the slide of warm skin against his own.

He stepped back because he sensed danger. Ian's instincts had served him well in the past, and he would not ignore them now. For the first time in his life, a woman confused him. And confusion was a danger. She had clearly traveled far, but not in search of the Pleasure Master. Then why?

Mayhap Gordon Mackay had sent her. God's teeth, did the man never give up his quest to capture Ian? But then, Ian didn't think Gordon canny enough to send a woman such as this.

"I've answered yer question, lass, now ye must answer mine. What potion did ye use on my brothers? Ye spilled a wee bit on yerself, and ye didna seem worried, so I dinna think their man parts will fall off."

Curiosity. Ian had more than the normal man, and his father had often warned him it would bring him grief. But Gordon Mackay or not, he must know more about Kathy of Hair.

It was curiosity that held him now, helping a woman whose strangeness should have sent him fleeing as his brothers had fled.

She shrugged. "Oh, that was mousse. It makes hair more manageable."

He smiled. "Men also, 'twould seem."

Was the woman mad? Most would think so, but Ian Ross didn't think like most. She had told the truth about being from another place. Her clothes, her speech, and the strange things she carried with her were like nothing he'd ever seen.

Beyond that, she was clear-eyed and sharp-tongued. Her tongue reminded him much of Mad Mary, the clan healer, who told any who vexed her that her red hens passed on the secrets of healing along with the eggs they laid each day. He knew some who believed the tale.

Kathy of Hair. 'Twas a strange name. Who was she, and where had she come from? She had a boldness about her that fascinated him, and no woman had fascinated him in a very long time.

"Pleasure Master? What's a pleasure master?"

He'd started walking again and could hear her struggling to keep up with him.

He slowed his pace, not only because of the woman, but because he remembered Malin was following. Why *had* Malin followed him today? The cat was old and had not wandered far from home for many years. But Malin *knew* things, had always known when Ian needed him. Why today?

"Yer speech is different from any I've heard. Where is this New York?"

"New York is a state of mind, and it's here somewhere if I can only find it. Now what's a pleasure master?"

Her answer made no sense, and her questions were like buzzing insects you could swat away but never discourage. Mayhap it would be safer if she fell behind, then faded into the mist from whence she'd appeared.

Ye lie, Ian Ross. He taught others so much, gave so much of himself and enjoyed the giving, but there was a sameness to his feelings, a joy only of the senses and mayhap satisfaction in having helped someone. But *this* woman. This woman was different. For the few moments he'd been close to her, *touched* her, he'd felt a pull, a connection that went beyond the body's heated need. The sensation puzzled him, *excited* him.

He heard her labored breathing as she drew level with him, still holding her strange toy. "Where're we going? What place is this? And I want to know what a pleasure master is." She punched him on the arm to emphasize her demand.

Ignoring his better judgment, he slowed further, then glanced at her. Her face was flushed from trying to keep up with him, and her blond hair lay damp and curling from the mist against her cheeks. She glared up at him with eyes as wide and blue as the firth on a sunny day. But beneath her anger, he sensed the fear, the confusion, the *truth* of what she'd told him.

"Even though 'tis yet summer, 'tis no day to be wandering the hills. Ye'll come to my dwelling where ye can dry off. Then mayhap we can find a way to return ye to yer land." *And I can find a way to make sense of how ye make me feel.* "Ye can also tell me about the things ye carry wi' ye. What I've seen so far is passing strange."

"Summer? This is summer? You've gotta be kidding." She shivered. "Okay, question one answered. Now, where *are* we? And don't run that firth stuff past me again." She cast him a considering look. "Do you have a lisp? Maybe you meant *first* not *firth*. That would explain why nine-one-one couldn't find us."

"I dinna know what ye blather about, woman. Ye're in Scotland, as ye must well know."

His budding frustration disappeared as he watched her grow pale, then clasp her lower lip between small white teeth in an attempt to still its quiver. She was a brave lass, and he admired bravery. " 'Tis not such a bad place to be. Once ye're warm and dry, ye can tell me what I need know in order to return ye to yer land." His attempt to console her came out gruffer than he'd intended, but then he'd had no need to console a woman for many a year. Women came to him for other things.

"That might be a little hard. I don't have any ruby slippers to click." She seemed to have gained control over her quivering lip and was now blinking quickly to keep back the tears. But he could see the tell-tale sheen.

Luckily, they'd reached his home. "Welcome to my dwelling, Kathy of Hair."

"Where? Where?" She swung in a circle.

"Here." He pulled aside the brush that hid the entrance.

"You live in a *cave?*"

"Aye. None have come here—"

"Of course they have. I'm here."

"—and lived." He should not have said that, but he was frustrated with his uncertain response to this woman when he'd never known uncertainty with *any* woman.

"Oh." Silence. Then a mad scrambling. "Feet don't fail me now."

Exhaling wearily, he turned and caught her arm before she'd gone three strides. "Ye're safe wi' me, lass. 'Tis no secret where I live. I was but teasing ye."

"Sure. I knew that." He could see her pulling her composure around her. "But why would anyone live in a cave? Shouldn't you be living in a castle with a drawbridge and a moat full of piranhas, stuff like that?"

He sensed her hesitancy as she followed him down the dark tunnel leading to his living area.

"Not that I believe . . . Hmm. Hypothermia. I wonder if I have . . ."

"A castle is cold and drafty, exposed. This place suits me well. 'Tis large, ne'er grows too cold, and stays dry. 'Tis easy to defend and also . . . private. I know of none other like it." His curiosity had swelled to monstrous proportions. He must know the meanings of the words she used. He must know—

"But . . . I thought wolves and things like that lived in caves." She'd drawn closer to him, probably for protection.

He felt the brush of her body against his back, and it was as though no clothes separated them. He drew his breath in at the thought of her lying naked on his furs. Waiting. It wasn't a comfortable thought. He'd grown used to being the one creating images for others.

Glancing over his shoulder, he grinned at her in the darkness, knowing his grin had little to do with humor. "Aye. Wolves live in caves." *And not all run on four legs.*

The widening of her eyes told him she'd understood his message.

He stepped aside so she could enter his living area, visible in the dim light from a hole that opened to the surface. Then he quietly lit candles and added fuel to the small hearth, bathing the room in a warm glow.

"I . . . didn't expect this." She ran her hand over one of the heavy tapestries lining the walls.

At least his home had diverted her for a moment

41

from worrying about her plight. "Ye expected a wee hovel wi' a dirt floor and mayhap a few wild dogs fighting for scraps from my table?" He smiled.

"Of course not." She sighed. "Yes. That or some dreary castle crouched at the edge of the Cliff of Doom." She frowned. "Isn't that the name of a video game or something?" She swayed slightly.

"Sit by the fire." He set her things down, then watched as she carefully placed the strange toy she carried on the rug close to the hearth.

He smiled as she scanned the room. "Ye'll find no chairs in this room, but the cushions are verra comfortable."

Sinking onto the pile of pillows next to her toy, she glanced at his rugs. "These are Oriental. What would Oriental rugs be doing in the wilds of Scotland in . . . 1542?" She flinched as she said the date.

"My great grandfather traveled to many places and brought the best of what he saw home wi' him." *The power of the Pleasure Master.*

As she skimmed her fingers across the nearest rug, her gaze turned pensive. "Not to change the subject, but how can I be in the year 1542 if my cell phone still works?" Frantically, she dug through her purse for the phone, her one connection to her real life, her sanity.

No 911 this time. Who to call? Mom and Dad were on their cruise. Besides she'd never worry them with this . . . whatever. Coco would ask too many in-depth questions she couldn't answer. Finally, she punched in the numbers for Pampered

Life, her work, her salvation. Of course, it was Christmas Eve, so Dawn had probably left by now.

When Dawn finally answered, Kathy almost sobbed with relief. "Dawn, you've got to help me. I'm in 1542. Allegedly." She frowned at Ian Ross.

"Kathy? Fifteen Forty-Two? Is this some hot new club you didn't tell me about?"

Kathy shifted her frown to the phone. "Club? I'm talking about the past, the *year* 1542. I'm between two damn firths." *Remain calm. Do not shout at co-worker. Shouting solves nothing.*

"Got it. You're hung over. Bet there's a man, too. I knew it had to be something like that when you didn't show up for work."

"I'm *not* hung over." Kathy shouted. "Furthermore . . . Work? I don't work on Christmas."

"You do on December 26. Clara Stone was really ticked when you weren't here to do her color. Better show up tomorrow."

"Dawn, there's this guy, Ian Ross. He lives in a cave—"

Giggles.

"Fine. The least you can do is make sure someone does Mrs. Tierney's hair." Confusion clouded her thinking. December 26? How had she lost two days?

"Hey, anything for a friend." Dawn's voice turned uncertain. "You're okay, aren't you?"

Okay as compared to what? Okay as in she wasn't being stalked by a saber-toothed tiger? Kathy glanced at Ian. Maybe not. Anyway, it wouldn't do any good to worry Dawn about her mental health, and Dawn would definitely think Kathy was crazy if she told the truth. "I'm fine, Dawn."

"Look, I gotta run. Got a customer waiting. Let me know if you need something else."

Kathy sighed. "Sure."

"See you tomorrow."

"Right. Tomorrow." With a groan of despair, she shut off the power. When she could think again without fighting the urge to break into hysterical tears, she'd figure out whom to call for help.

She turned her attention back to Ian Ross. "Okay, what's *really* happening here?"

"Nothing, but if ye wish something to happen I—"

She didn't like the sudden gleam in his eyes. "Forget it. What I mean is, why am I here with you? Maybe I'm not here. Maybe you're just a brain-blip caused by inhaling too many hair chemical fumes."

"Hair chemicals?"

"Maybe not. No one else complained of taking unbooked flights to Scotland after doing Mrs. Henley's gray roots. Anyway, I need proof that this is 1542. New Yorkers don't buy the Brooklyn Bridge. We're street smart. You don't pull the wool over our eyes." Amazing how a few clichés made her feel better. This had to be some clever scam, and she wasn't going to fall for it. *What about his clothes, the land, his speech?* No, she wouldn't believe it. This was some kind of gigantic hoax. *But who'd want to bother?*

He frowned, and she watched the lines in his forehead deepen, his lips tighten. A dangerous man, a man who'd lived life and not always found it gentle. She suppressed a shiver.

"I dinna know this Brooklyn Bridge. And what purpose would pulling wool over yer eyes serve?" In two strides, he reached the spot where she'd collapsed, then sat down facing her. For the first time, she noticed the sword he carefully set beside him. She peered more carefully. Was that a knife hilt sticking out from his sock? Sure, New Yorkers had to protect themselves, but this guy was into overkill.

She was alone in a cave with a very strange man who carried a sword and stuck knives in his socks. He relaxed against one of the cushions, then smiled. A man who, in her world, would make her heart pound and her mouth grow dry.

But she was in *his* world, and she was too confused, too scared to react to any man. *So what do you call what happened when you first met him?* She chose to ignore that thought.

He settled himself deeper into the cushions, then ran his gaze from the top of her head to the tips of her tingling toes. Her heart pounded and her mouth grew dry.

Desperately, she searched for a subject that would put him on the defensive, give her time to pull her scattered wits into some semblance of order. "About this pleasure master stuff? What's a pleasure master?" Darn. She couldn't stop the stupid flip-flopping of her stomach.

Food. When was the last time she'd eaten? "Maybe I passed out from hunger. Maybe you're just my brain's attempt to remind me I haven't had a good prime rib for a while." That hadn't come out exactly as she'd intended. "What I mean is, if we're talking pleasure, I'd like—"

"There are pleasures greater than food, lass." His voice was a husky murmur.

"Uh-huh." She knew better than to ask what.

He didn't answer. Instead, he pulled off his belt, then the wool plaid he wore, until he was left with only a shirt that barely reached the top of his muscular thighs. Once again relaxing back against the multicolored pile of pillows, he bent one leg at the knee, then smiled at her. "The fire makes it verra warm. Dinna ye feel the heat, lass?"

She knew if she allowed her gaze to follow the path of his inner thigh to where his shirt ended she'd see . . . No, she wouldn't go there even if the rest of her body was yammering for a peek. She was above cheap thrills.

His skin glowed golden in the fire's light. So *much* bare male skin made her feel prickly and . . . Sweat formed between her breasts, then trickled across her stomach, but she clutched her coat more tightly around her. "No. Absolutely not. All comfy cozy here."

Abandoning his relaxed position, he sat up, then edged closer to her. "Ye want to know about a pleasure master."

She gulped. He needed a T-shirt with "Danger—explosives" printed across his chest to warn innocent New York women. Okay, so New York women wouldn't need a sign to get this guy's message. "Well, not really. I mean, you've probably got better things to do."

"No." He moved closer.

"All this pleasure master stuff can wait till tomorrow." If she hadn't had the pillows bolstering her, she would have scuttled backwards like a frightened crab.

"No." He moved closer still, close enough for her to feel his heat, to inhale the mingled scents of crisp misty morning and warm male flesh.

"Ye must be comfortable while I explain."

He reached for her coat, and she sat unmoving, unable even to blink as he slipped it off her shoulders, then down her arms. She couldn't summon the will to pull her sweat-dampened silk blouse away from her body, even though she realized it outlined in detail her breasts, nipples, and heavy breathing. What was wrong with her?

"I know the secrets of what brings a woman pleasure." He leaned closer toward her, and his raven-wing hair fell forward, a dark curtain of mystery.

Kathy believed him, and recognized that a change of subject was in order. "Personally, great hair brings me pleasure. It wouldn't take me a minute to get my scissors, snip off those dead ends, do a little shaping and . . ." She willed her hands to remain still, denying the urge to reach out and run her fingers through the tangled strands. "Well, maybe not right now."

"Dead ends? Shaping? Ye make no sense at all, lass." He didn't back off.

With an instinct she didn't question, she knew

47

that to touch would be to lose. But what else was there to lose? She'd already lost her sanity; that was the only explanation she could think of to explain her feelings.

"I show women the joy they may know from touching a man's body. . . ." Reaching out, he slid his finger across her lips. "And the unimagined pleasure they may feel when a man touches them."

She jerked her head away. If she'd been an oyster, she would have snapped her shell shut on his finger. He was just like her ex, reaching for every pearl in the oyster bed, then happily trotting off to find more oysters. Well, this was one oyster who didn't intend to lose another pearl.

"I don't need anyone to teach me about joy, thank you very much." There must be millions of women who lived happy, productive lives without experiencing the big O at the hands of some jerk.

Hmm. Hands. Ian Ross had a man's hands— large, capable. But capable of what? And his finger? She could still feel its pressure, its warmth.

"Ah, but I think ye do, lass." He drew his bottom lip into his mouth as he studied her, and when he released it, her gaze was drawn to its damp sheen, its fullness. What would it be like to touch those lips with hers?

She had to get out of here. Find her way back to good old New York. Back to New Year's Eve in Times Square and yelling at the Knicks when they blew it in the fourth period. "Hey, joy is way overrated. A few times a year is enough for me." How about once in a lifetime? That'd be nice.

He frowned at her, and she noticed the small lines that fanned from the corners of his eyes. Eyes that gave away no secrets, that seemed like the hidden Adirondack mountain lakes she'd visited on childhood camping trips— deep, distant, and cool— even as his words spread warmth through her.

" 'Tis sad. Ye need me badly."

He smiled, and she forgot his eyes, their secrets. She'd seen good-looking men in her life, but none could smile like Ian Ross. His smile reached inside and touched every dark, confused part of her. And that scared the heck out of her New York soul.

"Look, mister. I was married to a man who knew all there was to know about women's joy. Lord knows, he practiced a lot. So don't tell me what I need. What I need is to try my cell phone again."

He reached down and touched her hand, effectively stopping her from grabbing for the phone.

"Are ye saying ye were wed to a pleasure master? 'Tis impossible. A pleasure master canna wed and remain a pleasure master."

"Yeah, well Peter likes the best of both worlds. He's a marine biologist and believes if the scientific approach works with plankton, then it should work with humans. He studied everything on human sexuality, then practiced on me. When his hypothesis didn't match his test results, he concluded I was incapable of having an orgasm and therefore unable to reach sexual nirvana." *I was incapable of being a complete woman for him.*

She cast Ian Ross a speculative glance. "You know, this whole conversation could be really freeing. I usually wouldn't talk about stuff like this with a total stranger, but since you don't really exist, it's okay. I mean, talking to a brain-blip is no big deal."

He frowned at her. " 'Tis a strange tongue ye speak. What is an . . . orgasm?"

Hmm. "I'll explain later. Anyway, Peter was convinced that if he and his love gun couldn't bring me sensual ecstasy, then I was hopeless." Her fear? Maybe Peter was right. She'd thought she loved him, so why couldn't . . .

"His love gun?"

"Later." Kathy narrowed her gaze. "The end wasn't pretty. I came home from work one day to find Peter and his love gun testing Peter's hypothesis with my friend Joan Gates in our bed. Joan's orgasm results were a smashing success." It had hurt, God how it had hurt. "*My* hypothesis is that Peter and octopuses are sibling species. And before you ask, that's marine biologist-speak for—they're closely related species.

" 'Tis the way of many men, lass."

"Tell me about it." Did that sound casually unconcerned? There were some feelings she couldn't even share with a brain-blip.

She brightened. "Hey, a hair stylist comes prepared. I whipped out my butane curling iron, heated that sucker up, then told good old PMS his tomcatting days were over. He and Joan were so anxious to leave, they forgot all about their clothes when they ran out the front door. I locked the door behind them, then called the local paper to come get pictures."

"Butane curling iron?"

"Later." Afterward, she'd thrown herself onto the couch and cried—for the love that hadn't been love at all, and for all her shattered dreams. Then she'd dried her eyes, pulled out her wedding album, and cut her scumbag husband out of every picture. Then she'd cut him into tiny pieces and flushed him down the toilet. A symbolic gesture, but satisfying.

"If pigs could fly, my ex would be leading the hog flock south for the winter. Can you believe he's suing me for mental anguish? Can you *believe* it?"

Ian Ross was looking at her with a dazed expression on his face. "I canna believe many things."

Kathy glared at him. "Well ditto here, mister."

"What does the word 'sue' mean?"

"Later." She'd *never* let another womanizer into her life. If she ever decided to try again, she'd look for a virgin, a man who'd love her and wouldn't point out her shortcomings in bed, wouldn't blame *her* if she didn't have an orgasm. "Old PMS says I compromised his credibility with his colleagues, held him up to ridicule, and that I drove him to other women because I couldn't . . ."

"Have an orgasm."

"Right. Anyway, the judge set the court date for February fourteenth. Valentine's Day, for heaven's sake. Is that the pits, or what? I'll be there if I have to crawl on my hands and knees." He'd taken everything else from her; he wouldn't get her money.

"PMS? What is PMS? And dinna tell me 'later.' "

Kathy glanced away from Ian Ross, only to meet the malevolent stare of Malin, who'd planted himself on top of Peter. Fitting. They both had three sturdy legs.

" 'Tis an answer ye owe me, lass. What is PMS? And dinna tell me 'tis yer husband's name because I ken it stands for more."

"Umm . . . well . . ." Now would be a great moment for her to be whisked back to New York. *Hint, hint.* Nothing. "PMS is . . . plumbing made simple."

His gaze was disbelieving. "That doesna make sense."

"Nothing makes sense." She was pitiful. Connie Dare, the stylist who worked in the cubicle next to her at Pampered Life, wouldn't be sitting here feeling sorry for herself. Connie would have already called her lawyer and filed a lawsuit against someone for something. It was the now thing to do.

"Ye havena told me what an orgasm is."

"An orgasm is . . . like . . ." It's like what she'd never had with her ex-husband. "Uh, it's like an . . . explosion." Great imagery. She hoped he didn't want something more specific.

"Explosion?"

Arrgh! "Explosion. Boom." She made some vague motions in the general direction of her "boom" area.

"Aye." A smile tugged at the corner of his mouth.

The rat. He knew exactly what she was talking about. *Calm down. Any minute now you'll blink and be back in New York. Then you'll never see Ian Ross again.* It'd be great if she could take him back with her. He was the most spectacular man she'd seen in years.

She stared into his eyes. Eyes that suddenly swirled with emotion, heat. That willed her to enter his world. That seemed to drain her own will to resist.

"Heed me, Kathy of Hair. A woman's need and fulfillment start *here.*" He placed only his index finger against her forehead, yet she felt the connection all the way to her toes.

"Not here." He ran his finger down the side of her jaw, her neck, then stopped as he touched the tip of her nipple.

Could've fooled me. She sucked in her breath at the sizzle of sensation that spread like honey on a hot day. Why couldn't she move away, break the connection? Why didn't she *want* to?

"Nor here." He drew his finger between her breasts, down over her stomach, then laid his palm flat against her skirt, and her thighs clenched as though no material separated his flesh from hers, as though she could hold his touch warm between her legs.

She breathed in gasping pants, tried to battle past sensations so strong she felt like screaming, tried to remember . . .

"No!" With her last ragged shred of willpower, she rolled away from him.

He let her go.

"Pleasure Master, my foot. You're just like my ex. You're nothing but a womanizer with a fancy title. I bet you never met a woman you didn't love."

53

He leaned back and stared at her. He seemed truly puzzled. " 'Tis not about love, lass. 'Tis about joining wi' another for pleasure. I teach women how to take a man's body and enjoy the taking."

"Huh." She scrambled to her feet, needing to distance herself from him, from whatever strange feelings he seemed able to generate. "Sounds like the same old testing-in-the-name-of-science scam my ex-husband ran past any woman who'd climb into bed with him."

She walked over to stand beside Peter and tried to ignore Malin's low growl. "But I dropped out of the scientific community a long time ago." She directed a determined stare at Ian Ross. "You'll never get a chance to practice on me, Pleasure Master, because I'll never let you touch me again."

He smiled. A smile of wicked temptation and sweet promise.

"I dinna need to *touch* ye, Kathy of Hair."

Oh boy.

Chapter Three

Ian watched her reaction—her unease with what he'd revealed about himself, with the things she'd told him about her life. Restlessly, she clasped and unclasped her hands in her lap. Her need to flee beat at him in waves of silent panic.

Once again, she reached down and pulled the strange object she'd spoken into out of her bag. "So now that we've kind of explored your job description, I guess it's time for me to get on home. I mean, it's Christmas. Everyone should be home on Christmas." She gazed forlornly at the object in her hand.

Surprised, Ian realized his sympathy for her overrode his desire to hold the object in his hands, to hear what she heard when she spoke to it.

The women who came to him were challenges, and after he'd solved their problems, he thought no more of them. Sympathy was a soft emotion, and the Pleasure Master could allow no soft emotions to interfere with his life.

She looked up at him, and he saw defeat in her eyes for the first time. "I . . . I don't know whom to call. What do I say? It's 1542 and I'm stuck in Scotland? Send a taxi?"

He didn't try to hold her. After her reaction to what he'd told her about himself, he didn't think she'd welcome his touch. "Ye seem verra upset wi' the year. What year would please ye?"

She ignored his question and moved over to stare at his hearth. "You know, I really think I want this to be a brain-blip. With a brain-blip I can go to a state-of-the-art facility where they'll do an MRI, locate the problem, and fix it. That way I can still be in—"

"God's teeth, woman, ye make no sense at all. What year do ye think ye're in?" What had she done to him? He *never* lost his temper with a woman. The lass looked as though she'd break into pieces if he touched her.

Emotion flooded her eyes. Shock, desperation, fear. "I'm pretty sure this is just a brain-blip. Probably too much stress in my life. And finding out that old PMS is suing me must've set everything off. Sort of like a panic attack. That means I'm still in 2001, and you don't exist."

He didn't know which confused him more, her belief that she came from a future time or her assertion that he didn't exist.

Mayhap his earlier suspicions had been right.

Gordon Mackay had already gone to foolish lengths to capture him for Fiona, and this might be another such effort. Gordon knew Ian's curiosity was his weakness. What better way to lure him into a trap? But could Gordon even conceive of things as strange as the toy the woman carried with her, the object she spoke to, and the "mousse"?

Ian shook his head to clear it. He could only deal with what was happening now, and not worry overmuch about possible conspiracies. "What does this New York look like?"

She blinked at him. "It has buildings that reach into the sky, millions of people, and traffic jams that give me migraines."

He didn't believe there were buildings that reached into the sky, but then lasses often enlarged things beyond the limits of truth. Had not rumors spread about the size of his—?

"So, I guess you've never spent any time in the Big Apple."

Big apple? Where might they grow a fruit large enough to shelter a man? And what was a traffic jam? Mayhap she meant only to mock him.

"Ye want proof that this be 1542? Come wi' me." Frustrated, he spoke more harshly than necessary. "Then I'll have yer true story, not the tale ye've told me."

Her eyes widened. "You don't believe me?"

He raked his fingers through his hair. "Ye name me a brain-blip and say I dinna exist, yet ye expect me to believe ye've traveled from some future time."

57

She seemed to wilt before his eyes. "Right. You have a point there."

"Still, I will give ye the proof ye crave. Mayhap ye werena sent by the Mackays."

She pursed her lips, and her gaze grew puzzled. "Who are the Mackays?"

He forced his attention from the ripeness of those lips. "Fiona, the sister of Gordon Mackay, desires me. She doesna want to share, but the Pleasure Master canna belong to only one woman." He shrugged. "Gordon willna accept that. He is ever plotting to capture me for her."

"I feel your pain. Hey, sticking with just one woman would be a real bummer. So many women, so little time." She narrowed her eyes to blue slits of contempt.

"Dinna judge. Ye're strange to the ways of the clan."

"But not to the ways of men with testosterone overload." She glared at him. "And don't ask what testosterone is."

Enough. "We'll leave as soon as I don my plaid." Drawing the wool around him, he rose, then turned his back on her as he finished. He felt her gaze touching him, moving across his shoulders, down his back, leaving a trail of phantom fingertips that drew a shiver from him.

He strode toward the tunnel, but stopped when he reached the spot where Malin still lay atop the strange toy. He grinned. "Wi' only one front leg, Malin canna leap verra high. Yer toy suits him."

"Great. Peter lives to please."

Her grouchy sarcasm widened Ian's grin. Women he knew were always sweetly compliant. A touch of sour intrigued him.

Wordlessly, she followed him back down the dark tunnel and out into a now sunny day. He sensed her pause, her startled gasp.

" 'Tis beautiful when the mist clears and the sun shines on the mountains and burns." Startled, he realized he was speaking to her as he would any stranger to the Highlands, not the trickster he half believed her to be.

She took a deep breath. "I can smell the sea."

"Aye." The sea. He'd often stood gazing at the gray endlessness of it and wondered what lay beyond. He knew something did because of the tales passed down from his great grandfather. If he accepted those tales as true, that men could travel to strange places across a sea that seemed to have no end, could it not be true that men might travel across a sea of time? But he could see the water, he couldn't see time. And so he didn't believe.

He walked at a slow pace, allowing her to keep up with him.

"I don't mean to sound nosy, but . . . Okay, I'm nosy. It's a weakness."

He exhaled a sigh of resignation. She wasn't going to leave him alone.

"How does this pleasure master job go? Do you work a forty-hour week, with an hour for lunch each day? What about overtime? Oh, and do you have health insurance and a retirement plan? Hmm. I guess you have to have malpractice insur-

59

ance too. I mean, what if a client doesn't attain her desired level of joy? Do you just give her money back, or does she get credit toward her next shot at joy? Do you advertise in the yellow pages, or—"

She tripped over a small rock and fell against him.

He drew in his breath at the searing connection. Her small gasp as she righted herself assured him she'd felt it also. And wanted it no more than he did.

Somehow, that annoyed him, and he took it out on the ridiculous things she wore on her feet. "Can yer King Clairol not put something on yer feet that will allow ye to walk a short distance wi' out falling all over a man?" He would have to get her something to . . . No. She wouldn't be here long enough for him to need to worry about her footwear.

"Falling all over a man?" He heard the anger in her voice and immediately felt better. "Look, buster, if I were going to fall all over a man, it wouldn't be you."

He was annoyed again. Why wouldn't it be he? No man could bring her the pleasure he could. He smiled at her, a practiced smile that he long ago had learned softened women, made them open to him. "A night on my furs would cure yer shrewish nature."

"It'll never happen. I'm one hundred percent seduce-proof, mister." *Ignore the way he made you feel when he touched you, looked at you. This isn't real, so the feelings aren't real.* "The only thing a night on your furs would bring me is a sore back."

Okay, so she wasn't being fair. No man could bring her pleasure. Her ex had huffed and puffed like The Little Engine That Could, and gotten zip for his trouble. "You haven't answered any of my questions about your work."

She looked up at Ian Ross in time to catch his take-off-your-clothes-and-we'll-do-it-right-here smile. "I dinna *understand* any of yer questions. The Pleasure Master isna about *work*. 'Tis a sacred duty."

Kathy sighed. "Sacred duty. Gotcha."

He frowned, reminding her once again that she was alone in a strange place with a man she didn't know. It paid to watch what you said, even to a brain-blip.

"Look, I'm sorry. When I get upset, I get sarcastic. I guess it's sort of a defense." She smiled weakly.

He nodded. "What do ye care about, Kathy of Hair?"

She blinked, surprised by the question. "I . . . care about being a good person and raising women's self-esteem by giving them great hair. Why?"

"Then ye must understand what *I* care about, lass." He paused at the top of a low hill where a sudden cold wind whipped his hair away from his shoulders in a dark cloud. "My great grandfather was carried off by pirates while still a lad and taken to the East, where he was sold to a powerful woman who kept many men for her pleasure."

"A male harem?" Intriguing concept.

"I dinna know what ye call it. My great grandfather was her favorite, and she taught him the secrets of the Pleasure Master. At her death, my great grandfather was freed. He returned to the clan wi' a bed, two cats, and a knowledge of how to pleasure a woman like no other man."

A hard smile touched his lips. "The duty of Pleasure Master falls to the first-born son. My brothers would deny it, but I am the first-born."

His smile softened, warmed. " 'Tis a duty I enjoy."

"I bet you do." Kathy drew in her breath. Wow, he was good. A five-alarmer with barely a lift of his lips. No false alarms here.

His smile faded. "My father has fallen in love and married. 'Tis forbidden. Now I am the Pleasure Master."

"Right. Don't want any pesky love and commitment getting in the way." She suspected her smile was bitter.

"Ye dinna understand. The Pleasure Master belongs to the clan. He canna serve the clan wi' a jealous wife getting in the way of his duty."

"Well, pooh on her for not understanding. Jealous wives are the pits." Ian Ross was *not* endearing himself to her.

His smile returned. "Ye must try me before ye mock."

Try me. Even the thought sent shocking ripples of heat to an area her ex-husband had left ice cold. "Think I'll pass on the offer. So, if your father is the *official* Pleasure Master, why've you been doing his duty?"

He shrugged. "A Pleasure Master must prepare for years, know all there is to know—"

"Got it. Practice makes perfect."

"But now my brothers have convinced the laird that they also have a right to the title, and though my father favors me, he must agree to a trial to see who is most worthy."

"Sure. Gotta have the most worthy." Kathy was barely listening as she processed the information and came up with a startling conclusion. "I think I missed something here. Your father has just now married for the first time?"

"Aye." He lifted his gaze to the darkening sky, his hair tangling around the face of a dark angel. "I am a bastard, as was my father before me."

"And how do you feel about that?" God, she sounded like her ex-husband in his sex counselor mode.

Ian stared at her. " 'Tis expected."

"Oh." This whole thing was growing more bizarre by the moment. "So, do you have a son to—"

Suddenly, his attention shifted to the path behind them. Grabbing her hand, he pulled her behind several large boulders. "Someone follows us."

No, no. She'd wanted him to keep talking. Somehow, it was important to know—"Following us? Who'd want to follow us?" Lost in his story, she'd forgotten for a while where she was, what had happened. Now the fear rushed back.

He put a finger to his lips, and they waited.

It didn't take long. Over the rise of the hill came Peter with Malin stretched majestically across his top. Peter's three short legs propelled him along at a surprising speed. When he finally reached the spot where they hid, he stopped and his amber lights blinked a welcome.

" 'Tis magic," Ian whispered.

"No, it must be some sort of tracking system." Sighing, Kathy walked over to Peter. "My . . . kingdom makes toys that react to light and motion. Peter's pretty sophisticated. I'm surprised I got him so cheap." She glanced nervously up at Ian, who'd emerged to stand beside her. "But it's not magic. No sorcery here. And I'm not a witch. Wouldn't recognize a witch if she whacked me over the head with her broomstick."

A smile touched the corner of Ian's mouth, whimsical and totally sincere. And totally take-me-to-bed dangerous. Kathy stomped down hard on all and sundry soft feelings toward him. Sacred duty, my foot. Nice life. Pass on the secret of joy, make a child, then move on. After all, Pleasure Masters don't marry. Convenient.

"Dinna fear me, lass. I wouldna care if ye had a caldron tucked beneath yer arm and a familiar attended ye." He cast Peter a thoughtful glance. "My great grandfather told of many things that couldna be explained."

He continued his trek down the path. Kathy followed wearily behind him, Peter chugging along cheerily by her side.

Where was Ian Ross going, and why was she going with him? *Because he's the only person you know, and what else do you have to do?*

Now on top of everything else, she had to put up with a tiny tin man following her. *No Emerald City down this path, Peter.* Maybe he was looking for a heart. Maybe she'd give him Ian Ross's. Oops, mistake. Ian Ross didn't have a heart either.

Engrossed in her thoughts of doom and gloom, she smacked into Ian's solid back with a grunt. "Hey, give me a break. Warn me when you decide to stop." Okay, she was being bitchy, but this situation called for a little bitchiness.

"Ye have a sharp tongue on ye, woman. I meant only to show ye the proof ye've demanded."

He'd stopped at the crest of a hill, and the wind plastered his clothing against his hard body. His wide shoulders seemed to dare the elements as the gale swept his hair in dark streamers from his face. A face that matched the grim beauty of the stark hills surrounding them and the roiling storm clouds gathering overhead.

The primitive power of man and nature frightened her, and she looked away, down the hill to—

No. It couldn't be. But it was. A village of stone cottages that could have burst from the pages of a history book. The few men visible wore the same belted garment as Ian Ross. No cars. No wires proclaiming electricity. No sign announcing: HISTORICAL REPRODUCTION. AUTHENTIC PRIMITIVE SCOTTISH VILLAGE. YOUR TAX DOLLARS AT WORK.

"Does yer New York look as this does, Kathy of Hair?"

Inexplicably, Ian's soft question acted as the lit match held to the powder keg of her denial, her brain-blip theory, her belief she'd wake and everything would be as it was before.

The trembling began in her soul and worked outward. Panic she'd managed to control behind a wall of logic exploded in waves of nausea. Her legs refused to support her and she sank to the rocky ground, still staring at the scene below. Tears streamed down her face, and she didn't care—not about the puffy eyes she'd have later, nor her loud embarrassing sniffles.

She sensed him. His heat, his scent. His arms wrapped around her, and he pulled her back against his chest. She heard the scrabble of his knees on the ground behind her, and her misery lifted for a minisecond while she worried about the pain of bare knees on pebbled earth.

The agony returned, and she clenched her arms tightly across her chest and rocked back and forth. She felt him move with her, then he turned her into his embrace and pressed her head to his chest as he sat back on his heels.

She burrowed her face into the rough wool and sobbed loudly, uncontrollably. Slowly, she slid down his body until her head rested on his lap. His voice murmured husky words of comfort in a language she didn't know.

And when she lay exhausted, drained of all the

tears she felt she could ever shed in a lifetime, he wiped her eyes with a cloth.

Only when she felt bare skin beneath her head did she realize he'd hiked up his wool garment, then used it to dry her eyes.

With her head pillowed on his bare thighs, she felt almost comfortable, safe.

Safe? With Ian Ross? *Never.* She was suddenly aware of the flex of hard muscle when he shifted his weight, of what lay beneath the edge of his shirt, of the scent of male, and the realization . . . *She was lying in the lap of a man who was more than 400 years old.*

He offered no help, didn't try to stop her when she scrambled awkwardly to her feet. She'd shown him weakness not even old PMS had seen. Ian Ross wouldn't see it again.

She stared down the slope at the village, anywhere but at the man who now stood beside her. She tried desperately to think of something other than the truth. Blinking, she finally registered what she saw. "Aren't those your brothers? Why're they standing naked in that stream?"

His bark of laughter startled her. "Ye must truly have put the terror in them. They think 'tis an abomination before God to bathe more than twice a year. But 'tis preferable to having their manhoods drop off at an inconvenient moment." He shrugged.

Suddenly, someone shouted and gazes turned up to where they stood. People poured from the cottages and Ian's brothers scrambled from the stream.

Kathy heard Ian's muttered curse.

"There's nothing for it. We must speak wi' them." Grabbing her hand, he started down the hill with her in tow.

"Do you think that's wise? I mean, your brothers didn't seem to have well-developed senses of humor. Uh, can you explain to them that I don't have any witch genes anywhere in my family? Mom wouldn't even let Aunt Betsy bring her tarot cards into the house." She could hear Peter clunking along behind her. Great. She might as well have a black cat slinking at her side.

The villagers met them halfway down the hill. The two naked giants had managed to wrap themselves in their plaids. Kathy noted that their love guns were well covered.

" 'Tis the woman! The one who would steal our manhoods," the one named Colin announced to the huddled masses behind him.

Why would any thinking woman want to do that? "Look, I'm not interested in men or their hoods. Definitely don't want any part of a man."

"And she brings a demon wi' her," Colin continued, unfazed.

Demon? Where? Kathy followed the horrified gazes down to . . . *Peter?* Uh-oh. Peter's amber lights blinked happily. He obviously didn't understand the situation.

The brother named Neil puffed out his chest and stepped forward. Cautiously. "We must destroy the woman and her wee spawn of hell."

Wee spawn of hell? Not in her wildest imagination would she classify Peter as anything more than a little pain-in-the-butt. In fact, she . . . Hmm. What had come right before the spawn of hell bit? She widened her eyes. *Destroy the woman. Ohmigod! I'm outta here.*

Her legs were already in running mode when someone lifted her from her feet and pulled her against a rock-hard body. "Calm yerself, lass. Ye'll come to no harm," Ian Ross assured her in a low rumble.

Easy for him to say. No one was trying to turn him into a toasted marshmallow. The whole scruffy mob looked like it was just itching to have a witch burning. Okay, so the itching part probably came from all the freeloaders living on their infrequently washed bodies.

"Ye willna harm her. This is Kathy, Princess of Hair. She has traveled far to learn the secrets of the Pleasure Master so that she might find joy in a man's touch. Her father, King Clairol, has ruled that she must marry, but she canna abide a man's lovemaking. In return, she has brought strange and wonderful things from her kingdom to pay for my service. Ye'll welcome her as a guest to the Highlands." Ian smiled, obviously pleased with himself.

What? He'd said she was *what?* "Uh, I beg to differ with—"

"Hold yer tongue, lass, if ye expect to live through the day."

Put that way, she supposed—

Colin stepped forward, a sly grin splitting his bearded face. " 'Tis the woman we've waited long for, Ian. A true challenge for the Pleasure Master. A woman who canna be wooed, and one who when angered carries deadly potions that may unman the bravest warrior." He looked pleased by the thought. "If she willingly joins wi' ye, Neil and I willna argue yer right to be Pleasure Master. Ye owe the clan proof that ye be worthy."

Ian's lips thinned, and his gaze narrowed to gray slits of danger. "And what proof will ye give the clan that Neil or ye are *more* worthy?"

Those in the crowd nodded their heads, acknowledging the fairness of Ian's question.

Ian's lips tipped up in a smile that never reached his eyes. "As ye have chosen for me, I will choose for ye. 'Tis fair."

The mob mumbled its agreement. Colin and Neil looked worried.

"I must think for a while on who to choose for ye." Ian's smile was pure evil.

Kathy had had enough. "You have to be kidding. This sounds like a script from the World Wrestling Federation. In this corner we have the Great Seducer, defending his Pleasure Master title against all comers." She stood on tiptoe to glare at him. "Well, let me tell you, Ian Ross, you've just met Kathy the Unseduceable, so get ready to lose—"

She got no further. Lowering his head, he kissed her. There was no softness in the kiss, no tentative first touching of lips. It was a brand, pure and simple. Ian Ross's sold sign, like the one she'd plunked in her front yard two weeks after PMS and Joan had done their thing in her bed.

She wasn't sure at what point the kiss changed. She just knew his lips softened, tempted in a way she'd never thought a kiss could tempt. The tip of his tongue traced her lips and when she parted them, slid inside.

Opening to him, she explored his mouth as he did hers, wondered at the sudden rush of need, her pounding heart and a heat that had her wishing she could stop long enough to shed her coat and every other darn thing she wore. His kiss was liquid lightning, crackling along her nerve endings and exploding in white-hot desire.

When he finally released her, she stood staring blindly at him, knowing in her heart she'd never experience a kiss like that again. And wondering how he'd done it. How had he wrung a response from her in thirty seconds that her ex, who'd read every book ever written about women's sexuality, hadn't achieved in five years of marriage?

And Ian Ross had done it with just his lips and tongue. What greatness could he rise to if he used the rest of his body? The thought was frightening, *intriguing*.

Suddenly, she grew aware of the silence. Glancing around, she met the avid stares of the villagers, who waited with bated breath to see whether the Pleasure Master had triumphed with just one kiss.

No way. She'd sat through every Mel Gibson and Brad Pitt movie, even a Ricky Martin concert, and lived to tell the tale. No Highlander from 1542 was going to reduce her to a whimpering puddle with just a kiss.

71

He was only a medieval copy of her ex, and she had more important things to think about. Like how to get back to New York by February 14 so she could destroy Peter Matthew Stone in court.

Appearance is everything. She stepped away from Ian Ross. She yawned. "That was adequate. Not great, but adequate." *That was a nuclear explosion, and I was standing at ground zero.*

A loud "oooh" of admiration swept through the crowd. Colin and Neil looked gleeful.

Ian's expression of concern was belied by the amused glitter in his eyes. " 'Tis a difficult task ye've set me, Colin. The lass must stay wi' me so I may give her my full attention."

"Aye," the crowd agreed.

Colin and Neil didn't look quite so pleased now.

Kathy wasn't pleased at all. "Hey, wait just a minute—"

Ian leaned close. "Do ye wish to stay wi' them, lass?"

"Umm." She glanced at the villagers. One toothless old man grinned at her and winked. "Maybe not."

Nodding, he turned and started walking back up the hill.

" 'Tis a lucky woman ye be," a female voice murmured.

"Aye," another agreed.

Kathy thought it all depended on your perspective, but right now Ian Ross seemed the lesser of two evils. Turning, she hurried after him.

He was walking too fast again. Since she couldn't

get close enough to berate him, she made do with something closer. "This is all your fault, Peter."

Peter clattered along beside her, still wearing Malin as a hat, totally oblivious to all the trouble he'd caused.

"If you hadn't followed me, I might've convinced those very strange people that I was just like them. Okay, maybe not. I've never seen so much bad hair gathered in one spot before." She shuddered at the thought of all those sun-bleached split ends.

And that, of course, reminded her of home. *Don't think of that now.* Maybe tonight, in the comforting darkness where she could pretend nothing had happened, she'd take out today's horror and examine it.

She quickly shifted her thoughts back to Peter. "Now I have to live with Mr. Pleasure Master in his cave. And it's all your fault." Good. She'd found a scapegoat.

Beside her, Rhett Butler drawled, "Frankly, my dear, I don't give a damn."

Chapter Four

Ian listened to the woman's restless movements in the darkness and waited. Silently. He'd learned the power of silence, whether lying in wait for an enemy when a sound could mean death, or beside a woman, touching her with quiet, allowing her desire to build. Seducing her in all the ways that needed no words, no glide of flesh against flesh. And there were many, as Kathy of Hair would soon know.

But tonight was not the time. Tonight she thought only of this New York she believed she came from. *And what if what she says is true?* He did not close his mind to all things different, but this seemed overmuch to believe.

No, even with her strange speech and the odd things she brought with her, he could lie beside her now, run his fingers the length of her smooth body, touch her as he'd touched so many women, and she'd be like all other women.

She moved again, and he drew in an impatient breath. There was nothing for it. He must speak with her or neither of them would sleep this night.

Pulling his plaid around him, he rose and walked to where she lay. He sat beside her, letting her feel his presence.

"Ian?"

His aloneness, his oneness with all things physical, opened him to the things that other men could not see. The woman's fear and confusion broke over him in waves of tortured feeling. A canny hunter would strike while the prey was weak. He thought about it, then dismissed the idea. Not tonight.

"Ye canna sleep."

"I never sleep well in a new place. And your bed isn't exactly floating-cloud quality. Besides, it's too quiet. I'm used to traffic, people." The darkness softened her voice, rounded the sharp edges of her complaint.

She sighed. "I'm sorry, Ian. Forget the last whine. It's not the bed, it's . . ."

He could hear the tears in her voice, knew she'd cried in the darkness, muffling the sound so she wouldn't wake him. " 'Tis the darkness that feeds yer fears. When ye canna see, ye turn yer thoughts inward."

"But how did I get here? How will I get back? *Why* am I here?"

He had no answers, so instead he rose and used the still-hot remains of the hearth fire to light a candle, then returned to her side. In the flickering light, he searched for the truth.

"Hey, I've got it." Her choked laughter held no happiness. "The Great-Hairdresser-in-the-Sky couldn't stand looking at dry split ends here for another century so She sent me."

He sensed the silent scream behind her words.

He watched her turn onto her side, then prop herself up on one elbow. Listened to the rustle of her clothes. Caught his breath at the blue glitter of her eyes in the candlelight. Felt the first familiar stirrings.

"You know, that whole idea is funny. There was this . . . God, I'm already talking in the past tense." The thought seemed to upset her. He could see it in the aimless patterns she traced on his fur, recognized it in her uneasy pause.

"I watched *Ghostbusters* on video last week. You have to understand, I'm a huge movie fan. Anyway, all through the movie they kept repeating, 'Who you gonna call?' I guess that's me. No offense, but your friends have to have the worst hair in the universe." She shrugged. "Desperate times call for desperate measures. So someone or something yanked me into your time to fix it."

"Ye believe this?" What was a video? What was a ghostbuster?

"No." Her voice was small, lost. "Look, I don't want to deal with my problem tonight. I don't know *how* to deal with it."

"Aye, well since ye must stay here for a time, I could tell ye about the people, about—"

"Tell me about *you*, Ian."

"What would ye know?"

"Everything."

He smiled. "Ye dinna ask much, lass." Without thinking, he pushed back a lock of her hair that had fallen across her forehead. Her sudden flinch made him wonder. "Ye're not comfortable wi' men."

Her glance turned defiant. "I'm fine. I just don't want anyone touching me."

Ye will, lass, ye will.

Her gaze dropped beneath his stare. "Anyway, we're not talking about me. Let's hear about you, about your family."

Would ye have me speak of those who come to me in the night, of their secrets, their fears? Would ye know of the blood shed in the name of the Pleasure Master?

He smiled. He would tell her what she expected and let the darkness keep its secrets.

Shrugging, he stared into the shadowed corner where Malin slept peacefully atop Peter. " 'Tis a short tale. Since I was the first-born, I was taken from my mother at nine years to begin learning my duties as Pleasure Master." *'Twas pleased enough she was to rid herself of a bastard Ross.* "I fight for the clan when need be." He narrowed his gaze. "And I spend overmuch time avoiding the Mackays."

"You know, I wasn't much of a history buff in

77

school, but I would've remembered this Pleasure Master stuff."

Puzzling. She spoke as though she truly did live in a future time. "We are a small clan, and few brave the Highlands to find us. We dinna have visitors other than the Mackays, and they only to raid our cattle." *And the women who come to me. So many of them.* He could close his eyes and feel their warm bodies moving beneath him, inhale the scents of exotic oil and desire. Veiled women, who when the night ended returned to London or farther with a gift none other could give, a secret they dared never share.

"We are the only clan wi' a Pleasure Master." How had *she* found them? She could not have survived such a harsh journey carrying only her strange "toys." The Mackays?

He watched a line form between her eyes, confusion fill her gaze. "Funny, but I wouldn't expect a primitive isolated society to bother with something like a Pleasure Master."

He didn't understand many of her words, but he could guess their meaning. "The clan has gained fame from the Pleasure Master, and those who come from afar enrich the villagers." Ian found it amusing that a bit of gold and fame would make him a source of pride to the clan, when without those things he would probably be damned as an abomination.

He saw her need to ask more about the fame and enriching, but other questions pulled at her.

"How does your mother feel about this Pleasure

Master stuff? Doesn't she want you to fall in love, have a family of your own?"

He shrugged. "My mother is dead. I ne'er saw her again after my father took me."

"Oh."

He recognized the glint of sympathy in her gaze and wondered at it. " 'Tis no matter. I didna need my mother." *Any more than my mother needed me.*

She offered him an uncertain smile. "Well, at least you had your father's love."

Now he was truly puzzled. "My father hasna e'er loved me. Love isna important. He taught me what I need know to be the next Pleasure Master. 'Twas his duty."

Her expression turned frantic. "Your brothers. You're triplets, for heaven's sake. You have to be close to them."

He grinned. "Ye dinna understand us, lass. We havena e'er agreed overmuch about anything. They wouldna grieve if I were gone."

Her look of horror wiped the grin from his face. "Ye're too tender, Kathy of Hair. Accept that love has no part in my life. The clan must know that I canna love any that come to me, that I can only teach them what needs teaching, then return them wi' their hearts untouched, their secrets safe. 'Tis the only way the Pleasure Master can exist. He must be beyond love for any one woman."

He gentled his voice. "But if ye desire to know joys of the body such as ye've ne'er known before, mayhap I can show ye the power of the Pleasure Master."

She'd forgotten. He'd made that stupid bet with his brothers. He had to seduce her to be the Pleasure Master. So why this panic? He hadn't a prayer of lighting her fire. She should just let him try, get it out of his system.

No. She couldn't. And she *wasn't* afraid. Fine, so he'd made her feel something earlier, but she'd been in shock then. People didn't act normally when they were in shock. "Forget it. No joys of the body tonight. Let's play a game."

"Game?"

She could feel his confusion. Good. A confused Pleasure Master wouldn't have time to plan seduction.

"Play?" His voice turned warm, husky.

Okay, nothing to worry about. This was probably his sitting-with-woman-in-darkness voice. Automatic. He wasn't even thinking about touching her.

Touching her. Imagine. His fingers sliding across her flesh, circling each nipple. Then his lips on her breasts, drawing each nipple into his mouth. Hot, demanding.

She dragged in a deep breath. It was steaming in here. Who'd turned up the thermostat? She'd just turn it down. . . . Problem. No thermostat.

She glanced up, met his silver gaze across the flickering candle flame, and *knew.*

"Stop it." She couldn't control the wobble in her voice. "Stop it right now."

"Stop what, lass?" His lips tilted up in a smile that invited. Promised.

"Stop what you're trying to do to me." She

wasn't so sure now. What *had* he been trying to do? Maybe nothing. Maybe shock was causing her to imagine things. "Oh, never mind. I'll get a game."

She scrambled to her feet, putting distance between herself and any possible pleasure field that might surround him. Of course, the whole idea was nonsense. *What happened to you today should be nonsense, too.*

Rooting around in the large plastic bag, she pulled out a checkers game. Safe. Easy for him to understand.

She wondered . . . She stuck her head into the bag. "Send me home. Someone in here send me home."

"Ye begin to sound much like Mad Mary. She speaks to her hens. Ye speak to a sack."

Before drawing her head from the bag, she grabbed a small yellow sunflower. She had no idea what it was supposed to do.

Closing the bag, she turned to glare at Ian. "If I can talk to someone who's been dead for more than four hundred years, I can talk to a bag."

"Aye, but—"

"Besides, I wasn't talking to the bag. I was talking to the toys."

He shook his head. " 'Tis a great need to talk ye have. Mayhap I can speak wi' Mad Mary. She might gift ye wi' one of her hens and—"

"Not funny, Ross." Holding the flower and the checkers box, she hurried over to Peter. "Okay, the game's up, Peter. Send me home."

Malin growled his displeasure while Peter's amber lights flashed happily. "E.T. phone home."

She sighed. "Right. Phone home."

" 'Tis sorcery."

The sudden tension in Ian's voice startled her. Kathy turned to catch him staring intently at Peter. She indulged in some mental head-slapping. Ian hadn't been close enough before to hear Peter speak. "No. Definitely not sorcery. Just some wires, circuits, and a computer chip thrown in there somewhere. Someone programmed him with a bunch of movie quotes, and he spouts them at totally inappropriate moments." She cast Peter a meaningful glare. Then she dared a glance at Ian. Nope, he hadn't understood a word she'd said.

Trudging back to her glorified cot, she sat down. "Where's H. G. Wells when you need him?"

"Who is H. G. Wells, and why would ye have need of him?"

She sighed. "He was a writer who wrote about a time machine and . . . Oh, never mind. Who sent me here, Ian?" She couldn't keep the despair from her voice.

"I dinna know, but I wouldna think one of yer toys could do so." He pulled the checkerboard from the box and set it between them.

His voice sounded relaxed, but she still sensed his unease over Peter's speech.

"Well, *something* did." Absently, she put the sunflower on the cushion next to her and studied it.

Huge blue eyes blinked open. Waving its leaves

madly and wiggling its stem to an imaginary beat, the small flower announced, "I loooove you," in a high-pitched little-girl voice.

"Great. Just great," Kathy muttered. Scrambling to her feet, she picked the flower up and transferred it to a ledge beside the hearth. "Don't want to mention the *L* word around here, honey."

The flower's eyes closed, and it fell silent as Kathy returned to her seat across from Ian. "It must have motion sensors like Peter, but Peter's technology seems a lot more complex. I still can't figure out why he was so cheap. The price tag must've . . ."

Her words trickled into silence as she glanced at Ian.

He sat transfixed, his gaze riveted on the sunflower. His hands shook as he grasped the checkers box in a crushing grip.

Uh-oh. Major mistake. From the look on Ian's face he intended to stomp the hapless flower into tiny plastic pieces. Why hadn't she thought before she—

"I dinna ken how ye make things move and talk that havena life."

"Not me. I don't make them do anything. They come that way from the toy factory. All I do is push the button. Anyone can push a button. *You* can push a button." She wanted to make that perfectly clear. No way was she going to end up the featured attraction at a Highland wienie roast. Make that a witchie roast.

She smiled brightly. "Go right on over to the bag

and stick your hand in. Push a button, any button."
From the look on his face, he'd rather stick his hand
into a bag of vipers. "I don't blame you for being
afraid because—"

"I dinna fear ye or the things ye brought wi' ye."
His gaze turned hard, and for a moment she saw
the stranger he really was.

Something niggled at her subconscious, a feeling
that beneath his sensuality lurked the heart of a
dark predator, moving silently through the frightening world that wasn't *her* world, stalking her.

She'd let him see her weakness today, but she
wouldn't do that again, wouldn't turn her back on
him again.

"Oh, come on, Ross. Give me a break. Your
brothers were terrified, and you're trying to tell
me—"

" 'Tis why my brothers willna be Pleasure Master."

He was as strange to her as any fabled creature
rising from Loch Ness's depths, and she knew her
expression revealed her thoughts.

"You don't love. You don't fear. What do you
feel, Ian Ross?"

"*I* dinna feel, lass. I make *others* feel." But he *did*
feel with this woman—unease with her toys that
seemed much too alive, frustration with his desire
to know the meanings of all her strange words,
and . . . uncertainty with her. Of all his feelings,
uncertainty was the most unsettling.

He must put all emotions aside, though, if he intended to remain Pleasure Master. He had to join

with this woman, and he would use his power in any way necessary. Tonight would be the beginning.

Absently, he pushed the game aside and reached for her foot. She'd kept on all her clothes, removing only her footwear. Wise lass.

Grasping her ankle, he lifted her foot onto his lap. He felt her sudden tensing. "Ye're safe, lass." *Ye'll ne'er be safe from me, Kathy of Hair.* "I mean only to warm ye. When the hearth fire burns low, a chill creeps in."

She remained stiff, unyielding. But she didn't pull her foot away. He smiled. It mattered not. The vixen could run from the hunter, but in the end she'd find no hiding place, would want none.

Cupping her foot in his palms, he rubbed a rhythmic pattern. Slow, deep strokes. " 'Tis wondrous, the feel of flesh against flesh. Close yer eyes and give yerself to the heat, the pleasure. Dinna think of today, the morrow. Think only of now, of the touching." He purposely lowered his voice to a murmur.

He'd meant only to lull this time, but her unblinking, wide-eyed stare told him she felt the change even as he felt it. The tightening in his groin, the pressure of his growing erection.

Strange. He'd learned control of his own body even as he learned to control the bodies of others. He must work harder to guard his reactions with this woman.

Holding her gaze with his, he slid her foot tightly against his erection, gasped at the pleasure-pain of the pressure, and wondered why she didn't seek to free herself. Knowing he would gain no release on this night, he still increased his torture by rubbing her foot over his flesh, until his groin's throbbing pulsed in every part of his body.

"No."

Her one strangled word was enough. He released her, but she didn't jerk her foot away.

Instead, she clenched her foot, tightening the pressure until he couldn't suppress a groan of agony at his own need, at the anticipation of pleasure.

Then slowly, she slid her foot from his lap. "I . . . I think I'm warm now."

He knew his smile was one of triumph even as he forced his breathing back to a normal rhythm. "Ye felt the power, Kathy of Hair."

"Power?" She looked uncertain, but beneath the uncertainty he saw the beginnings of realization.

Aye, she would learn. "I freed ye, yet ye didna move away. Ye pressed yer foot more tightly against my flesh. Why?"

"I . . . I don't know." She glanced away, but not before he saw her confusion.

"Ye do, lass." He allowed his thoughts, his desire to move over her.

She turned back to him. "What're you getting at, Ian?"

"The joy to be had between a man and woman has many layers. Ye just experienced one. Ye held the power to do what ye would wi' my body, to give pain or pleasure. Didna ye feel the clenching in yer own body even as ye pressed against mine? Didna this man ye left in New York allow ye power over him?"

"No."

He didn't know which question she answered, but it didn't matter. She would think about what he'd said, and that was enough.

"Sleep, lass. I'll not touch ye again." *Tonight.*

"It wouldn't do you any good. I'm seduce-proof. Remember?"

"Aye." He heard the defiance in her voice and smiled. Mayhap she'd prove a challenge, and he loved challenges. "But still, I wouldna wish to send ye running into the night like a deer from the wolf."

"You're no wolf, Ross." Her laugh sounded breathless. "A wolf mates for life."

She lay down and turned her back to him, leaving him with the unsettling knowledge that she thought him less than a beast that ran on four legs.

But what she thought of him didn't matter. He must remember that. The only important thing was that he meet his brothers' challenge, that he seduce this one woman. And the pleasure he'd give her would be hers to remember when she returned to New York.

He strode to the hearth fire and stirred up the dying flame.

"I loooove you."

He glared at the wiggling flower as he added wood to the fire. His brothers. He must pay them in kind for their challenge. He would find women for them who truly couldn't be seduced, at least by men who knew so little about a woman's pleasure.

He paced away from the fire, then back.

"I loooove you."

But he couldn't concentrate on his brothers tonight, could only think of the woman who lay so close, could only imagine her heat surrounding him, welcoming him. He continued to pace.

"I loooove you."

He pictured the moment she would look into his eyes and *know,* what he truly was, what they would share. His step quickened at the thought.

"I loooove you."

Clenching his fists, he swung to face the wee yellow demon. "God's teeth, will ye cease yer blathering about love!"

And surprisingly, the flower was quiet.

Breathing deeply, he turned to see if the woman had noticed his loss of control, but her loose-limbed stillness told him that she slept.

Exhaling sharply, he crouched and stared into the heart of the flame. "I give ye tonight, Kathy of Hair. Rest well. For not even a score of strange minions will save ye from me."

"I loooove you."

Chapter Five

The sounds woke Kathy. From the muted clicks and scrapes, she guessed maintenance workers must be in her apartment hallway. They could at least wait until nine o'clock. And she must be getting the mother of all colds because it felt like an elephant was sitting on her chest. No wonder, after standing in the sleet last night waiting for . . .

The elephant purred.

She opened her eyes to meet Malin's unblinking yellow stare, and the horror of yesterday came pouring back. She groaned.

"Ye dinna sound well, lass. Do ye have a pain?"

"It's lying on me." She turned her head enough to see Ian seated on a rug with pieces of something scattered around him.

The sheer power she felt when she looked at him

again forced her to draw a deep breath. Malin growled at the sudden rise of her chest.

Ian's hair, a dark tangle of temptation, framed his face as he leaned over his work. *His hair.* Before she went back to New York, and she would go back, she had to run her fingers through those strands.

She'd start with a shampoo, some conditioner, then snip off a few ends. . . .

Kathy turned on her side, and Malin plopped off her stomach onto the fur. He ratcheted his growl up a notch. "Sorry, Your Nastiness." She braved Malin's wrath by offering him a brief head scratch, and his growl subsided to a grumbling complaint.

"Malin has decided he likes ye."

"Could've fooled me." And after she memorized the texture of Ian's hair, she'd go home, because she had too many things to do.

" 'Tis a great honor. Ye dinna want to be one whom Malin doesna like."

"Bad things happen?"

"Aye."

Forget Malin. Kathy had some major issues to address. She could deal with the toilet situation, but there was something even more important. "Coffee? Tell me you have coffee in 1542."

"Coffee?"

No. She couldn't function as a rational human being without her two cups of coffee. Only one thing could help her cope with a world sans coffee. "Okay, I'll settle for a piece of chocolate."

"What is chocolate?"

Kathy stared at him. Impossible. She knew her history. When old Noah had loaded his ark, he'd taken two of every animal and a bag of Hershey Kisses. How to explain the wonder of chocolate to one who'd never tasted it? "Chocolate is . . . smooth, rich, and sweet. It makes a bad day good, and a rotten date okay. It's . . . chocolate."

"This chocolate sounds wondrous, but I havena any to give ye."

No coffee? No chocolate? She couldn't stay here.

"What're you doing?" Okay, she'd keep a positive attitude today. This time-travel stuff had to work both ways. So all she had to do was figure out how she got here, then figure a way to go home. Not impossible for an intelligent, twenty-first century woman, right?

Before her positive attitude could spring a leak, she climbed to her feet and padded over to where Ian was still engrossed in his work. She narrowed her gaze. Those small yellow pieces looked familiar. They looked like . . .

"Suzy Sunshine. Those are Suzy Sunshine pieces. What've you done to her?"

He raised his gaze to hers, and the intensity of his silver stare almost made her forget New York and the unfortunate Suzy Sunshine.

"I took the wee flower apart to see how it worked." He slid his gaze the length of her body, and a heated sizzle followed its path. "I have a great curiosity about *all* things."

Hah. She could fling innuendoes as well as the

next guy. "Well, I hope you don't expect to run around taking apart everything you don't understand? One of those *things* might rear up and sock you in the jaw."

"Mayhap." He grinned, dissolving her crusty morning attitude like warm water melting snow.

Speaking of warm water . . . "Umm, any chance of my getting some water to clean up with?"

"Aye." He nodded toward a tunnel branching off from the main room. "Ye'll find a small pool of water there."

Translation: water colder than Arctic ice in a tunnel darker than a New York alley. Not inviting. She shivered.

His gaze softened. "I could bring water from the pool and heat it over the fire. Ye could bathe by the hearth."

"And where would you go?" She already knew the answer, but it was always good to get verbal confirmation.

"I would sit and watch ye. 'Tis a thing to be enjoyed, *shared*." His lids drifted half closed, but that did nothing to hide his hot anticipation of all that sharing.

Fine. At least cold water would get her circulation moving and wake up the old brain so it could contribute its share toward her going-home plans. She grumbled her way back to the bed, mumbled as she slipped her socks and boots back on, then paused in her chant of discontent long enough to ask, "What do I wash with, leaves and sand?"

She didn't mistake the glitter of amusement in

his gaze, and she also didn't mistake her own re-action to his magnetic pull on all things female in her. When the Power responsible for sex and temp-tation handed out pheromones, She must have lost her place after getting a look at Ian Ross because She'd given him a double dose.

Ian rose in one lithe movement, strode to a small wooden chest, and lifted out several items. He brought them over to Kathy. "Ye have a poor opin-ion of me, lass."

She took the items gingerly, making sure she touched no part of him. Touching Ian would not be something a thinking woman should attempt be-fore her first cup of coffee. *No coffee.* She'd for-gotten.

She glanced up at Ian. Of course, there would be compensations. She looked back down at the things he'd given her. "Scented soap and real cloth?"

His smile flowed over her—teasing, inviting, *dangerous.* "Women like to gift me wi' small re-membrances of them. 'Tis kind of them."

Kind? She didn't think so. All six feet plus of him towered above her. Raw masculinity and smooth seduction. Harsh beauty and hidden depths. Com-binations most women would find irresistible. Ex-cept Kathy Bartlett. She'd have no problem resisting him. She glanced up at him again. Sure. No problem at all.

"Well, I'll just trot on down this tunnel. Be back in a flash." Then she'd call the smartest person she knew to help her get the heck out of here.

She'd taken only a few steps when her cell phone rang.

Ian's nostrils flared like a wild stallion scenting danger. Hmm. The stallion image needed to be explored. *After* she begged whomever was on her phone to find New York for her.

She walked to her purse and pulled out her phone. Taking a deep breath, she spoke. "Hello." Did she sound calm, serious, *sane?*

"You have papers to sign, girlfriend, so we can kick your ex's sorry butt all over that courtroom. Where are you?"

Kathy closed her eyes. *Yes.* The smartest person she knew. Coco—friend and attorney. "I'm tied up. . . . Well, not literally. I'm . . . Oh, what the hell, I'm in Scotland."

There was a moment of silence while Coco digested this. "Scotland."

"Scotland in 1542." Kathy watched Ian edge closer so he could listen.

"Scotland. 1542." Long silence. "I guess that means you won't be able to make our meeting today. I could reschedule."

"I'm not joking, Coco. Something happened yesterday. I don't have a clue what, but I ended up here. Believe me." Forget calm. Concentrate on sane.

"Here? Here like in Scotland?"

Kathy listened as Coco rustled papers. Probably looking for the number to her local mental health clinic. "I know it sounds crazy, but I'm really in Scotland."

"I hope this is about a man, because if it isn't, we've got real problems. Do you have a man there?"

"Yes, there's a man, but—"

Kathy had no time to say more. The phone was taken firmly from her.

Ian gazed at the phone, then put it to his ear. "If it's a man ye desire, I can help ye. Ye must know that a man doesna want a lass who talks overmuch, so ye must curb yer need to blather."

"And *you* are?"

Uh-oh. Coco's thunder voice, discernible across entire continents without the benefit of modern technology. Kathy winced. Coco had been known to reduce tough men to tears with that voice.

"Ian Ross. And ye sound like a bonny lass."

"Cut the crap. Are you holding Kathy against her will? If you are, I'll charge you with kidnapping, unlawful transportation across state lines, intention to—" Ian held the phone away from his ear and blinked.

He glanced at Kathy. "What does 'cut the crap' mean?"

Kathy rolled her eyes.

He put the phone back against his ear. "Yer voice would entice the strongest man if ye didna deafen him first." Ian closed his eyes. "Ye should wear black, lass. One wi' yer boldness must have hair the color of flame. Red hair trailing down yer back and a brawny man to run his fingers through it. Ye're a woman of fire, Coco. Ye deserve a strong man."

There was complete silence on the other end of the line for so long that Kathy feared Coco had fainted from the shock of a man talking back to her. She pulled the phone away from Ian. "Coco? Are you okay?"

"Who *is* that man?" Coco actually sounded . . . bemused. "He's right, of course. I need a strong man. How'd he know I have red hair? When you get back in town, maybe I could meet him. If that's okay with you, of course?"

"Sure. No problem." Kathy stared blindly at the far wall where a tapestry filled with fantastic winged creatures hung. *Fantastic.* Who would ever believe her story? No one. "My car's sitting on I-95 near my exit if no one's stripped it or towed it away yet. And would you check on my apartment until I get back, Coco?"

"You're not going to tell me what you're really doing?" Coco sounded serious suddenly. "Strange time to take a vacation. You aren't the impulsive type. Are you sure everything's okay?"

"Wonderful." No one in either time would ever believe her. "Do me a favor. Find out if anything important happened in Scotland in 1542."

"Really into this Scotland thing, aren't you?"

"More than you'll ever know. I—" Kathy's concentration was shattered as the sound of footsteps in the tunnel signaled a visitor.

She took the phone from her ear and turned in time to see one of Ian's brothers burst into the room. Hard to tell which one with all that facial hair.

"Have ye chosen for me, Ian? 'Tisn't fair that ye have more time to woo yer lass than I have." He strode over to stand beside Ian, then cast a startled glance at Kathy's phone. "It doesna matter which wench ye choose. There isna a lass I canna have." He leaned close to the phone, then put out a tentative finger to touch it.

"There's another man there. I can hear him. Sounds like an arrogant macho jerk. Put him on." Kathy winced as Coco's demand carried clearly to the two men.

Ian grinned. "I dinna know what a macho jerk is, Neil, but it doesna sound like ye've won Coco."

Neil turned pale and swallowed hard, and Kathy could almost feel his need to run from her phone. But she had to give him credit. Seeing that Ian didn't run, Neil stood his ground. Barely.

"What demon's tool is that, Ian?" His voice was strangled.

" 'Tis one of the wondrous things Kathy of Hair has brought from her land. She can speak wi' those she's left in her kingdom."

" 'Tis passing strange." Neil reached for the phone with fingers that shook. "I would speak wi' this Coco. She has insulted Neil Ross. It isna a thing I take lightly." He glanced at Kathy uncertainly. "Who is this Coco?"

Kathy was having a hard time keeping a straight face. Maybe she was getting used to the idea of being in this place, because it was the first time she'd felt like laughing since her expensive lemon had overheated. "Coco is my . . . dragonslayer."

Neil looked suitably awed. " 'Tis impossible for a weak woman to do such deeds."

"I heard that, bozo." Coco's voice dripped icy venom.

Neil's gaze narrowed as he put the phone to his ear. " 'Tisn't seemly for a woman to speak so to a man. Ye must learn to respect those stronger and wiser than ye."

Kathy backed away from the phone. *Massive explosion imminent.*

"And that would be . . . ? You sorry piece of dog doo-doo. I'll respect those *stronger and wiser* than me when I meet them. You're not it, buster. I'd chew you up and spit you out if I had you in court. I *hate* Neanderthal boneheads who think that just because they have a penis, it makes them gods."

Neil looked shocked.

"Gotta give you credit, though. You have balls. No man has talked to me like that in years and kept them."

Neil glanced down. Probably to check that the body parts in question were still attached. Coco had that effect on men.

"Oh, and I'm only Coco to my friends. You may call me Ms. Jones, Attorney at Law. Tell Kathy she doesn't have much more play time. It's already January fourth. I'll talk to her later, and you can go to hell."

Everyone stood in frozen silence as the disconnect click announced Coco had hung up.

January fourth? How could it be January fourth

when—? Kathy felt Ian move closer. She didn't have to see him to know where he was, *what* he was. Even if her mind suggested this Pleasure Master stuff was all nonsense, her body, her senses recognized him.

She glanced up in time to catch his wicked grin.

" 'Tis an unfortunate first meeting, Neil, but ye'll do better next time."

Neil narrowed his gaze. " 'Twould give me more joy to talk wi' one of Mad Mary's hens than to speak wi' that woman again. 'Tis glad I am she dwells in another kingdom, or I might throttle the bold wench."

Kathy tried to tamp down her growing uneasiness. She didn't like the glitter in Ian's gaze or his expression of false sympathy.

" 'Tis sad I am to hear ye say so, Neil, because I've chosen Coco as yer challenge. 'Twill take a *true* Pleasure Master's skill to win such a lass."

Ian shifted closer to Kathy, close enough for his arm to slide along the silk covering her arm, close enough to feel her quiver at his touch, close enough to silently show his brother that Kathy was his.

"Ye wouldna do such a thing to me, Ian." Neil gingerly handed the phone back to Kathy. "No man could seduce a demon voice coming from yon devil's toy. It isna a true test. I canna see or touch the lass."

Ian narrowed his gaze. "Was it fair to choose for me a woman who proclaimed she had no interest in any man?"

99

The woman in question seemed to be enjoying their argument overmuch. "Well, at least you can touch me, Ian."

Ian smiled at her. "Aye, that I can. And will." He allowed his lids to drift half closed, imagining his hands, his mouth, on her smooth body. "Ye'll ne'er forget Ian Ross's touch."

"Arrogant." She moved away from him.

"Truthful." It didn't matter how far she moved, how far she ran, he'd find her.

"I'm not going to argue over something that doesn't matter. I won't be here long enough for you to seduce me, and when I leave I'll take Coco with me." She offered him a parting glare as she scooped up the soap, cloths, and a small object from the thing she called her purse, then headed for the tunnel leading to the pool. "Oh, and don't take my phone apart while I'm gone."

Neil cast him a sharp glance. "She doesna sound like a lass whose father sent her here to learn the pleasures of a man's body."

Ian shrugged. "She doesna wish to marry and doesna believe any man can bring her joy. 'Tis a difficult task Colin and ye have set me."

Neil looked uncertain, but forged ahead. "Ye should prepare another to take yer place, Ian. What if Mackay captures ye? Or what if those from the kirk who wish ye dead succeed?"

"The Pleasure Master has been a part of the clan for nigh a hundred years. The people wouldna allow it." *But what about Kathy of Hair?* The kirk could accuse the lass of witchcraft without fear of retaliation. He must guard her well.

"Ye keep the secrets of many families, Ian. Their secrets would die wi' ye. 'Tis a tempting thought to some."

Ian nodded. "No matter. There can be only one Pleasure Master."

Neil's gaze turned calculating. "But ye could train another, just as Father trained ye. Ye have no son of yer own to pass the secrets to, so ye should train Colin or me to take yer place. 'Tis common sense."

"Ye've given me much to think on, Neil." He grinned at his brother. "Mayhap I'll do what ye wish. . . ."

Neil's eyes lit with triumph.

"After we've decided who is the true Pleasure Master." He clapped Neil on the back. "Ye may visit often to speak wi' Coco. Tell Colin I'll speak wi' him today about his challenge."

Neil drew in a deep breath and stared hard at his brother, then cast a meaningful glance at Peter and the phone. "The woman is verra strange, and the things she carries wi' her seem bewitched. Dinna forget I was there when ye first met. She appeared out of the mist wi' no sound. How did she reach us wi' no sound, no warning? Who really sent her, brother?" He smiled, then strode from the chamber.

Ian narrowed his gaze on Neil's departing back. Would his brother betray him if given the chance? Ian didn't know. But he trusted no one. Those who trusted often ended up dead. Ian Ross intended to live a long, fruitful life. *Fruitful.* He smiled. Grabbing two candles, he headed down the tunnel Kathy had taken.

Drat it. Pen flashlights were not meant to illuminate stygian pools of water that probably housed any number of nameless nasties. No way was Kathy Bartlett climbing into that water. She'd bet its murky bottom was cluttered with the skeletal remains of foolish bathers.

Kathy dipped her hand into the water. Cool, but not as icy as she'd expected. Quickly, she knelt at the edge, took off one piece of clothing at a time, and washed as best she could. If she were still here tomorrow, she'd opt for the tub beside the fire. *Without* Ian Ross as resident voyeur.

She'd just finished rebuttoning her blouse when something stopped her. She heard nothing, but she still knew. Ian was coming. She shivered. It was crazy. She was the same person who had fallen asleep during a Metallica concert, yet she could *sense* when Ian was near.

Turning her head, she could see twin glowing lights moving down the tunnel toward her. In this place she could almost imagine a fairy-tale dragon with glowing eyes seeking her by the darkened pool.

She shook off her fanciful thoughts as he drew closer, and she could make out his dark silhouette. Narrowing her gaze, she stared at something small moving behind him. It was hourglass-shaped, with a cat perched atop it. *Peter.*

Great. Make this a three-ring circus. Couldn't a woman have any privacy in this blasted time?

"Have ye bathed yet, lass?" He strode to the side of the pool and placed his candles along the bank to illuminate it.

"Yes. Now go away." How embarrassing. Now that she could see the pool, she realized it was only the size of a small pond. In the flickering candlelight, the pool and chamber looked innocuous.

Ian ignored her. " 'Tis unfortunate I didna arrive sooner. Mayhap we could have bathed together."

He didn't look at her, but she knew what he was thinking. "When frogs fly. Go play your bagpipe or storm a castle, but go away."

" 'Tis a cruel woman ye be." He didn't sound very crushed. "But I must bathe before I slay my daily monster." He shrugged, then took the soap and cloth from her. "If ye willna bathe wi' me, I must bathe alone."

Kathy barely had time to close her gaping mouth before he'd undressed. She ought to look away. She slid her gaze across broad shoulders, muscular back, and buns to cry for gleaming golden in the candles' flames. But she couldn't. An experience like this came once in a lifetime. Good thing. Hyperventilation couldn't be healthy on a regular basis.

He strode into the water and stopped when he reached the middle of the pond. The water only reached his hips. He turned to face her.

Now she would look away. But there were some things you couldn't turn from. She remembered her first trip to the Bronx Zoo. The tiger. Mom had warned her not to go near the cage, but she'd been hypnotized by the animal's untamed power. She'd inched closer. Then the tiger had looked at her, and she'd known that if he wanted to eat her, nothing could stop him. Not bars, not her mother. Nothing.

She felt that way now. In the shadows cast by the candlelight, Ian stared at her, silver gaze promising that when the time came, nothing she said, nothing she did, would make a difference.

Sleek, beautiful, dangerous. He stared at her across the chasm of more than four hundred years, and it was as though she looked into the eyes of that tiger again.

She shivered with delicious fear. Delicious? She had to be crazy.

Leaning back, she watched him splash water over his body, then soap himself. He slid the cloth over his arms, shoulders, torso.

Her breathing quickened as he washed lower. Now she'd look away. Okay, so she'd wait a little longer.

She held her breath as his hand paused over the shadowed part she couldn't quite see, *wanted* to see. Amazing. She'd never cared very much about seeing any part of old PMS.

"Ye're a bold lass, to watch a man so." He didn't sound upset at the thought.

"Yes, well this is sort of like a virtual reality trip.

It's primitive here, so I figure it's okay to act a little primitive. I mean, I wouldn't do this back in New York." *Weak, Bartlett.* "Umm, aren't you going to finish?"

His smile flashed white in the dimness. He drew the cloth slowly, lingeringly over himself. What she couldn't see, she imagined. She licked suddenly dry lips.

"Come to me, lass. Touch me. Know how much I want ye." His voice was a low murmur, pulling her, making her want to throw her clothes off and wade into the pool.

And just when she felt she couldn't resist another moment, he laughed and broke whatever had stretched between them.

"Ye're not ready yet. But soon. Verra soon."

"I wouldn't bet on it." Her voice sounded weak, wimpy. How did he do that to her?

He splashed water over himself to rinse off, then waded to the shore.

Kathy tried to focus on his eyes, but his full lower lip, sensuous and kissable, kept distracting her. So she looked at his chest. His nipples were pebbled from the cold water, and she had an almost overwhelming urge to touch one with her tongue. Imm, not a safe area. On to his stomach, which was only a short drive from his . . .

She looked quickly, then glanced away. He really *did* want her. The thought frightened and excited her.

He moved close. "Ye'll lay wi' me, Kathy of Hair.

When the time is right, when ye want me, ye canna deny me."

"That'll be never, Ross." No matter how crazy he made her, she had to keep up appearances, because as tempting as he was, Ian Ross was only about sex. Been there, done that.

But she wished he wouldn't stand so close. Close enough that she could feel his damp heat, smell the scent of clean male animal. *Close enough to feel his erection pressing against my hip.*

Before she had time to react to the contact, he moved away. " 'Tis time for Malin's swim." He walked over to a patiently waiting Peter and scooped the cat off the toy's top.

She forced herself to focus only on his upper body. Below lay personal loss of composure. "Swim? Cats hate water."

Ian waded back into the pool carrying Malin. "The cats brought back from the East by my great grandfather have a love of swimming. Malin is of their line, but he doesna do well wi' only three legs, so I help him."

An important truth nudged at her until she couldn't ignore it. "You claim you don't love anyone, but you love Malin."

He was silent as he lowered Malin into the water and supported the cat as he swam.

She thought he wasn't going to answer her until he finally spoke. "Ye're right. I hadna thought of it."

Nothing more. He evidently wasn't going to explain. After a few minutes, he lifted Malin from the water and made his way to the bank.

"Walking around naked in front of everyone doesn't bother you, does it?" *Don't come near me. Please don't come near me.*

His gaze was puzzled. "In front of *everyone*? I see only ye."

"There's Malin and Peter." Said aloud it sounded sort of dumb, but dumb seemed to be an apt description for her this morning.

His lips curved in that particular smile that made her swallow her heart. "Malin doesna care, and Peter isna alive." He glanced at Peter and his smile widened. "Besides, Peter's eyes are on top of his head. He canna see more than the ceiling, so I dinna need to feel shame."

"I suppose so." She cast Peter a sideways glance. Maybe it was his ability to move and speak, but there were moments when good old Peter made her uncomfortable. Not afraid, but . . . uneasy. Of course, everything in this strange time made her uneasy.

Ian rubbed one of the cloths over Malin to dry him, then set him back on top of Peter. Picking up the other cloth, he moved toward Kathy. To her relief, he stopped several feet away.

He held out the cloth. "Dry me, lass."

It wasn't a request. It wasn't exactly an order. It was simply something he expected.

Well, he could drip-dry all day before she'd touch him.

"Ye want to, lass." His voice lowered to that tempting murmur. "Run yer hands over my bare body. Know me. Ye willna be harmed. I wouldna touch ye if ye didna want it."

"Right. No harm." Was she crazy? No, *she* wasn't crazy, but her hands were because they took the cloth. Her feet were because they stepped close to him. "We have a situation here."

"What?"

"Nothing. I was just explaining something to my mind." Her mind had better deal with it. This was insurrection on a major scale. If her brain couldn't control her hands and feet, what *could* it control?

"Turn around." When he obeyed, she slid the cloth across the smooth expanse of his back. Marveled at the delicious indentation at the base of his spine. Considered all the interesting things a woman could do with that indentation.

She abandoned the cloth long enough to trace with her fingertip the white line of a scar that slashed across the middle of his lower back, to wince at the imagined pain. "I fell off my bike when I was ten years old. Landed on a piece of glass and needed stitches in my leg. I still remember how much it hurt."

"I fell off a horse onto the knife of an enemy. 'Tis not something soon forgotten. It has made me overly careful about falling off horses."

She moved the cloth lower and rubbed the fabric over each marvelous bun. Her body clenched on a need so strong that she froze. She couldn't believe the things her mind was suggesting she do with those buns. No wonder it didn't have time to keep her hands and feet in control. It was too busy thinking up erotic activities involving Ian's . . . lower extremities.

As she stood frozen, doing a bang-up imitation of a wax figure, Ian turned. Her hands were still poised over his . . . lower extremities.

She swallowed hard. Speaking of hard . . . No. Not even her wayward hands had the nerve to go *there.*

Kathy raised her gaze to Ian's.

His eyes glittered a silver challenge. "Ye canna tell me, Kathy of Hair, that no man can make ye feel. If ye touch me now, I will lay ye down beside yon pool and teach ye the truth of yer own body."

The cloth dropped from her nerveless fingers. Forcing her gaze the long gleaming length of his body, she admitted the truth.

She didn't know whether Ian Ross could help her achieve the long sought after, ever elusive orgasm, but he certainly made her want to try.

Another truth coughed politely, gaining her attention. She couldn't try with Ian Ross, because if he succeeded where her ex-husband had failed, she'd be forced to feel something for him. And he was a man for whom no woman should have feelings. The ultimate love-'em-and-leave-'em guy.

"I . . . I have to do something." Without even trying to make her retreat seem anything other than the escape it was, she turned and hurried down the tunnel with her puny pen flashlight casting its tiny beam.

Behind her, Peter clattered along, happily chanting, "Follow the yellow brick road. Follow the yellow brick road."

Chapter Six

Ian smiled as he donned his plaid and followed the woman back to the main chamber. Fear had prompted her retreat, but she would soon realize that he was not the enemy, that the enemy lived within. Her own desire would bring her to him. 'Twas always so.

His smile widened when he emerged from the tunnel to find her trying to put pieces of the flower together.

"What did Suzy Sunshine ever do to you? I'll never get her back in one piece again."

She cast him an accusing glare that made him laugh. His laughter surprised him. Between the Mackays, the kirk, his brothers, and his need to satisfy so many, he had found little time to laugh in recent years.

"Go ahead, laugh. See if I care. Maybe Suzy Sunshine was my only way back to my time. Now I might be stuck here forever. And if you ruined my only chance to go home, I'll make your life a living hell, Ian Ross."

" 'Tis a threat to make a strong man tremble." He strode to her side and gently removed the pieces from her hand. "I'll make her whole again for you. Dinna fear." *I'll make ye whole again.*

"Why did you want to know how Suzy worked, anyway?" She moved to her pack and pulled out several items.

He peered to see what she held. " 'Tis wise to understand all that surrounds ye. Those who do live to be old men."

"Maybe I'm wrong here, but I get the feeling that everything's a kind of battle to you. Like it's you against the world."

She held a brush and some sort of container. Fascinated, he watched her run the brush through her hair. She had beautiful golden hair that curled in a way that tempted him to slide his fingers through it. 'Twas shorter than most women's hair, but a temptation to men nonetheless.

"Did you hear me, Ross?"

"Aye." What would she do with the container? "Ye come from a safe land. Ye wouldna understand."

"Try me."

He would try her very soon. He would taste every part of her wondrous body. But he suspected that was not the meaning of her words. "I have battled the Mackays for many years. Fiona is determined to have me."

"She must love you very much."

"Fiona loves no one. She wants only my body and the pleasure it can bring her."

Her gaze slid over him, and his body tightened in response. Yes, he would enjoy this woman.

"Sounds like you and Fiona were meant for each other. No love, no commitment, just sex. But if you're really tired of being hunted, why don't you let her catch you, then be a real dud in bed? When you don't live up to your reputation, she'll just throw you out." Kathy smiled, obviously pleased by her solution.

"Like yer husband did to ye, lass?"

Her eyes widened in shock, then narrowed to angry slits. "What makes you think any man could throw me out?"

He shrugged. "Well, mayhap not throw ye out. 'Twould take a strong man to do such, and yer kingdom must have many weak men to allow their women to speak to them as Coco and ye do." He watched her face flush. He was enjoying himself mightily.

"You primitive savage. Barbarian . . ."

She obviously searched for harsher words to throw at him.

"Ye need not compliment me so." Her angry response to his teasing and things she'd said before about her husband told him much. But she must trust him more before she'd tell him all.

She took a deep steadying breath. "So why not

try my plan? Get her to throw you out?"

"Fiona would geld me first."

"Hmm. A woman of action."

Her words were cold, but Ian watched her swallow hard. He waited with pleasure for her next solution to his problems.

"So who else do you have to worry about?"

"The clergy. The priest who rules the kirk thinks me an abomination. He would see me dead if he could. He canna act openly because 'twould anger the people, but he can send hirelings to kill me."

A small line of concentration formed between her eyes, and he forced himself not to reach out and smooth it away with his finger. He rarely kept himself from touching a woman, but he didn't want to distract her. Her speech was much too entertaining.

"Okay, let's move on. How about your friends? Can't they protect you? I mean, you could move down to that village, live next to a friend." He could see the confusion in her gaze. She was as innocent as a lamb. He must guard her well.

"The Pleasure Master doesna have friends. 'Tis like the clergy, lass. I canna speak of those who come to me, trust me wi' their secrets. 'Tis not allowed. If I claimed a friend, the people would suspect I told their secrets to him. The Pleasure Master must hold himself apart, live apart from others."

"Wow. The Pleasure Master sounds like such a great job, I can understand why you and your brothers are fighting over it. I mean, who wouldn't?"

He recognized her sarcasm, but didn't understand it. " 'Tis a great honor. Many know about our clan because of the Pleasure Master. 'Tis a source of pride. And those who come share their wealth wi' the village."

She frowned. "The village? Don't they pay *you*?"

It was now his turn to frown. She didn't understand the Pleasure Master at all. "I wouldna take payment for teaching others."

"Why not? You're the one doing the work. That's the basis of good old capitalism."

She seemed truly outraged for him. "Lass, if I took payment for what I do, 'twould make me a . . ."

"Right. It would make you a . . ." She quickly glanced away. "So what're we going to do today to help me go home?"

He smiled at her obvious change of subject. "We canna *do* anything 'til we've formed a plan, but I thought ye might go wi' me to visit Colin. I must tell him of my choice for his challenge."

"Poor Colin," she muttered as she raised the container she still held and sprayed a vile mist into the air around her head.

He'd leaped back before he could control himself. "God's teeth, woman, ye poison the air we breathe wi' yer noxious vapors."

She shrugged, then smiled. Obviously, his reaction amused her. The vixen.

"Hey, it's a small price to pay for great hair." She cocked her head and studied him. "Why don't you let me work on your hair a little? I mean, you have

115

wonderful hair, but I could even the ends, do a little of this and that—"

"I would rather cut off my head and offer it to the Mackays."

"I don't think that's the part they're interested in." She cast him a scornful glance. "Well, if you want to go around looking like Braveheart Unchained, hey, who am I to interfere?"

"What is braveheart?"

"A movie."

"What is a—"

"Forget it."

He did some glaring of his own now. How could he learn if she'd never explain the strange words she used? Then he allowed himself a smile. Once she was in his bed, there would be time afterward for talk. She would explain all to him then.

Kathy eyed him suspiciously. She didn't trust the way he was smiling at her—sexy, confident. "What? What're you thinking?"

"I'm thinking of ye in my bed." He raked his fingers the length of his still-damp hair.

"It'll never happen." But even as she said the words, her gaze followed the path of his fingers through his hair, and she wondered what it would feel like to do the same with *her* fingers, what she would feel with his bare body touching hers.

"Come, lass, 'tis a long walk to the village." He started toward the cave entrance with Kathy tagging reluctantly behind. " 'Twould be easier if I had my horse, but the Mackays took him in their last raid, and I have yet to get him back."

"Why can't I stay in the cave? I have to figure out how to get home." She also had a few other things to figure out. Like what she could use to replace her deodorant. And toothpaste? She'd never gone one day in her whole life without brushing. She *had* to brush. Then there was coffee. Kathy wouldn't even think about the agony of caffeine withdrawal. And kick her if she ever took a flush toilet for granted again. Her one positive thought? She had at least three weeks before she'd have to worry about dealing with . . . No, she wouldn't even go there.

He paused and glanced back. "Ye need to be seen by the villagers so they dinna imagine things about ye that are not so. Ye'll also need some proper clothing and footwear."

She questioned his logic. Mingling with the local folk would simply reinforce their belief that she was "passing strange," and "passing strange" was *not* a healthy thing to be in this time.

"I think I'll just stay home and talk to my toys. Besides, I won't be here long enough to need new clothes and shoes." Even as she said the words, she realized they were a mantra she had to keep repeating to retain her sanity.

"Ye'll come wi' me if I have to carry ye."

She didn't doubt for a minute that he'd do it, and his smile promised the experience wouldn't be all that unpleasant. "If you put it that way . . ."

Huffing angrily, she tagged after him. A clatter behind her reminded her that someone else wanted to go. "I don't think Peter will create exactly an I'm-plain-folk-just-like-you image."

"Canna ye make him stay here?" He sounded exasperated, but even in exasperation he looked incredibly edible. The man was a phenomenon.

Once again, Kathy walked over to Peter and picked him up. She studied him from every angle. "Nope. No off switch."

"Mayhap I will take him apart next. I could learn how he works."

Peter's amber lights blinked rapidly. "You've got to ask yourself one question. 'Do I feel lucky?' Well, do ya, punk?"

Kathy almost dropped the toy. Peter must be programmed with every famous movie line known to man. But how was it that his remarks always seemed to fit the situation? Peter could be downright creepy sometimes. Putting him firmly on the ground, she turned to Ian. "Do you have something to block the entrance so he can't get out?"

"Aye." Ian sounded distracted as he stared at Peter.

"He's a toy, Ian. Just like my other toys."

"Suzy doesna act so strange."

Kathy couldn't help herself, she grinned. "Listen to yourself. Yesterday morning you would've run screaming from Suzy."

He scowled at her. Uh-oh, wrong comment.

"I wouldna run from a wee flower." His scowl softened into a smile. "But I would have wanted to. All fear what they dinna understand, the same way ye fear laying wi' me."

"I'm not afraid of you." *Liar.* His smile made her want to explore his tempting mouth, his unspoken promises. His eyes drew her, making her blood heat, making her forget all the ugly accusations old PMS had thrown at her, making her want to crawl inside his body. And if that wasn't scary, nothing was.

"Yer denial hasna the sound of truth in it." His voice was a low murmur of seduction. "There is naught to fear in pleasure. I will teach ye all that is wondrous, all the feelings the body can know. And when ye return to yer land and the men ye've known, ye'll search for one who can make ye feel as I've made ye feel. If ye find him, take him as yer own forever."

"How can you be so sure?"

"Because I *know,* lass." He moved close, sliding his fingers along her jaw, tracing the shape of her lower lip, lowering his head until his lips skimmed hers, a warm brush of sensuality.

His power frightened her. He was the pause at the top of the highest roller coaster. The fear of the uncontrolled plunge, and the simultaneous longing for it. Ian Ross was the danger, the power, the elemental force, and nothing in her New York life had prepared her for a man like him.

"Come wi' me, Kathy." His voice held the flavor of smooth whiskey. Just the memory of it would warm her on a cold New York night.

"Fine. We'll go to the village, I'll blend in with the local populace, and you can deliver the bad news to your loving brother. Simple." There was nothing simple about it, and Kathy knew Ian hadn't been asking her to come with him to the village.

Ian's soft chuckle mocked her attempt to ignore what he'd meant, what he *was*.

Peter's lights flashed as he added his own words of caution. "Be afraid. Be very afraid."

"Give me a break, Peter. Don't you have any quotes that aren't oozing melodrama?" The truth? She thought Peter's comment was right on the money.

As she followed Ian out of the cave, then watched him block the entrance, she considered the mental stability of someone who'd talk to a toy.

The long walk to the village gave her plenty of time to try to figure out why she was in sixteenth-century Scotland. In fact, she thought about it until she started to get a headache. With only a few Advil in her purse back in Ian's cave, she thought she'd better discourage unnecessary headaches.

So she thought about Ian. That gave her an ache in an entirely different part of her body. How could he do that without even touching her, without even *looking* at her?

Maybe old PMS's research into all things sexual really meant squat. Maybe reading a bunch of books and then proclaiming yourself sexy didn't matter if you didn't have sexy equipment and a sensual aura. Kathy didn't know what kind of aura Ian Ross had, but she could feel it even as she walked five feet behind him.

She admired his smooth confident stride, the lift of his long hair in the light breeze, the sense of controlled violence about him. Controlled violence? Yes, it was there. Kathy considered herself a millennium woman, but she had to admit that in this place, in this time, a dangerous man excited her. He was a beautiful animal at home in his environment. *But it isn't your environment, remember.*

They'd reached the top of a small hill, and Ian paused to look in every direction. Kathy puffed as she finally caught up with him. She was used to being on her feet all day, but all this walking was making her legs ache.

"What're you looking for?" All she could see were more green hills, rocks, and small streams. Scenic but bleak, empty.

"I must guard against those who would attack me."

"Okay, so I'm not familiar with your particular situation, but you seem a little paranoid to me. Don't you trust anyone?"

"I trust Malin. I trust my horse, e'en though he didna battle overmuch when the Mackays took him. I dinna trust any humans."

"Don't you think it's a little strange that you ask women to trust you with their bodies, their secrets, and yet you don't trust anyone?" *Gotcha.* Let him try to wiggle out of that one.

His smile was the sun on an ocean beach. Beautiful, warm, but dangerous if you made the mistake of allowing it to lull you to sleep. "I ask women to trust my body, my knowledge, and my promise as

Pleasure Master to guard their secrets. 'Twould be foolish to trust further."

She knew she shouldn't take it personally, that his mistrust was Ian Ross's character flaw, but it still rankled. "I know you don't think I come from the year 2001. What would it take for you to believe me?"

His gaze seared her, looked into her soul and found it wanting. "I'd need to trust ye, lass." He shrugged. " 'Tis a thing that willna happen."

"Right. No trust. Foolish of me to ask."

Seemingly satisfied with his search, he continued along the path.

Kathy groaned as she tagged along, stumbling over small rocks and grumbling about the cold.

He glanced at her and grinned. " 'Tis a fine summer day. Ye're lucky 'tis not winter."

"Hmmph." She knew she was being bitchy. She knew this wasn't his fault. But he was convenient, and she wanted to complain. "Right now, I should be finishing up Mrs. Kierney's hair, then going to Coco's for dinner."

"If it's hunger ye feel, we'll eat at Mad Mary's."

She caught a glimpse of the village in the distance. "Mad Mary? Umm, that's a . . . distinctive name."

"Mary is our healer. Many find her strange." He cast Kathy a wicked smile. "Ye'll have much in common."

"I don't think so." She was in no mood to agree with anything Ian Ross said right now. She was tired, she was cranky, and she wanted to go home to her cozy apartment.

"Aye, ye will. Mary speaks wi' her hens, and ye talk to yer toys. 'Tis alike ye are." He guided her down the rutted, muddy road leading to one of the cottages.

Kathy would have delivered a to-the-point New York reply, but she was too busy staring at the people who were staring at her, particularly the women, particularly their hair.

No one spoke to her, and everyone seemed anxious to keep a safe distance away. Ian prayed she'd say nothing foolish. The people accepted him because the Pleasure Master had been part of their lives for so long. They had no reason to accept Kathy's strangeness.

Ian exhaled sharply when they'd finally reached the safety of Colin's cottage. His brother didn't rise early unless there was pressing need, so he had no fear that Colin wouldn't be within.

Bleary-eyed, Colin opened his door and allowed them to enter. " 'Tis past time ye told me my challenge, Ian. 'Tisn't fair that Neil and ye have already started yer quests."

Kathy moved around the room, missing no detail. She paused at Colin's words. "Don't worry, Colin. No one's made it to first base yet."

Colin blinked at her. "First base? What is—"

"Forget it," Ian suggested.

Kathy grinned at Ian. "You're learning, Ross."

"I've decided yer challenge, Colin."

Colin smiled smugly. "It canna be more difficult

than the one ye gave Neil. 'Tis not likely he'll triumph."

"I'd give him a zero chance," Kathy offered as
she ran her hand over the bagpipes sitting in the
corner. "Do you play the bagpipes, Colin?"

"Aye." He turned his attention back to Ian.
"What say ye, brother?"

Ian couldn't remember a time when he'd enjoyed
the telling of anything more. "Yer challenge is to
woo Mad Mary."

Colin's face lost all color beneath his beard. "Ye
jest. No man has e'er bedded Mad Mary."

Ian shook his head in mock sadness. "I dinna
think ye need worry overmuch about bedding her.
I doubt ye'll live that long."

Colin made a choking sound. "Ye canna—"

"I can, Colin. 'Tis my right. As ye've chosen for
me, I've chosen for ye." He turned to where Kathy
stood staring, fascinated at Colin's now flushed
face. " 'Tis time to leave, Kathy."

Colin said nothing as they left. Ian suspected his
brother was incapable of speech.

"That was pretty mean, Ian." Kathy trotted to
keep up with him. He'd liked it better when she'd
trailed behind. "I mean, choosing an old wrinkled
crone for Colin. At least Coco's attractive. And
how's Colin supposed to get anywhere with someone who's crazy?"

"Ye talk too much, Kathy of Hair." He walked
faster, hoping she'd fall behind.

"You answer too little, Ian Ross." She trotted faster to keep up.

Relieved, he left the village and climbed the hill to where Mary's house stood alone. He didn't bother knocking on the door because he knew Mary would be tending to the small herb garden behind her cottage. Rounding the corner of the house, he saw Mary bent over one of her plants.

"I mean, how do you communicate with someone who talks to chickens? At her age, I'd suspect senility. The poor woman probably needs to be in an assisted living facility, with medical help available. . . ."

Mary straightened, then smiled when she saw Ian. "Welcome, Ian."

Ian turned to where Kathy stood with an open mouth and unfinished sentence. "Kathy of Hair, meet Mad Mary."

Chapter Seven

Mad Mary was young, she was beautiful, and Kathy was embarrassed by all the preconceptions she'd voiced. Loudly.

Mary approached them, brushing the soil from her hands. "Ye've brought the woman to me, Ian."

The woman. Mary's words sounded impersonal, but the gaze she fixed on Ian was anything but. Kathy felt a twinge of something she wasn't ready to identify.

"Aye. This is Kathy of Hair." The smile he offered Mary was open, devastating.

"Welcome to my home, Kathy of Hair."

Mary's greeting sounded sincere, her smile was warm, and her gaze was clear and sane. Kathy felt the heat rising to her face. She'd prejudged Mary just as the villagers were probably doing to her.

"Thanks. Ian says you're a healer. I guess you've treated him for a few aches and pains, maybe a few battle wounds?"

Okay, so she was fishing, but if Ian wouldn't tell her much about himself, maybe others would.

"Aye, a few. Though not all wounds can be treated wi' my herbs."

Great. What was that supposed to mean?

"I've come to warn ye, Mary."

Ian's comment effectively ended the fascinating discussion of his wounds. Probably his intent.

"I've given Colin the task of wooing ye as his challenge. He wasna overly pleased."

Mary frowned. "Ye're a wicked man, Ian Ross. I dinna need Colin following me around like a wee pup."

Ian's smile made wicked look awfully inviting. "He'll need to fortify himself wi' some strong drink before beginning his quest. Ye'll be safe for a few days."

While the conversation flowed over her, Kathy studied Mary. Pale skin, hazel eyes, and black hair falling to the middle of her back made for a striking combination. Clean, shining hair. A rarity. Ian and Mary were the only ones who seemed concerned with cleanliness around here.

"Kathy has need of clothing and footwear. Can ye help?"

Mary asked no questions, but merely nodded.

Ian smiled his special smile that promised even the depths of hell would be heaven with him, and

Kathy watched the change in Mary's eyes. The softening, the *desire.*

Kathy couldn't imagine any woman being immune to his brand of assault. Except her, of course. She recognized what he did with that smile, so she was safe. Sort of.

"I'll leave ye to yer garden. Dinna let Colin fash ye." Ian glanced at Kathy. "I'll wait for ye on the path." He strode away.

Kathy waited until he was out of earshot. "I guess you've known Ian a long time."

"Aye." Mary looked amused as she led Kathy into her cottage. Kathy glanced around at the herbs drying, the hearth, the few pieces of furniture, and wondered what she'd do if she had to live this way for the rest of her life. *The rest of her life.* She shuddered.

She couldn't go there right now. "Umm. He hasn't told me much about himself." *Subtle, Bartlett. Really subtle.*

Mary gazed in the direction Ian had gone. "If there were a thousand men gathered for a woman to choose from, she'd choose Ian. 'Tis his special gift to draw women to him." Her gaze turned pensive. " 'Tis also his curse."

Well, that was a big help. "Right. A special gift." She accepted the things Mary handed her. "Thank you for not asking questions."

"As ye have?" She offered Kathy a wide grin.

"As I have." She smiled back at Mary. "Oh, I was wondering whether you could help me with a few more little things."

A few minutes later, Kathy left Mary's cottage clutching the clothes, a piece of bread, and some leaves to use with a twig in place of her toothbrush. Colgate could make a fortune here. At least her teeth wouldn't rot and fall out. Mary had assured her that it didn't get warm enough for Kathy to worry "overmuch" about underarm odor. Kathy wasn't reassured as she waved to Mary. "I hope I'll see you again."

Mary smiled gently. "Ye will."

Kathy scarfed down the bread as she trudged after Ian. Why was she here? She didn't have any special gifts. Sure, making women's hair look great was a life skill, but not important on a saving-civilization-from-certain-doom scale.

A mistake? At this very moment could the heavenly host be searching frantically for that pesky human they'd misplaced?

She discarded possibilities, leaving a trail of despair all the way back to Ian's cave.

"I'm sorry I didna ask Mary to feed ye. If ye need to wash the bread down, ye may have whiskey or water. I'll get ye some milk when I visit the village next. If ye desire anything more, I'll show ye some leaves that were given to me. The woman said they would make a fine brew. I havena tried them."

Leaves? No beans? Dammit, she needed *coffee* in the morning.

"God's teeth, canna a man leave his dwelling wi'out fear of knaves?"

Kathy glanced up, startled from her misery. "Knaves? Where? Where?"

"Someone is in the cave."

He was already striding down the tunnel toward the main chamber when she finally realized the cave entrance had been open. Peter. Was Peter safe? She hurried after Ian.

Peter met her, amber lights blinking, just as she reached the living area.

Picking him up, she hugged him tightly. "Thank God you're okay."

"A bunch of hokey religions and ancient weapons ain't no match for a good blaster at your side, kid."

Kathy set Peter down, then frowned at him. "Right. Blasters. I'll remember that. Guess you've watched *Star Wars* a few times." She was doing it again, talking to a toy.

But all thoughts of Peter vanished as she glanced around the room. Neil sat on the cushions holding her cell phone and bellowing into it. His face was cherry red. He must be talking to Coco.

Ian was busy trying to disentangle Malin from Neil's hair while the cat growled his displeasure at being deprived of his prey.

Neil abandoned the cell phone long enough to glare at Ian. "Yer cat is a wee spawn of hell. And that shiny demon the woman brought wi' her speaks in the devil's tongue."

Kathy blinked. Looked like Neil had covered just about everything.

"Malin is a warrior. He was protecting his own against one who shouldna be here." Ian sank onto a cushion to watch his brother.

"'Tis ye who chose this shrewish vixen as my challenge, so ye must allow me to speak wi' her."

"*Shrewish vixen?* I heard that, you bombastic buffoon." Coco's shout made Neil wince. He held the phone away from his ear.

He glanced at Ian for help. "Bombastic buffoon?"

Ian shrugged.

"Men should be like Kleenex—soft, strong, and disposable," Peter offered.

Kathy smiled. She'd always liked that line from *Clue*.

"I didna ask yer advice, demon." Neil scowled as he gingerly returned the phone to his ear.

"Ye need to learn respect for men, Coco. If ye were here, I would bare yer bottom and redden it wi' my hand."

"Ohmigod," Kathy muttered. She edged away from Neil. Nothing could save him now.

Surprisingly, silence followed his pronouncement, then a soft chuckle. "You'd really try to spank me?"

"Aye." Neil's hand was clenched so tightly to the phone that his knuckles were white. "Then I'd make love to ye."

"Hmm. Put Kathy on the phone, hotshot."

Neil's gaze was glazed as he handed the phone to Kathy with shaking fingers.

Kathy had to know one thing. "How'd you reach Coco? I didn't give you her number."

Neil stared at her for a dazed moment. "I only

touched yer phone, and she was there." He stumbled toward the cave's entrance.

Peter followed him, offering advice. "Women need a reason to have sex. Men just need a place."

How could Neil have reached Coco if he hadn't punched in her number? Was someone controlling . . . ? No, she couldn't deal with that thought now. Drawing a deep breath, Kathy put the phone to her ear. "I'm sorry, Coco, but—"

"What's he look like, Kathy?"

"Neil? He's tall, broad shoulders, great buns—"

"You've seen them, his buns?"

"Well, yes."

"I won't ask how. What's his face look like?"

"I'm not too sure. He has this beard and—"

"Tell him to shave it off. I hate facial hair. Then we'll talk." Coco was quiet for a moment. "Sure you don't want to tell me where you're holed up? I know this whole thing with your ex has stressed you out, and I understand you have a new man, but it would help to know where you are."

"It wouldn't do any good, believe me."

She could hear Coco's sigh. "Okay. I guess you'll tell me when you're ready. Just make sure you're back by the court date."

"Court date. Sure. By the way, what *is* the date?"

Coco's silence was longer this time. "January tenth."

January 10? Kathy fought back a feeling of despair. Her job would be history by now. Thank heavens Mom and Dad were still on their cruise.

Kathy watched Malin jump back atop Peter.

"Oh, would you check out one more thing for me?
See if you can find a breed of cat that likes to swim
and tell me where it originated."

"Let me get this straight. You're with a man who
sounds like pure sin, and you want to know about
cats?"

Kathy sighed. "Humor me, Coco."

"Will do."

Kathy listened to the click as Coco hung up, feeling the disconnection to her time all the way to her
soul. There *had* to be a way back.

Wearily, Kathy pulled off her coat and dropped
it on top of Mary's borrowed things, then sank onto
a cushion. Ian was attending to the hearth fire.

Summer. It was summer in this time and place,
but it was still chilly. No chillier though than the
cold numbing her heart.

Silently, Ian knelt behind her, but she couldn't
summon the energy to move away from him.

Putting his hands on her shoulders, he massaged
her tight muscles. She stiffened.

She felt his harsh exhalation against her exposed
neck, where it sent tingles skittering down her
back. She shifted, uneasy with her body's instant
reaction to him.

"Ye're like the hare when it spots the wolf, lass.
I mean only to ease yer body."

She glanced warily back at him. "That's what I'm
afraid of."

"If I meant anything more, ye'd know it." His lips
brushed her neck and she drew her breath in a startled gasp.

"How would I know?" Nerve endings unused to male stimulation of any kind were happily gathering to discuss the possibility of the big *O*. They were doomed to disappointment. *Never* with Ian Ross.

His hands slid down her back, kneading spots that made her moan with relief. Damn him. Everything he did felt good.

"Ye'd know because ye'd feel it."

Big help. Didn't he know she *felt* it every time he was within shouting distance?

"And because I wouldna hide my intent. I'd speak of it."

"I don't know how smart that is. If you warn me, I can run." She *would* run, fast and far. Away from the temptation of trying for sexual nirvana with a man who, even though more sensually persuasive than her ex-husband, still believed that sex and caring weren't connected. Uh-uh, wouldn't catch her with that again.

"Ye wouldn't wish to run." He transferred his attention to her neck, squeezing gently, reminding her of his leashed power, of what he could do if he chose. She wasn't sure whether that thought frightened or excited her.

"Pretty sure of yourself, aren't you?"

"Aye."

Now *that* frightened her.

He moved away, and she almost slumped with relief.

"I must put yer wee flower back together again." He picked up Suzy pieces and bent over them, his hair shrouding his expression. "What do ye do in this place ye claim to come from?"

She watched his strong, capable fingers carefully repairing the yellow flower. And thought about those fingers. On her. "Uh, when I'm finished doing my princess stuff, I cut, style, and color women's hair."

He glanced at her from beneath dark lashes and smiled. "Yer hair is wondrous. Ye need do nothing to it."

Nothing except renew the wondrous blond color once a month. "Thank you. I think." Was this the beginning of his seduction? Did he start with compliments before launching an all-out attack?

"Ye dinna take compliments well, lass." He glanced down at Suzy again.

"That's because compliments aren't always sincere. They can be a ploy to get something from someone." *Like sex.*

"Is that what yer husband did to ye?" Suzy was now taking on a recognizable shape.

"My husband exploited my weaknesses—a desire for his love and a need for security."

Ian didn't take his attention from the nearly restored sunflower. "Those dinna sound like yer words. Ye speak more bluntly."

She laughed. "Right. That was Coco's lawyer-speak." Kathy relaxed as the laughter released her tension.

"What do ye do for joy, lass?" He held up the flower.

"I loooove you."

135

Yep, Suzy was back.

"Ye must do something in this New York that makes yer heart sing." He placed Suzy carefully back on her ledge, then reached into Kathy's sack and pulled out Baby Born. Tearing the packaging off, he stared thoughtfully at the doll.

Her heart sing. Shocked, she realized there was only one thing she did in her time that made her feel even remotely as alive as she felt with Ian Ross. "I skydive."

He set the doll in his lap and stared at her. "I dinna understand."

She smiled, remembering all those times Ms. Wilson, her fourth-grade teacher, had told her to write as though she were trying to describe something to aliens from another planet, painting a picture for them in their minds. And here she'd thought Ms. Wilson's picture-painting for aliens had been a waste of time.

Ian offered her his come-and-take-me grin. Leaning forward, he traced the outline of her lips with the tip of his finger. "I must learn yer smile since I dinna see it verra much. 'Tis wondrous."

Kathy paused a moment to allow her senses to recover from his touch. Amazing how her breathing rate was affected by contact with any part of Ian Ross's body. "Everything is wondrous to you."

Suddenly, his eyes widened, then he grimaced. Unceremoniously, he dumped Baby Born off his lap to reveal a large wet spot. "Not everything. God's teeth, I canna believe ye make toys that do such things."

Kathy bit her lip, but it did no good. She laughed.

"Dinna laugh, woman. Now I must rid myself of this so it may dry."

Uh-oh. What did ridding himself of *this* entail?

She wasn't kept in suspense long. With no wasted motion, he stripped off his plaid, leaving only his shirt, then turned his attention back to her. "Ye havena explained this sky diving yet."

She'd have a hard time explaining her own name with all that golden skin to distract her. Temptation didn't just beckon as Ian bent one leg at the knee in what she now recognized as his *comfortable* position. It grabbed her by the throat and shook her.

She coughed to free her throat from temptation's hold. "Skydiving? Oh, skydiving. Well, you go up in a plane. . . ." What if she reached out and ran her hand up the inside of his thigh? Would she surprise him, or would he just smile that I-knew-you-couldn't-resist smile?

"What is a plane?"

"It's a machine that flies. People ride in it, and it takes them into the sky higher than birds fly." How high would he let her go? Would he open himself to her, allow her to glide her fingers under his shirt, touch—

He frowned. " 'Tis a hard thing to believe."

Hard. Her breathing quickened. When she finally touched him, would he grow hard beneath her fingers, would he thrust against her hand when she clasped him? "Hard. Right. Uh, where was I?"

His gaze turned thoughtful as he watched her; then his lips tilted up in a secret smile. "Ye were flying through the air."

"Okay. Got it. Air." Funny, she was having trouble getting any air into her lungs. "When the plane reaches a certain height, everyone except the pilot jumps out."

His frown returned. "It doesna seem a wise thing to do."

"Huh? Oh, yeah. I forgot something." She slapped her forehead in a symbolic gesture meant to indicate that her brain was scrambled, and she was trying to knock all the pieces back into their correct slots. "You have a parachute strapped to you. It's like a giant umbrella that you open part way down and it slows your descent so you can drift to the ground." *Down.* What would he do if she slid her hand down his length, cupped his—

"What is an umbrella?"

Arrgh! "Forget it." She forced her gaze away from the place no sky dive could take her.

"Ye seem overly fond of those words. Do ye escape all that bothers ye by using them?" He lowered his leg.

She didn't feel capable of logical reasoning, so she shrugged.

"It matters not. If I visited yer kingdom I would try this skydiving." He picked up Baby Born and set her safely on the rug between his spread legs.

"You would?" She didn't try to hide her surprise. It didn't take much gray matter to know that this wasn't a normal response for someone from his time.

"Aye. I've always had an uncommon curiosity about all things." He slanted her a challenging smile. " 'Tis a great weakness and will bring grief to me in time. Many have told me so."

Kathy could have told him he was uncommon in many ways, all intriguing to any woman breathing. Okay, so maybe the woman didn't even have to be breathing.

Ian picked up Baby Born and examined her. "How does this toy work?"

Poor Baby Born.

The voices reached her in the night—soft, secret. About the same time her bladder informed her that it didn't give a hoot whether there was indoor plumbing, she'd better *do* something or else. It was the "or else" that made her struggle from her bed.

What to do? A short hospital stay that involved unpleasant bedpan memories made her determined *not* to use the chamber pot, but she darn well wouldn't go outside in the dark by herself. Anything could be outside at night—marauding barbarians, land-dwelling offshoots of the Loch Ness Monster's family.

By herself. Hmm. Maybe Ian would walk her to the entrance, then stand guard while she went.

The voices reached her again. She searched for Ian in the faint glow of the fire. She didn't see him, but he had to be somewhere in the cave because she recognized his voice.

She'd never mistake his voice. Made for the night-deep, dark, filled with hidden meanings. She followed the sound.

Kathy finally traced the murmurs to a tapestry-covered doorway she hadn't noticed until now. She hesitated only a moment. The night was the Pleasure Master's time, but if she didn't interrupt him she'd explode.

What were they doing in there? Their voices sounded normal, no passionate whispers, no heavy breathing. Should she call out? Maybe she should just stick her head in and beckon to Ian.

Maybe she should do something fast because all she could think about were phrases like "water balloon" and "broken water main."

Be honest. You want to know what the Pleasure Master does, catch him in the act, whatever that might be. Ian wasn't the only one with too much curiosity. She sighed, giving in to the temptation that would land her in hot water for sure. Water. Damn the consequences. She pushed aside the tapestry and peeked in.

She had time to register only basic things. Ian, a strange woman, an incredible bed. The woman seated in a chair by the fire turned her head from Kathy. Ian rose from his chair and strode to the door.

"Ye'd better have good reason for interrupting so." His body filled the doorway, blocking out the light from within, hiding the woman.

Kathy stared up at his shadowed face. His eyes

gleamed silver even in the dim light, and she felt his anger like a physical blow.

Maybe this hadn't been such a great idea. She'd been so worried about the creatures of the night outside the cave that she'd forgotten Ian Ross fell into the same category.

"I . . . I have to go."

He frowned. "Ye've found a way to return to yer kingdom?"

"No, I mean I have to *go.*"

She wasn't sure, but she thought she saw a glimmer of amusement in his eyes.

"I wouldna stop ye."

"Um, I really don't want to use the chamber pot, so I thought maybe you'd walk outside with me and sort of stand guard while I . . ."

"Aye. Stand guard." He turned his head back to the woman, and an unspoken agreement must have passed between them because Ian stepped out of the room.

Wordlessly, Kathy followed him out of the cave.

A few minutes later, Kathy emerged from the undergrowth. Damn and double damn. She'd never pass the bathroom tissue section of a supermarket again without expressing her heartfelt appreciation to the unknown inventor.

She pulled a twig from her hair, then brushed leaves from various parts of her body. She'd *never* adapt to this. Kathy Bartlett wasn't an adaptable kind of person. She didn't do the back-to-nature thing. Dad had learned that on their first camping trip. She wished Dad were here now to bundle her into his car and drive her back to modern plumbing and electricity.

Okay, finished whining. Drawing a deep breath, she started back to where Ian waited. *Not* patiently.

Relieved, Kathy saw the woman standing beside him. He wouldn't yell at her in front of company, would he? Her relief disappeared when the woman walked away from him toward a grove of trees. A dark silhouette separated itself from the shadows to meet the woman, and they disappeared in the night.

Great. Just great. Alone with Mr. Dark-and-Furious.

He said nothing when she reached him, only led her back to the main chamber. She stopped. "Thanks a lot. I can sleep now."

He kept walking. "Come."

Kathy Bartlett didn't answer to one word commands. "I don't think so. I'm really tired." She plunked herself on her furs.

Wordlessly, he returned to where she sat, scooped her up, carried her to his room, then set her on her feet. She was too shocked even to kick and threaten him with legal action.

"Okay, now that you've shown me how big and strong you are, I'll go back to sleep." She tried unsuccessfully to control her voice's slight quaver.

"Ye willna."

Well, that was pretty clear.

She tried pushing past him to the entrance, but it was like shoving against a wall. "What're you trying to prove, Ross?"

"Ye didna call out."

Kathy sighed. "Okay, I didn't call out. I'm sorry."

"Ye were curious."

Truth time. "Yes."

He reached for her wrist, then dragged her farther into the room. Uh-oh. Time to worry, *really* worry.

"Ye wish to know what the Pleasure Master does. 'Tis time ye learned." Dropping her wrist, he moved past her, and she followed him with her gaze.

"Come to me, Kathy of Hair."

Her eyes widened, her heart pounded, and she tried unsuccessfully to swallow as her gaze shifted from Ian to what stood beside him.

The Bed.

Chapter Eight

"You have a *gold* bed?" she whispered.

" 'Tis gilded. This was the only thing besides Malin's ancestors that my great grandfather brought home wi' him." Ian slid his hand down the post, which was carved into the shape of a writhing snake.

The bed glowed molten in the candle flame, its silk hangings a shimmering crimson flow of sensuality.

"Are those paintings on it?" She still couldn't force her voice above a whisper because the bed felt like . . .

"Aye. Come closer."

She didn't want to, but the bed drew her, *he* drew her. She moved closer and peered at the many scenes painted in deep rich detail. She saw a man who looked very much like Ian and a woman. They were . . . "Ohmigod. In every painting they're . . ."

"Enjoying each other's bodies. The woman who owned my great grandfather had this bed made to celebrate their joinings. Each time he pleased her more than the last, she had a scene painted on the bed."

"Is this where you . . . ?"

"Nay. I use the outer chamber, but ye were there, and I didna wish to disturb ye."

Kathy watched, fascinated, as he ran his fingers across one of the painted scenes. She'd never known there were so many ways to . . . enjoy a man's body. "Why is there a blank space here near this post?" She pointed. No way would she touch.

"The woman died, and my great grandfather said there were none that came after her worthy of a scene." He shrugged. "It has remained so since then."

"He must have loved her very much." She still couldn't speak above a hushed whisper.

Ian frowned. " 'Twas not love. She gave him more pleasure than any other. She taught him the secrets of the Pleasure Master."

"Sorry, didn't mean to mention the *L* word." *What are those secrets?* No, she didn't want to know. Ian was as foreign to her as a man could be. A beautiful, sleek creature of the night. "Do you ever sleep in the bed?"

He shook his head, and his hair caught and held the candle-glow. "No one has slept on it since my great grandfather. My father and grandfather said 'twas too strange and would make those that came to them uncomfortable. I have kept it because 'tis a symbol of what I am."

"Will you ever sleep on it?"

His lips curved in a mocking smile. "I'll bed the lass I love on it."

In other words, never.

"Why have ye been whispering? There are none to hear us." He slid his hand over her hair, curled a strand around his finger, then pulled. He held the strand up to the light. "Yer hair shines gold like the bed."

Like the bed? Maybe she needed a little more ash in her color. "Have I been whispering?" She forced her voice to a normal volume, but it sounded almost disrespectful in the presence of the bed.

The bed was of the night, just like its owner. Funny, but she'd always pictured a bed made for sex as being built of dark wood and velvet.

It wasn't. This golden bed with its erotic paintings, crimson silk hangings, and posts carved into sinuous snakes was sex, sin, and all that was carnal. It scared the hell out of her.

"Well, thanks for showing me the bed. I'll go back to sleep now." She edged toward the entrance and held her breath, praying that he'd allow her to escape. She frowned. Escape didn't have a good sound to it.

He followed her, trapping her in an aura she knew must be as red as his bed hangings.

"Ye still dinna understand what I am."

She glanced past him at the bed. "I get the general concept. Now can I leave?"

"Nay."

He spoke the word softly, but he might as well have shouted it, because the force of his utterance flattened her against the wall. She held her hands stiffly at her sides, knowing that if she raised them to ward him off, she'd end up with her palms splayed across his wide chest, feeling the solidness of muscle and flesh, the strong pounding of his heart.

His lips curved up—secretive, sexual. "Ye may touch me, Kathy."

With a distant part of her mind, she noted his abandonment of her title. "Touch you? I don't want to touch you. Why would I want to do that?" She clenched her fists to keep her hands at her sides.

"Ye dinna lie well, lass." His gaze never wavered from her face. "I want to touch *ye*. I want to touch the fear in ye and change it to hunger."

"I'm not afraid of you." Which wasn't exactly true. Her senses were already gorging, but the excess baggage she'd toted behind her to this time would keep her on a strict diet. Fear of being hurt, of being a failure again, were strong appetite suppressers.

His smile widened as he reached past her and pulled the tapestry aside. The brush of his chest against her nipples dragged a gasp from her. "Go and sit by the fire while I tell ye more about the Pleasure Master."

She heard only the word "Go" as she hurried

back to the main chamber, then sat down on her furs. Safe. He sat down beside her. *Maybe not so safe.*

"The woman ye saw came only to speak of how to please a man. She is a widow who was married to one who wanted only compliance. She will soon marry a man who expects her to know much about pleasuring him."

"What did you tell her?" *Did you give her a hands-on demonstration?*

He acknowledged her unspoken question with a grin. "I told her of places to touch a man that would drive him mad wi' want of her and how to gain her own release when she held him deep inside her—"

"Okay, heard enough, don't want to hear anymore." *Where* would you touch a man? She supposed he didn't mean the obvious places. But she wouldn't ask, didn't want to know.

"I don't understand why she'd come to you, though. She looked as though she'd traveled a long distance. Couldn't she have found someone closer to tell her those things?"

He studied her from under half-lowered lids, and she resisted the urge to squirm. "There are those who could tell her about the touching, but the touching comes last. She has wealth and can afford to travel to one who knows what comes before."

"And that would be . . . ?"

"In time, lass." His smile was full of wicked promise. "I'll teach ye of what comes before and the places ye may touch a man." He stopped smiling. "And the places a man may touch *ye*." He left her. Left her to dream of his hard body, spread for her enjoyment. His hands, his mouth touching every part of her, wringing a response from her that she ached for, *feared.*

She opened her eyes to morning light shining through the roof opening and Baby Born sitting whole on the shelf beside the hearth.

Shifting her gaze, she saw Ian seated by the fire. He was dressed, but his hair was still damp. He must have visited his cave pool. No pool for her this morning. She wanted warm water.

"You're up early, Ian." She rose, thankful for the gown Mary had given her. It covered her from neck to toe, and after her conversation with Ian last night, plus her vivid dreams, she felt the need to hide behind an armor of cloth. As if that would make any difference to Ian.

"Aye. I was speaking wi' Peter. He has told me that life is like a box of chocolates and that I'll ne'er know what I'll get. 'Tis a wise thought."

"But not totally original." She sidled over to Ian and sat down beside him. First she'd lull him with ordinary conversation. "I noticed that you didn't take Baby Born apart."

He glanced at the doll. "When I looked at her, I knew I wouldna be able to put her back together again. I dinna take things apart if 'twill destroy them."

A deeper understanding arced between them. "Remember that, Ian. Please remember that."

149

He nodded, then returned his attention to Peter. "Yon toy is stranger than the others."

She wasn't interested in Peter right now; she was interested in a warm bath. "I don't know. Toy technology has really skyrocketed. You'd be surprised what toys can do."

She glanced at Peter, but the toy's lights remained dark. "I was really desperate for toys, and I needed them fast. So I stopped at this strip mall with a bunch of stores that had only a few toys left. The store where I got Peter didn't even have a sign outside. But there he was, sitting on the shelf with a price underneath him. He was the only one left, and I didn't see any salespeople around, so I left the money on the counter and ran to the next store. I wasn't even sure what he did, but I couldn't be picky."

"Mayhap he can do more than ye know."

His gaze shifted to her, and she felt the shock as though it were the first time. How did he do that? "I've already asked him to send me home, and I'm still here."

"Mayhap he doesna wish to send ye home." His gaze slid the length of her gown as though it were invisible.

She didn't want to think about not going home. "You mentioned yesterday that I could have a warm bath if I wanted." After getting the warm water, she'd worry about getting Ian Ross out of the cave.

He smiled and his gaze heated. Uh-oh. She

wanted hot water, not hot gazes. "If it's too much trouble, don't bother."

" 'Tis no trouble."

He rose, and before she could even close her gaping mouth, he'd stripped, then tied his shirt around his waist. "I dinna want to get my plaid wet when I draw yer bath. 'Tis verra uncomfortable traveling wi' wet clothing."

"Sure. Uncomfortable." The light from the hearth highlighted wide shoulders, muscled chest, powerful thighs, and strong legs. He oozed potent sensuality, and kick her if she ever asked for warm water again.

With unblinking intensity, she watched him carry water to the tub he'd placed in front of the fire. She noted the sweat from his exertion that made his body glisten, the smooth slide of muscles as he moved, the tantalizing view of firm buttocks as he bent over the tub.

When he'd finished, he stood in front of her, his feet planted wide. She slid her gaze up the long length of his body only to discover a knowing grin.

"Did ye see all that needed seeing?"

"I wasn't paying much attention." And to think she'd always prided herself on telling the truth, even when telling Mrs. Jenkins that no, long blond hair did *not* make her look like Britney Spears lost her a client.

He didn't seem to think the lie worthy of a reply because he gestured toward the tub. "Ye may bathe now. Then ye must dress and come wi' me to Neil's dwelling."

"Why can't I stay here while you visit Neil?"

"I dinna want to leave ye alone. There are dangers ye know nothing about."

Dangers? That didn't sound comforting. But she had something more pressing to take care of. She had to get him out of the cave while she bathed. "I dropped my ring outside last night. Do you think you could look for it? It belonged to my grandmother, and I'd hate to lose it." She tried for an inspired look. "Gee, now would be a great time to search while you're waiting for me to finish my bath."

He frowned as he put on his plaid. "Ye had no rings on last night. There is no need to make up tales. Ye need only ask me to leave while ye bathe."

"Well, dumb me for thinking you intended to stay and watch. Wasn't that what you said yesterday?"

His smile lit the dim interior. "Aye. But yesterday I wasna in a hurry. If I watch ye today, I willna get done what needs doing. We wouldna leave the cave at all."

Maybe it was time to remind him of a basic fact. "Forget what you think you know about women. I don't want to be seduced. Yes, I find you physically attractive, but I have a mind. And my mind tells me that making love with you would be a mistake. So no matter how you make me feel, my mind will always override my senses. Give it up, Ross."

"If ye say so."

She didn't for a minute think he believed her as

he placed Malin on top of Peter and headed for the cave entrance. "Ye must come wi' me, Peter. Only women may stay."

Peter paused, his lights flashing. "My first day as a woman and I'm already getting hot flashes!" Then he tagged after Ian.

Robin Williams? *Mrs. Doubtfire*? Kathy grinned at Peter's parting shot.

Ian sat on a rock outside the cave and thought of the woman bathing within. She'd be easing into the water now, the ripples lapping at her breasts. He'd seen enough to know her breasts would fill his hands. He longed to feel their weight, their texture. Her pale shoulders would gleam as she drew the cloth across them and down over her breasts.

Would she touch her nipples and moan softly, imagining his mouth on them? Would she slide the cloth beneath the water, dragging it across her smooth stomach, along her inner thighs, and think of his fingers tracing the same path?

God's teeth, but 'twas a hot morning. He lifted his hair from the back of his neck, letting the cool air touch him. It wasn't much help.

He'd saved the best thought for last. Would she draw the cloth between her thighs, touching herself and imagining his fingers stroking the spot that brought her pleasure? Would she breathe his name?

"Winter must be cold for those with no warm memories."

Startled, Ian glanced at Peter, then smiled. "Ye'll

153

ne'er find Ian Ross wi'out a warm memory." He turned his gaze to the cave entrance. " 'Twould please me mightily to add Kathy of Hair to my memories." Only she would never be a warm memory. He knew when they joined it would be the crackle of a hot fire, the steam from a boiling caldron. 'Twould be a memory to heat the coldest night.

He frowned. It seemed he thought overmuch of the woman and not enough of his brothers' challenge. He must keep in mind the reason for this joining.

"She'll be dressing now, Peter, putting on layers of cloth to protect her body from me. 'Twill do no good." He rose and walked toward the rocky path leading away from the entrance. It was always wise to make certain no Mackays were near.

"Ian Ross, I want to talk to you now!"

Turning, he hurried back to the cave entrance. What manner of beast could make her shout so? He drew his knife from his sock in readiness.

He reached the cave to find Kathy standing at the entrance with hands on hips and the gleam of battle in her eyes. Glancing around, he saw no danger.

"You don't play fair, Ross. I don't know how you did it, but you were touching me when I was taking my bath." As her initial anger cooled, he sensed uncertainty creeping in. "I closed my eyes, and I *felt* you touch my breasts, and . . . other places."

He knew not what to tell her. His power was such that when his response to a woman ran strong, he could will himself into her imaginings. But he'd felt nothing that powerful for any woman since the first stirrings of his undisciplined youth. *Why now?*

Mayhap Malin had been right to follow him that first day. Malin had sensed danger, and any woman who affected him so was a grave threat. The Pleasure Master must feel no emotion so strongly, not even physical need. "I dinna understand ye. I did nothing but speak wi' Peter about the coldness of winter."

"Oh." She shifted her gaze from him. "Well, it sure felt like someone was touching me."

"The shock of what happened to ye has made ye imagine what isna there." *And what is yer excuse, Ian Ross?*

"Maybe." Her expression brightened. "So why're we going to Neil's place?" She picked up her cloth bag and put its strap across her shoulder.

"What have ye in yer sack?"

He didn't miss her guilty start. "Oh, this and that. Nothing much."

"Be verra careful to whom ye show 'this and that'" He wanted to order her to take the sack back to the cave, but she would argue, and he had no time to waste.

They walked down the path, with Peter clattering behind. "Aren't you going to lock Peter and Malin up?"

He shook his head. "I have decided 'twould do no good. Neil has seen Peter, as have the others.

155

His strangeness might prove a protection should anyone accost ye."

"Accost me?" He saw a flicker of fear in her gaze.

"Ye must stay wi' me whene'er possible. There are those who would destroy what they dinna understand. I must leave ye for a short time, but Neil will keep ye safe."

She nodded, but remained silent for the rest of their walk.

They'd almost reached Neil's cottage when a man stepped into their path. Malin jumped from Peter and hobbled to stand beside Ian.

Kathy's first impression was that God the Father was out taking a stroll. The stranger was a walking stereotype complete with long flowing white beard and piercing gaze.

"Ach, the very spawn of the devil I hoped to meet." He even had the deep, booming voice she imagined God having.

She frowned. Maybe his robes were a bit overdone—green velvet trimmed in gold. Wouldn't basic black be more appropriate for an area with so much poverty? And maybe he was a little too . . . plump to be an exact replica of the Almighty. She'd never pictured God as needing to visit a fitness center.

Strange. He'd mentioned spawn of the devil and hadn't once looked at Peter.

" 'Tis the good father out tending his flock of sinners, no doubt. It must have sore grieved ye to leave yer mistress's bed so early."

She heard Ian's sarcasm and took a second look at the stranger. Father? A priest? What had happened to his vow of poverty? The rings on one hand would have paid her rent for five years. And mistress? He must have forgotten the Church vow of chastity.

The man smiled and destroyed his image. Sly and evil weren't godly expressions. "God rewards those who do His work and punishes blasphemers. Ye'll burn in Hell, Ian Ross." The thought seemed to satisfy him.

Peter's amber lights flashed, immediately drawing everyone's attention. Kathy wanted to clap her hands over her ears.

"Life after death is as improbable as sex after marriage."

The priest's eyes widened; sly and evil gave way to good old-fashioned terror. " 'Tis a demon."

Say something. "He's only a machine. The people who made him put those words into him. See, he's not the demon, *they* are. I'd give you their address, but I've lost my address book."

Peter's lights flashed happily. Evidently, he felt the need to take part in the conversation. "I always like sinners a lot better than saints."

The good father abandoned the field to the damned as he turned and fled, his robes flapping in the breeze.

Kathy stared at Peter. "*Last Man Standing*. Poor programming choice. What we needed was a more God-like quote. Maybe something from those God movies that George Burns made. Charlton Heston would've been a nice touch."

Ian was studying the toy with narrow-eyed suspicion.

"Ye have done what no other has e'er done. Ye made him run from ye."

Kathy couldn't keep quiet. The priest, Peter, everything was dissolving into the kind of dream she'd have after eating a pepperoni pizza right before going to bed. "Listen to you, Ian. You're talking to a toy. Every one of his lines is from some movie, for heaven's sake. I know because I watch tons of movies, and I recognize every quote."

Peter's lights flashed. "Incredible! One of the worst performances of my career and they never doubted it for a second."

"See? That's from *Ferris Bueller's Day Off.*"

Ian turned his gaze on Kathy, and she shivered at what she saw there. "I've ne'er seen a movie, and I dinna know what Peter is, but he isna a toy." His smile didn't reach his eyes. "Mayhap our priest has finally met one who canna be cowed by threats of eternal damnation."

She wouldn't believe Ian because if she did then she'd have to fear Peter, and she didn't need one more thing to fear. "You didn't seem too afraid of the priest."

Ian shrugged. "I have known him for twenty years. Our good Father Gregory has always condemned the Pleasure Master as a tool of Satan. He believes God has ordained that only *he* have pleasure."

"Do the people believe him?" When she got back to New York, she'd show more appreciation for Father Deleone's kindness and gentle sermons that didn't include fire and brimstone.

"The Pleasure Master has been in this glen longer than Father Gregory. He canna turn the people against me, but that hasna stopped him from trying to find one who would kill me. He doesna care who does the killing, so long as it canna be traced back to his holy self."

Kathy had never met evil up close and personal. This wasn't a random mugging reported on a sound byte as she drove to work.

"Father Gregory wants no competition for the ear of the laird. 'Tis not about God; 'tis about power."

Malin returned to his resting spot on top of Peter, and they continued to Neil's. But Kathy's world had been knocked a little more out of kilter.

She cast Ian a sideways glance. He was a man who survived knowing that he faced possible death or capture each day, and accepted the possibility with courage. Survived without benefit of a close friend or one who loved him. She realized Ian Ross was the strongest man she'd ever met.

And that disturbed her. She didn't want to admit Ian was different from her ex-husband. "You mentioned the laird. Will I meet him?"

"Mayhap." He turned up the path that led to what Kathy assumed was Neil's cottage. "He has traveled to speak wi' James, but if Henry sends his army across the border, the laird will return to

159

gather us to defend the king. My father travels wi' him."

James? Henry? She should have paid more attention to her British history.

Neil met them at the door. As he led them inside, she glanced around the bare room. A table and a few chairs. A hearth. Martha Stewart could spend a lifetime trying to make this place homey. Kathy was starting to appreciate the comfort of Ian's cave.

Ian stood by the door. "I would ask ye to keep Kathy of Hair safe while I'm gone."

Neil cast him a sharp glance. "Ye go to take back yer horse from the Mackays?"

"Aye." He turned to leave.

"Do ye need Colin and me to go wi' ye?"

She could see the light of battle in his eyes. Still, his offer of help didn't sound like that of a man who cared nothing about his brother.

Ian shook his head. " 'Tis best I go alone. One man risks less chance of discovery. I would borrow yer horse though."

Neil nodded, and they watched Ian leave. As she turned back to Neil, Kathy tried to ignore the heavy feeling in her stomach, the feeling that she was now truly alone. Funny, no matter how upset she'd been by her sudden launch into this time, she'd always known that Ian was there. What if he didn't come back?

"He'll be okay, won't he? He'll just get his horse and ride home, right?"

Neil didn't meet her gaze. "Aye. 'Tis nothing that Ian hasna done before."

She tried to push back the first twinges of panic with words. "I brought my cell phone so you can talk to Coco. I need to talk to her, too."

She dug the phone from her pack and dialed Coco's number. Coco answered on the first ring.

"Okay, where are you? You haven't called for five days and I've been worried. I tried to have your last call traced and came up with zip. Talk to me, Kathy." Coco's concern washed over her and made her feel like crying. But there was nothing she could do, absolutely nothing.

"I'm perfectly safe, Coco." *You haven't called for five days.* "It's . . . January fifteenth?"

"All day. Guess you still aren't going to tell me what's going on."

"There's nothing to tell. I'm with a man. I'm safe. Did you find any information?" She noted that Neil had edged close. Coco's sigh carried a world of frustration. "Wait a minute while I get it." She heard the rustle of paper. "Okay, James the Fifth died in 1542. Mary Queen of Scots was born the same year and was proclaimed queen. Henry the Eighth was king of England. Oh, and that cat you wanted to know about. It's a Turkish Van. Associated with the Lake Van area of Turkey, loves to swim, and God knows why you wanted to know all that."

"I would speak to Coco."

Too late, Kathy realized Neil was close enough

161

to hear everything being said. Great. Just great. She handed the phone to him.

"Explain what ye meant, Coco."

Kathy knew if Neil used that tone of voice to her she'd blurt out everything she'd ever known.

"Ye say that King James is dead and that some Mary is queen? Ye dinna know what ye say. James is alive and there isna any Mary."

"Is everyone crazy there? I took this straight off the Net."

Kathy could see Neil's face pale above his beard. "What year is it, Coco?"

"I wish you wouldn't ask that question. It makes me nervous."

"What year is it?" Neil's voice had risen to a roar.

"Okay, okay. It's 2001." Kathy could hear the growing fear in Coco's voice. "Put Kathy back on."

Neil handed the phone back to her with fingers that shook.

"Kathy, you've got to get away from that place. Everyone's crazy. Just tell me where you are, and I'll come get you."

Kathy felt a tear slide down her face and didn't bother to wipe it away. "I'll be in touch, Coco." She hung up with Coco's frantic questions echoing in her ears.

She turned to Neil.

"Ye canna be from the future." He looked bewildered.

"That's what Ian said." She sat down on the chair by the table.

He pulled the other chair over to sit beside her.

"But these things she said about James and this Mary . . ."

"What if you find out they're true?"

He shook his head. "I would think both of ye witches."

"And . . . ?" If Neil told everyone she was a witch, would even Ian be able to protect her?

Neil shrugged. "I would say nothing. Coco is my challenge, and I will win her, witch or no."

Kathy breathed a long sigh of relief.

"Ye must tell me what sort of man Coco favors."

"Hmm. She doesn't like facial hair, so lose the beard. And she likes a man with good hair and a clean body. I can do a little with your hair, but you're going to have to bathe every day." Lost in thought, she barely noted his look of horror.

"Coco willna know whether I do those things."

Kathy grinned at him. "I'll tell her. I don't lie to my friends. And after we take care of those little things, we can work on your sensitivity."

He glared at her.

Well, maybe not. Some men just weren't cut out to be sensitive.

"Do what ye must." He'd probably walk to his execution with that expression. "Ye dinna have any noxious potions wi' ye?"

"Not a one." *Yes.* Kathy unzipped her backpack and pulled out her supplies. Finally, a chance to do what she did best. She'd start quickly while he was still enthralled with the zipper on her backpack and before he realized what she was doing.

One man would walk the Highlands with good hair and a new understanding of personal hygiene because Kathy Bartlett had passed his way.

She felt like a sixteenth-century Johnny Appleseed.

Chapter Nine

Would she be waiting for him at Neil's door, her golden hair blowing in the cold wind that had whipped up? Would her eyes that could hide nothing be clouded by worry? Would her lips be parted as she scanned the hills looking for a sign of him?

The thought of her warmed Ian. He would run his fingers through her hair, and pull her into his arms. He'd taste her soft lips, which could heat his blood as even the most potent brew could not.

They'd go home, and he'd tell her of what he'd done, of his satisfaction at outwitting the Mackays.

He could not remember ever being so eager to reach a woman before. Ian frowned. He enjoyed women's bodies, but that was the extent of his involvement with them. If he was to win the challenge, he could not allow thoughts of speaking with her by a warm fire to intrude. His thoughts must only be of seduction.

Ian couldn't suppress his disappointment to find Neil's door closed. He got off his horse, then led both Neil's and his horse around to the back of the cottage, where they could graze.

Finished, he pushed open the door . . . and froze. The man staring back at him *wasn't* his brother. His beard was gone, and the only reminder it had ever existed was the pale skin that hadn't been exposed to the sun since Neil was old enough to sprout hair on his chin. His hair still hung past his shoulders, but barely. It looked . . .

Ignoring the woman who was obviously responsible for the changes, he strode to his brother to take a closer look. His hair didn't look tangled and windblown. It looked shiny and *clean.*

Ian was both amazed and angry. He'd spent the day braving the cunning and wrath of the Mackays, and Kathy had thought only of his brother. Ian had no idea why the thought infuriated him so. It was not as though he'd returned to find them in bed.

He tried to recapture the attitude he should have as Pleasure Master, thinking only of how this would affect the challenge, but his fury would not allow him to think clearly.

He swung to confront the meddling wench. "What have ye done to Neil?" *What have ye done to me?*

"Ye needna bellow, Ian. I asked her to make me such as Coco would desire. 'Tis an improvement.

What say ye?" He grinned at Ian, then returned his attention to a small mirror he held.

"I can't believe how great Neil looks. Who would've thought all that hair was covering up such an incredible face. When I describe him to Coco she'll"—Kathy frowned—"want to see him."

Ian felt the stab of betrayal almost as a physical blow. "I wouldna have believed it of ye, woman. While I have risked death from the Mackays, ye've been here trying to help my brother win the challenge."

"Death?" Her eyes widened in horror. He felt some of his anger drain. "Neil said it was nothing, that you'd just get your horse and come back."

"And did ye think the Mackays would be waiting to give the horse to me wi' apologies for all my trouble? What did ye think they'd do if they caught me taking him?"

"I . . . don't know. I didn't think." She gazed at him, eyes dark with regret.

"She told me things I need know to win Coco. I must remember to speak of Coco's favorite French restaurant." Neil looked puzzled. "I dinna know why she wouldna eat good Scottish food."

Peter's amber lights flashed. "I think most Scottish cuisine is based on a dare."

Neil glared at Peter. "Ye should rid yerself of yon wee demon, Ian."

Peter seemed to be the only one Ian wasn't angry at. "I like him fine. He amuses me more than most." He glanced at Kathy. "Do ye ken what movie 'tis from?"

She nodded. *"So I Married an Axe Murderer."* She sounded subdued.

Momentarily diverted, Ian murmured, " 'Tis a passing strange name. I would see this movie."

Neil's gaze turned calculating. "I would thank ye, Kathy, for helping me win Coco. When I am Pleasure Master, I will remember what ye did." He slid his gaze to Ian to see his reaction.

"Dinna try to anger me more, Neil. I am tired and would go home." He turned to the door and could hear Kathy gathering her things together.

By the time he led his horse to the front of the cottage, she was waiting for him with Peter and Malin. "We'll walk home. I wouldna ask the horse to carry anyone after riding him hard all day."

She nodded, but said nothing. A part of him wanted her to apologize more, to look at him with eyes filled with remorse, to offer him anything if he would no longer be angry.

The reasonable part of him said he should forget his anger, that she had done nothing to really harm him. Reason said his feelings were hurt because she had not missed him, because she'd amused herself with his brother.

He didn't want to listen to anything reasonable though. He didn't want to think this woman could affect him so.

"Ian, someone is trying to get your attention." He felt Kathy tug on his sleeve and looked up.

"Aye, Jamie." He acknowledged the large red-haired man who was standing in front of the small stone cottage they were passing.

The man beckoned him inside, and Ian exhaled wearily. He couldn't ignore the man, but all he wanted to do was go home and sleep. "We'll stop for a short while. Leave Peter and Malin wi' the horse. Jamie will accept ye, but I dinna want to explain Peter."

"Fine." She followed him into the cottage.

He sat at Jamie's table, and Kathy sat beside him. "Has yer wife improved, Jamie?"

Jamie placed a drink in front of them, and Ian watched Kathy take a sip. For the first time that day he felt like smiling as her eyes widened and she blinked to stop their watering. She opened her mouth and drew in small panting breaths. His gaze was drawn to the rise and fall of her breasts. Mayhap he wouldn't go to sleep as soon as he reached home.

"She isna better. Since losing the babe, she willna do more than sit and stare at the fire. I dinna know what more to do."

Ian's gaze shifted to the woman half hidden in the shadows. She sat so still that if Jamie hadn't mentioned her, he wouldn't have noticed her.

"She lost a child?" Kathy's voice was warm with sympathy.

"Aye. 'Twas our first." Jamie folded his hands on the table and stared at work-reddened fingers. "I told her we would have more, but she wouldna listen. She grieves only for this one. The priest came, but he grew angry wi' her silence and said I should beat her if she wouldna submit. I dinna want to do such."

169

"Your priest is a bastard."

For once, Ian agreed with Kathy's blunt speech.

Ignoring Jamie's shocked expression, Kathy pulled open her backpack and rooted through its contents. "I stuck a few toys in here, thinking I might meet some kids who'd like them."

Ian huffed a breath of impatience. Would the woman never realize she was no longer in her land, where such things were accepted without suspicion? "Mayhap ye should leave all at home next time."

Ian's expression promised he'd have a lot to say about the things in her backpack when they reached the cave.

She grinned at him, knowing she was safe for the moment. He didn't dare say anything in front of Jamie.

Kathy pulled Baby Born from the pack and carried it over to Jamie's wife. The woman looked at her out of dead eyes.

Kathy reached out and laid the doll in the woman's arms. "This is Baby Born. She isn't real, but hold her, cry over her, then put her away and have another baby of your own."

The woman looked down at the doll, and Kathy feared she'd reject the gift. But slowly, the woman enfolded the doll in her arms, then looked up at Kathy. A tear slid down her cheek.

Oh shoot, she was going to end up bawling along with the woman. Quickly, Kathy returned to her seat beside Ian.

She blinked rapidly and tried to concentrate on what Jamie was saying.

" 'Tis the first tear she's shed since the babe died." He was staring at Kathy as though she'd created a miracle.

Kathy shrugged and tried for nonchalance. "Sometimes just having something to hold when you're feeling bad helps." She gazed thoughtfully at Jamie. "Have you tried holding your wife?"

Jamie looked uncomfortable. "I didna think she'd welcome my touch."

Kathy smiled. "I'd say she needs it now more than she's ever needed it." When her marriage and her world had collapsed, she had longed for someone just to hold her, comfort her.

"Would ye like a wee drop more to drink?" Jamie started to rise.

"Uh, no thank you." She looked at the drink in front of her. A few more sips and she wouldn't have a stomach lining.

"We've had a long day, Jamie. 'Tis best if we get home before darkness falls." Ian rose and put his arm across Kathy's shoulders.

She stiffened. Was this show of affection just for Jamie's sake? Would Ian be angry and disapproving again once they were alone?

Outside, Ian dropped his arm from her shoulders and retrieved his horse. When he returned, he grasped her hand in his, then continued along the path to his cave.

Night had fallen, the darkness intensifying Kathy's sensations. She could hear Peter clattering along behind them, but far enough away so that he couldn't hear what they said.

Listen to yourself. She was thinking of the toy as human. The thought made her uncomfortable.

"Ye wished to help Jamie's wife, but ye must be careful what ye show others." Ian's voice was low, with none of his former anger. "The Pleasure Master has been a part of the glen for almost a hundred years, but ye've been here only a short time. Many willna accept the things ye bring wi' ye. They will believe them tools of the devil."

She nodded, raising her face to a night sky filled with what seemed a million stars. She'd never seen a sky like this in New York. "I know you're telling the truth, but it's still hard for me to remember the differences between this time and my own."

His hand tightened around hers. A large hand, hard, comforting. "None will harm ye while ye're wi' me."

And she believed him.

"Ian, I noticed that Jamie was the only villager who invited you to stop at his home. Everyone else nodded, but then looked away."

She felt Ian's smile in the darkness. "Peter would discourage many. He doesna make a comfortable guest."

She stumbled over a rock, and Ian drew her to him, putting his arm around her waist. She felt wrapped in his solid strength, but there was something more. An awareness, a warmth that had nothing to do with body heat, quickened her breathing.

She hoped he thought she was just out of breath from climbing the hill to the cave.

"Okay, I can accept that, but I still had the feeling they were uncomfortable with you." She tried to relax, but relax wasn't part of her vocabulary where Ian Ross was concerned. "Except for Jamie. He seemed glad to see you."

Ian shrugged. "Jamie needed to speak wi' someone. I was passing by, and 'tis not a path many travel."

Kathy felt like Mrs. Martin's bulldog with a bone. She knew there was something he wasn't telling her, and she wanted to know. "But what about the others? They didn't seem too friendly, and don't tell me it was because of Peter."

"What if ye thought I'd lain wi' yer sister, counseled yer mother? Would ye feel comfortable speaking wi' me? What if I'd lain wi' *ye?* Would ye want others to see ye speaking wi' me, wondering?"

His bluntness was like the splash of a North Atlantic wave. "Then why do they let the Pleasure Master exist?"

The smile he turned on her was no smile at all. "The Pleasure Master brings wealth and fame to the glen. And those who come to me are desperate for help—women who have ne'er known joy of their bodies, women who wish to please their husbands, but need be taught how."

"I remember enough of my history books to know that in this time, women didn't think they were supposed to enjoy their bodies, and men didn't care about women's pleasure."

He frowned at her. "Did those who wrote yer books live wi' us to know all these things? There are always those who care about giving and receiving pleasure."

"I guess there can be exceptions in any age." She'd stopped in the middle of the path. "So why did Jamie accept you into his home?"

"Jamie is new to the glen. He has no family member who could have visited me."

"Oh." What more could she say? She understood men like her ex-husband, but she didn't understand a man like Ian Ross. Ian was as different from her ex as a tiger was from Jenny Clark's old orange tabby.

His chuckle was warm, amused. "Dinna look so horrified. I need only speak to many of the women who seek me out. I havena bedded all the lasses in Scotland." His smile faded. "But the legend of the Pleasure Master is such that most wouldna believe it. Since no one knows who has visited me, all are suspicious."

She glanced behind her. No Peter. He must've fallen behind. She'd stand a few more minutes and wait for him to catch up. "You'd have to work harder in my time. Women in 2001 are a lot more sexually aware. They know a lot more."

"Knowing and feeling are not always the same, lass." His warm breath fanned over her neck and she shivered.

She glanced behind her again. Where *was* Peter? The darkness closed in on her. This wasn't a New York dark, with street lights and lighted windows.

This was *dark*. And somehow, Ian Ross intensified the darkness, drew it to him, wrapped her in its blackness.

"Why do you keep doing it, if it alienates you from everyone?"

His glance was puzzled. " 'Tis who I am, who I've always been. I've been trained to be Pleasure Master since I was taken from my mother." His puzzlement gave way to warmth. "I enjoy women, and 'tis no burden helping them."

"I bet it isn't." Kathy had no idea why his last statement bothered her so much. "But I still say you'd have a lot rougher going in my time."

"Mayhap."

She couldn't read anything from his tone.

"Have ye ne'er had fantasies about men, Kathy?"

His question caught her by surprise, and she answered without thinking. "Bandits. I've always fantasized about being captured by bandits." She'd never told *anyone* that.

He dropped the horse's reins and moved closer, so close she could feel the heat from his body, see the rise and fall of his chest beneath his plaid. " 'Tis a fine fantasy." His low murmur barely reached her.

"Hear them, Kathy. Moving toward ye in the darkness. See them closing in on ye from all sides." His husky suggestions made her glance around.

What was that shadow beside the tree? And that scrabbling noise? Some small animal or Peter catching up?

"Feel the blood and evil they bring wi' them. Know what they want from ye." He reached across

175

her shoulders and slipped off her shawl. She didn't, *couldn't,* stop him.

"There is one who wants ye more than the others. He'll kill to make ye his, as he's killed many times before." He leaned down, a dark threatening shadow, and touched his mouth to the base of her neck. "Ye'll not deny him if ye wish to live."

This *wasn't* real. And yet she saw them, dark bearded men, with torn and bloodied clothing, leering at her out of the night. She heard their jeering laughter, felt their hot lust, knew that only their leader held them back. Because he wanted her himself.

Logic had nothing to do with her panic as she tried to turn and run from him. But he grasped both her hands, drew close until his body touched hers, forcing her back, back, until a wall of rock stopped her. "Hey, this isn't fun. You're scaring me."

Which wasn't completely true. Mixed with the fear was a growing excitement—fierce, wild.

"This isna about fun. This is about yer body and mine. I'll have ye here, and ye'll remember me always. When the darkness falls ye'll see me beyond yer window, and wonder what evil I'm about that night."

"I'll fight you." Her fear was disappearing, replaced by hot anticipation.

"Fight me till yer breath comes fast and hard, till yer heart pounds. 'Twill make no difference, but 'twill add spice to the taking." His voice was savage, *hungry*.

She kicked at him and made contact with his leg,

heard his muttered curse, and gloried in her fight against this bandit.

Her struggle to free her hands was useless as he grasped both wrists and forced her arms above her head. He pressed his body against hers, forcing her back until she could feel every ridge in the rock wall, every muscular inch of *him*. To avoid the rock digging into her, she pushed against his body.

"Ye canna escape me, lass."

With her arms stretched high above her head, she couldn't hit him. And as she tried to kick at him again, he shoved his knee between her legs, forcing her to spread them. Through the cloth of her dress, she could feel the strength of his thrust.

Even through her panties, she felt his knee pressing against her most sensitive spot. She clenched her thighs, riding his knee to increase the pressure. As he rubbed his knee back and forth, she felt the hot heavy feeling building. "I'll kill you for this."

"I fear ye already have."

She barely heard his soft response because some distant part of her mind was wondering how he'd pulled her so completely into the fantasy. But it wasn't a fantasy. He *was* a bandit, and she'd fight him until . . . "You're a dead man, you thieving—"

"I dinna think so." He transferred both wrists to one hand and trailed a path of hot kisses down the side of her neck.

With his other hand, he deftly unlaced her dress, then roughly pulled her arms down long enough to slip the dress to her waist and pull off her bra.

She was weak with something so strong she

hadn't the strength to fight. Every sense she had seemed centered in her breasts and between her thighs. She could hear the loud rasp of her breathing. Or was it his?

Bared to the waist, she felt him pull her arms high above her head again and secure her wrists in one large hand.

"Do ye feel my men watching ye, hungering for ye, knowing that your body is for me alone?"

The cold breeze played across her breasts and her nipples hardened in response. Without conscious thought, she arched her back, begging for . . .

With a groan, he lowered his head and put his mouth on one breast, sliding his tongue across her hard nipple, then gently nipping. She almost sobbed her pleasure.

"Ye'll give me much pleasure tonight, lass." He took her nipple into his mouth and suckled as he rolled her other nipple between two fingers, then gently squeezed.

She felt a tear slide down her cheek.

"My men draw closer. They want me to lay ye on the ground, spread yer legs, and take ye. They will draw pleasure from the watching."

"No." *No, don't stop. Please.*

"Aye, 'tis the way of bandits." He abandoned her nipples. Removing his knee from between her legs, he roughly pulled her dress up to her waist, then ripped her panties from her. "Ye'll not need these."

She didn't have the strength to close her thighs, and she knew his men were enjoying the sight of her bared body. She made a feeble attempt to free her arms, but he tightened his grip.

"Dinna struggle, lass. I willna free ye until I've thrust hard into yer soft body, filling ye . . ." He seemed to run out of words, and she could hear his sharp intake of breath as he slid his hand between her thighs, then rubbed one finger back and forth against the spot that already felt swollen, wet, and too sensitive to touch.

She did cry out then, and didn't care whether his men or every man in the Highlands heard her.

"Aye, let my men know what they miss."

His hand abandoned her, and she moaned her disappointment. She felt him pull up his plaid, then gasped at the hard pressure of his erection against her stomach. "I'll take ye here, wi' yer breasts bared and yer legs spread. I'll thrust hard and deep until ye scream wi' the pleasure."

She writhed against him—wanting, needing.

"Do ye want this, lass? Want it enough to live the fantasy to its end?" His question was low, harsh.

Yes. The word wouldn't come, she couldn't force it past her lips. She felt as though her hesitation lasted years, all the way back to the beginning of her marriage, all the way to the end of her hope.

He grew still. She could feel his breaths coming in huge gasps, felt desire shuddering through him. Slowly, as though each movement was agony, he released her. Pulling her dress down, he stepped back.

Her out-of-control senses began to right themselves. There were no bandits. She was standing in front of Ian Ross with her breasts bared and her emotions in shreds. Desire was slow to recede, and she could still feel small anticipatory spasms.

She picked up her bra, and put it back on. When Ian moved to help her, she shook her head. With unsteady fingers, she pulled up her dress, then laced it as best she could.

Shame flooded her. "Why did you . . . ? I don't understand."

She tried to ward him off, but he reached her in one step and pulled her into his arms. Then he just held her. "Dinna be ashamed. Ye enjoyed the fantasy. There isna shame in wanting another's body."

Finally, her shaking stopped. She looked at his face, shadowed in the night. She didn't know this man, nor the one she'd wanted deep inside her a few minutes ago. *Still* wanted deep inside her. "What was that about?"

"That was about the power of the Pleasure Master. I am what ye want me to be, what will bring ye the most joy."

She felt like one of the wild creatures of the Highlands. The scent of what had almost happened was still strong around them, the fight-or-flight instinct still warring within her.

"Why didn't you finish it? You would've won the challenge."

"Aye, but it wouldna have been fair. I want no fantasy between us when we join. I dinna want ye able to find an excuse to fool yerself wi'." His wicked smile flashed white in the darkness. "Do ye still feel ye canna have yer orgasm?"

She just looked at him. No answer was necessary. "Is that all?"

He shook his head. "Do ye still think I'd have no value in yer time, that women in 2001 know more?"

Kathy hadn't believed in the power of the Pleasure Master, but who could deny his vivid demonstration?

She turned from him. "You'd have value in any time." *But not to me.* Yes, he could make her respond, but it was just another form of manipulation, and she'd had lots of experience with manipulation.

He said nothing more as he turned and continued toward the cave, leaving Kathy to follow.

Kathy started to go after him, then paused as she heard a familiar clatter behind her. Great. Her two feet of shiny movie quotes had caught up. "Whatever you're going to say, Peter, don't. I'm not in the mood." The silence encouraged her. "Okay, so it might've been wonderful, but there's always a morning after the wonderful."

She turned her head enough to see Peter's flashing amber lights. Uh-oh, he wasn't going to stay quiet. You'd think carrying a fat cat all the way from the village would have sapped some of the zap from his smart mouth.

"I'd rather have thirty minutes of wonderful than a lifetime of nothing special."

"Shelly in *Steel Magnolias*. Think you're smart, don't you?"

Peter's lights flashed agreement. "Bill Gates wants my brain."

Chapter Ten

Approaching the cave entrance, he scanned the surrounding area, searching for signs of intrusion. There were none. He'd hoped the Mackays would be waiting, for he felt the need to crack some heads.

He could hear Kathy behind him, but she said nothing. Did she realize how close she'd come to completing her fantasy whether she wished it or not?

Striding down the tunnel, he paused before entering the main chamber. He must live with this woman until he seduced her. *Seduced,* not tricked into passion using a favorite fantasy. Then he would find a way to send her home. 'Twould not be as simple, though, as he'd thought in the beginning.

"Is everything okay?" She spoke from behind

him, but not too close. She'd learned caution with him.

"Aye. I was but checking that none had been here in our absence."

He walked into the room and lit several candles from the glowing embers of the hearth fire. She followed him and put her things near her bed, then picked up the nightgown Mary had given her. "I'll be back in a few minutes." She disappeared down the tunnel to the pool.

"I loooove you." Suzy Sunshine blinked her eyes, waved her leaves, and wiggled her stem in greeting.

He frowned at her. "Ye're bold for a flower, but then all seem so that come from yer land."

He exhaled sharply, allowing himself to relax for a moment. Never had a woman tested him so. He enjoyed being with women, but he'd never wanted one so badly that he'd lost sight of his purpose. Tonight he'd lost himself in his own pleasure, his own desire. Kathy of Hair was the most dangerous woman he'd ever known.

Even deep in his brooding thoughts, he knew when she'd returned. He sensed her like the wolf did his prey. *Or his mate.* The last thought left him uncomfortable. The Pleasure Master needed no mate.

He turned to gaze at her. She looked clean and beautiful. "I'll wash. If ye wish to sleep, ye may put out the candles. I dinna need light."

She met his gaze. "But it's early yet."

Mayhap 'tis too late. He shrugged. "Do what ye wish."

184

He strode to the pool, flung off his clothing, then waded in.

The cool water flowed around him, sliding past him like the smooth glide of her skin under his hands. But other women's skin had been just as smooth. Why did *she* affect him so?

He gazed into the water, watching it grow still, the ripples dying away as he stood without moving. It would stay thus, placid, if not disturbed. The pool had no wind, no currents, no *storms* to disturb it. The pool would never prove a danger to him. Such were the women he'd known. They'd acted and thought as women were expected to act and think.

But *Kathy*. He sometimes went to stand on the cliff overlooking the sea as a storm approached. His excitement would build as the waves crashed against the shore, then fell back into dangerous whirlpools and eddies, only to re-form and fling themselves against the rocks again. He'd close his eyes, letting the wind whip seaspray against his face, listen to the song of the waves. It was a Siren's song, and much like Kathy. Strong, unpredictable, *exciting*.

He washed quickly, then returned to the chamber. Kathy would test him as the sea would. But if he stayed on shore, secure in who and what he was, then she could do no harm.

She was seated in front of the hearth, peering intently at a game she'd placed in front of her. "Play with me, Ian. I think I've figured it out."

He wanted to refuse. 'Twould be best if he retired to his bed and tried to forget what he'd almost done tonight. But she looked up at him, smiling, *challenging*, and he couldn't refuse.

"What must I do to play this game?" He sat across from her.

"This is a hockey game. You use these buttons to control the figures. The idea is to get the puck in the net. It's pretty basic."

"Puck?" He frowned at the strange thing. "What do ye earn if ye win?"

"You get to push this red button. I don't know what it does because I haven't gotten that far in the rules. But I hate reading rules, so let's just start."

He blinked as she started pushing buttons on her side of the game, making the figures zigzag back and forth across the flat surface. He'd barely reached for his buttons before she knocked the puck into his net. A loud buzz sounded that almost made him leap away. Why must every toy either make a noise or soak you? At least this one wouldn't leave him wet.

"I won. I won." Her eyes shone with delight, and for a moment he forgot all about the game. "I get to push the button."

She pushed the button with enthusiasm, and a stream of water hit him in the face. His curses were varied and colorful. "God's teeth, woman, are all yer toys made by minions of the devil?"

Uh-oh. "Not really. I think this one was made by Linden Toy Company." She glanced at the box. "Yep. No devil's minions on the box."

He sat with water dripping down his face and a thunderous expression that probably would have driven a hundred Mackays back to their castle, but she couldn't help it. She started to giggle, let it build to a laugh, then lost control as it deteriorated into roll-on-the-ground guffaws.

A part of her responsible for protecting life and limb warned that her response was not receiving favorable reviews. Her laughter died away as she wiped the tears from her eyes, then chanced a glance at him.

His glare was silver fury. "Are ye done laughing at me?"

"Sure. All finished. Won't need to laugh for at least another month." He didn't look mollified. "Besides, I wasn't laughing at you. Not exactly. Okay, sort of. But if you could've seen your expression . . ."

"I wouldna have found it amusing."

"You know, Ross, you have a rotten sense of humor." Good. Now he was making her mad.

"I would play that game again." Wiping the moisture from his face, he gazed at the buttons with narrow-eyed determination.

"No."

He looked at her with the same expression he'd had when he first heard Suzy Sunshine.

An important revelation hit her. "People don't often say no to you, do they?"

His gaze softened, grew coaxing. "I dinna give women a reason to say no." He grinned at her, looking wicked, give-me-what-I-want enticing. "Play wi' me, Kathy."

She drew her breath in at his suggestion, his underlying meaning. "No."

He leaned back and studied her.

"Why will ye not play another game?"

"Because I bet you always have to win, don't you?"

"Aye." His smile suggested that losing to him wasn't such a terrible thing.

"Why can't you lose?"

His smile disappeared, replaced by a steady appraisal.

"I was trained to win. In all things. Ye dinna understand that 'tis the strong who survive."

"Okay, so you're competitive." There was more to this than winning; she knew it in her gut. "But it's not about winning, is it?

"You don't trust anyone enough to let them see weakness in you because trust is only a step away from those pesky human emotions, need and attachment. And human emotions make the Pleasure Master vulnerable." She narrowed her gaze to bring the truth into focus. "The Pleasure Master may not need emotions, but Ian Ross sure does."

"Ye know all this from the game we played?" His words were teasing, but his expression had turned wary.

She shrugged. "Hey, hairdressers know things. Talk to your hairdresser and you'll never need a shrink."

"I dinna know what this 'shrink' is, but 'tis not something I'd wish to need." Reaching across the game board, he placed his palm flat over her heart, and she felt the push of her breast against his hand with each breath she took. "I allow women power over my body when 'tis needed, but I trust no one. Trust is often betrayed. I am strong *here.*" He increased his hand's pressure, and it felt as though her heart was beating into his palm.

Leaning forward, Kathy placed her hand between his legs. "No, you are strong *here.* A heart isn't strong with no trust."

He looked startled. "I dinna understand all yer blather about trust." His lips curved into a smile. "But I know that ye must take yer hand away if ye wish to rest easy tonight."

She moved her hand. "You're changing the subject." She cocked her head to study him. "When was the last time you trusted someone?"

"I trusted my mother, but when my father came for me, she didna say a word to stay him. She was pleased to see the last of me."

Kathy looked down at the game, afraid her expression would show how his answer affected her, how badly she wanted to learn more.

He paused, and she thought he wouldn't continue.

"I didna trust *myself* tonight." He sounded as though the admission had been dragged from him.

She let out her breath. She hadn't realized she'd been holding it. "Don't be so hard on yourself. The night had its up side."

He lifted her chin to meet his gaze. "I willna lose control again."

There was one more thing she had to know.

"Could you ever learn to trust someone, Ian?"

"Never." His answer was immediate, decisive. "I could no more trust another than I could cease being the Pleasure Master."

"I guess it would be admitting someone was important to you. Wouldn't want to do that."

He didn't comment.

She slowly started to put the game away. "I learned something important tonight, Ian."

"Ye willna tell others yer fantasies so easily again. 'Twas a lesson hard learned." He watched narrow-eyed as she slipped the game into its box.

"My husband was my first real love, and when I couldn't reach satisfaction with him I thought I was . . ." Even now the word froze in her throat. "I thought I was frigid. And after my husband told me I was, well, I believed him. I mean, he said he was an expert. But tonight I came close enough to realize I could . . ."

His attention was riveted on her. "Ye're a warm, passionate woman, and yer husband was a fool."

She knew her smile was wavery. "For a manipulative guy, you say some really nice things. But what I meant was that I could, with *you*. I know my response was because of your . . . special gift, but maybe I can learn to have the same feeling with someone I love."

"Aye, wi' someone ye love." He didn't seem pleased at her confession. "And all people try to bend others to their will when 'tis needed." His smile turned calculating. "Or when it will get what they desire."

"I don't manipulate people." After what she'd gone through with old PMS, she'd *never* try to manipulate someone.

"Mayhap ye've ne'er wanted something badly enough."

Leaving her with that cryptic comment, he rose and blew out the candles. Sighing, she crawled beneath her furs. She had a lot to think about.

She listened as he lay down, then silence settled around her. Just when she thought he'd fallen asleep, she heard his soft chuckle.

"And we *will* play that devil's game again, lass."

She awoke to a babble of voices.

"I would speak wi' Coco. I have made myself look as she wished, and I can tell her how much I like her French restaurant."

Neil.

"I must speak wi' Kathy of Hair. Mad Mary willna allow me near her. How must I woo her?"

Colin.

"You're not too smart, are you? I like that in a man."

Peter.

"*Enough.* Ye've filled my dwelling wi' the blather of fools."

Ian.

It was nice to have the whole gang together again. She raised one lid to find four pairs of eyes peering down at her.

Neil looked frantic. "I must speak wi' Coco before Ian wins. I dinna worry about Colin. Mad Mary willna be won by such as he." He ignored Colin's angry grunt. "Ian hasna seduced ye yet, has he?" He cast her a suspicious glance.

Kathy glanced at Ian. His expression wasn't encouraging. For just a moment, she considered lying and ending this whole challenge thing. Because no matter what Ian thought, she had been a willing participant in her fantasy last night, even if he'd manipulated the situation.

"Umm. Not technically."

He won't need you anymore. If there were no challenge, he wouldn't need her to live with him; he might even send her to live with someone like Mad Mary. Mary was fine, but Kathy wanted to stay with Ian until she found a way home. She'd done some heavy thinking last night. There was something she had to do before returning to New York, and she had to be around Ian to do it.

Neil looked relieved. "Ye must be a strong woman. Ian hasna e'er taken so long to win a lass." He picked up her purse and pulled out her phone. "I will call Coco now." He walked to a far corner.

Kathy wanted to talk to Coco when Neil finished, but Colin grabbed her attention. "Ye've helped Neil, so 'tis only fair ye help me. What can I do to win Mary? I've cleaned myself and tried to woo her wi' soft words, but she willna listen."

"Why don't you ask Ian? He's the expert."

Colin didn't even glance at his brother. "Ian would be foolish to help me win the challenge."

Kathy shifted her gaze to Ian. He looked thunderous. She thought about refusing Colin, but he was right. She'd helped Neil, so it was only fair she help Colin.

"Have you tried playing your bagpipe outside her window?" Kathy couldn't control her smile. She could almost picture Mary's expression at being woken by the wail of a bagpipe.

Colin shook his head. "I only play the pipes when the laird leads us into battle. 'Tis meant to give us courage and strike fear in the hearts of our enemies."

"But wouldn't you make an exception for someone you loved?"

Colin looked at her as if she were crazy. "Aye. I would play for one I loved, but I dinna love Mary. I want only to seduce her."

Well, that was pretty specific. "Why don't you talk to her about her herbs? Women like to have something in common with a man."

"I dinna understand why we canna just go to bed and have sex." He looked truly puzzled.

"Have fun storming the castle." Peter didn't sound confident in Colin's abilities.

Ian looked amused. "Ye ken that Colin doesna yet have all the skills of a Pleasure Master."

Colin glared at him. "I'll learn." He looked back at Kathy. "I will talk to Mary as ye advised." He strode from the cave.

Kathy sighed. One down and one to go. She looked over at Neil.

"I dinna care what place ye choose to eat, but it must have good red meat. A man must keep up his strength."

Neil listened to Coco's response, then smiled. A sexy smile. "A man needs his strength to pleasure a lass all through the night."

Coco's response widened his smile. "The men of yer New York dinna have the endurance of a Scotsman. I would last until ye were so tired ye couldna lift yer head, nor any other part of yer body."

His expression grew puzzled as he glanced down to the part of his body that was obviously in question. "A lass has ne'er asked me such a question. I havena e'er *measured* it."

Peter's lights flashed. "We've got wee, not so wee, and frickin' huge."

Kathy grinned. *So I Married an Axe Murderer.* Great quote.

Neil glared at Peter, then turned away. "Let me tell ye some of the things I would do to ye." He lowered his voice so they couldn't hear any more.

Ian studied Kathy. "Ye've ne'er told me what these movies are that Peter speaks from. I ken they tell tales, but 'tis all I know about them."

Kathy shrugged. "They're large moving pictures with sound that tell a story." She felt frustrated. Movies were so much more than that. She wished she could show him one. *Uh, uh. It'll never happen. Don't even think about it.*

Ian looked intrigued, but said nothing more about the movies. "As soon as Neil finishes speaking wi' Coco, I'll get rid of him so ye may dress." His gaze grew thoughtful. "Ye thought of telling my brothers I'd won the challenge. Ye didna. Why?"

"Technically, you didn't. We didn't actually . . . You didn't . . ." *I wanted you to.*

His gaze slid over her, and even though she was covered up to her chin, she could feel the touch of his fingers, remember the pressure of his body, the coiling want in the pit of her stomach.

"But we will."

"If you're so confident, then why're you taking so long? If you wait, one of your brothers might win."

His lips lifted in the smile that turned her insides to mush. "Mayhap I enjoy the challenge. Mayhap I deny the pleasure so 'twill be sweeter when finally tasted." He glanced over at his brother.

"Ye would do *what* to me?" Neil looked truly shocked.

Ian returned his attention to Kathy. "I dinna need to worry about my brothers for a while yet."

Neil's laughter caught their attention. "Ye sound like a bonny lass. I would meet ye. When Kathy of Hair returns to her land, I will go wi' her." His voice lowered, grew husky. "Tell all other men they willna be welcome any longer. Ye'll need only me to warm yer bed."

Kathy glanced at Ian. "You can officially start worrying." She motioned to Neil. "Bring me the phone so I can talk to Coco."

She took the phone as she watched Ian guide Neil toward the tunnel. "What's the date, Coco?"

"And hello to you, too. It's January twentieth. I lied to the police and had your car towed to Mel's. He says you need a new radiator. You don't want

195

to know how much. I called your job and put them off for a while with a story about you being called away because of a sick relative. I've been going to your apartment and watering your plants. Your ivy looked lonely so I talked to it for a while. Your mom left a message on your machine from one of her cruise stops. I figured you didn't want their trip ruined with the piddling news about their only daughter disappearing to Scotland and living in a cave with a primitive Highlander. Did I forget something?"

"Sounds like you've covered all the bases. Thanks." She watched Ian crouch to stir the fire and enjoyed the flex of muscles across his back, the long line of his spine, the strong curve of buttocks and thighs. And thought about last night.

"So what's Neil look like?" The eagerness in Coco's voice surprised her. Coco's contempt for men was legendary. That was why Kathy had wanted her to take care of the divorce. Coco was like a piranha where cheating husbands were concerned.

"He shaved off his beard, and he's . . ." She cast Ian a worried glance. He didn't seem to be paying attention. "He's gorgeous. Dimples, green eyes, knife-edge cheekbones. Real model material."

"Hmm." There was a world of interest in the comment. "You know, I haven't had an alpha male in ages. Bring him along when you come home."

"Sure." Right. Like she didn't have enough trouble figuring out how to get herself home. "Talk to you later."

"Wait, Kathy." Coco's voice grew serious. "I don't know why you've made up this story, but I guess you need some time to yourself. If you decide to chuck the time-travel tale, give a yell, and I'll come get you."

"Thanks." She blinked back sudden tears as she put her phone back in her purse, then looked up to find Ian staring at her.

"What did Coco say?"

"She thinks Neil sounds like a really *fine* man. That spells trouble for you. By the way, how do you decide when someone wins? Coco wants me to bring Neil back with me."

"She must tell all that she will lay wi' him." He didn't seem overly concerned.

"That's not really fair. She won't know anything until she meets him in person."

His smile was wicked. " 'Tis a hard task I've set Neil, but if he is worthy, Coco willna need to see him." His smile softened. "Would ye not wish to take me home wi' ye?"

"Don't play games, Ian. I know you'd never come." She *wanted* to go home, but to go home without even a snapshot of Ian left her with a hollow feeling in her stomach.

"I know you don't believe I traveled from another time, but just for a moment assume I'm telling the truth. Help me brainstorm ways to get back. You don't think it was just a random blip in the universe, do you? Sort of like God burping?"

" 'Tis a wondrous moment when ye ask my opinion on any matter." His smile was open, a hint of

197

humor glinting in his eyes, and Kathy wondered how often he allowed himself to speak with a woman just for fun, with no agenda.

"I believe all things happen for a reason. I believe ye came from a distant land, but I dinna believe ye came from a distant time." He shifted his gaze to where Malin was taking his usual position atop Peter. "And if ye dinna remember traveling here on yer own, then someone or something brought ye."

"You think Peter's responsible." Not Peter, really. There had to be some intelligence, some life-force guiding Peter. But why?

Ian shrugged. "All yer toys seem strange, but only Peter speaks words that make sense wi' what's happening."

She nodded. "And there has to be something keeping my cell phone working. Talk about roaming charges."

Ian's puzzled frown reminded her how really far apart they were.

"Okay, suppose Peter *is* responsible for this whole thing. How do I convince him to send me home? I've already come right out and asked him."

"Tell me exactly what ye said right before ye found yerself here." He lowered his gaze and she studied the contrast of thick sooty lashes against tanned skin.

She guessed there was no way of avoiding the words if she wanted his help. "I wished for warmth, peace, conveniences, and a subservient man. At least Peter could've given me one of those."

"What does subservient mean?" He lifted his

gaze, and she reacted just as she did every time he looked at her.

"It means a man who'll do anything I want him to do, but won't want anything back."

His laughter startled her. It was deep and joyous, and it made her feel good all over. She would have said nothing could make her feel good all over right now. Go figure.

"Ye've come to the wrong place to find a man such as this."

He was making her grumpy. "Like I didn't know that already? Are you going to help me think of a way out of this mess or not?"

"Dinna fash yerself, lass. Mayhap ye need to tell Peter the opposite of what ye want. 'Tis what he seems to have given ye."

Kathy raked Ian's strong body with a considering glance. Maybe not.

Then she looked at Peter. She took a deep breath. She'd say it quickly before she could think of consequences, of how she'd feel if she never saw Ian Ross again. "I *don't* want to go home, Peter."

Nothing. She wondered at her small sigh of relief. No way did she want to stay in this time with a man whose whole purpose in life was to seduce her so he could win a contest. "I guess that wasn't it. So what do I say to him next?"

Ian looked distracted. "Ye seem to assume Peter's male. He has the contrary nature of a woman."

She narrowed her gaze. "He's aggravating and manipulative. Definitely male."

199

Laughter shone in Ian's eyes, lifted the corners of his expressive mouth, flipped her heart like an overdone pancake.

"Mayhap we should speak of something else ere we come to blows."

She shrugged. "Fine. Let's talk about you."

He shook his head, and his hair fell into another fascinating pattern across his shoulders. Just thirty minutes. She'd kill for just thirty minutes with her hands in his incredible hair. "What's to talk about? And don't ask me to explain all the words you don't know. I'd be old and gray before I finished."

"What do ye miss most about yer land?" His gaze grew intense, as though her answer was important to him.

"My parents." She could feel tears gathering at the thought of never seeing them again. "They live over in Jersey. Dad loves working in his garden, even if his tomatoes are never as big as Clyde Wilson's next door, and Mom is the world's best cook. No one makes a meatloaf like she does." She smiled through her tears.

He seemed uneasy with her emotion. "Aye, but I mean what *things* do ye miss."

She thought. Her car? Electricity? Hot water? "It's funny, but I don't really miss some of the big things I thought I'd miss. I think I miss some of the small things." The realization startled her.

"I miss the things that have sentimental value."

"I would hear an example."

"I miss . . ." The answer popped into her head. "I miss my shell necklace."

"I dinna understand."

It seemed silly, but there it was. "When I was about six years old, Mom and Dad took me to the beach. I lay in the sun too long and got the mother of all sunburns. While I was busy sniffling and whining, Dad went into a shop on the boardwalk and bought me this necklace made from pretty shells. He came back with it and told me that whenever I wore it, whatever was hurting would stop, that it would make me strong." She grinned. "I was six years old. I believed him. But that old necklace has always been special to me." Her smile died. "I hope I get to see it again."

He said nothing, simply stared at her. She glanced away, embarrassed. "I guess you never bothered with sentimental stuff."

"Nay."

Just the one word, but it said a lot about Ian's life. She felt sorry for him, and the feeling bothered her. On the surface, he seemed like a man who had it all. *But what do you have if you don't have any emotional connections?*

"Right. It was a silly story." She climbed from her bed and busied herself gathering the things she needed to get dressed.

He nodded toward the room that held the Pleasure Master's bed. "I'll be in there when ye finish dressing."

She dressed quickly, making sure Peter wasn't paying attention. For some reason, she was thinking of Peter as almost human. A manipulating male. And she didn't dress in front of strange males. She glanced in Peter's direction. A very *strange* male.

When she finished dressing, she wandered over to pat Malin's head. He greeted her with a friendly growl. She glanced down at Peter.

"You know, Peter, you're really messing up my world."

His amber lights flashed, a sure sign he was getting ready to mouth off.

"I am not under any orders to make the world a better place."

Chapter Eleven

Ian was still staring at the bed when he sensed her behind him. She didn't touch him, but he needed no touch to recognize her.

"I guess this bed is sort of like my necklace. You'd miss it if you had to leave." She was speaking in that hushed voice she'd used before when near the bed.

" 'Tis different. Yer necklace is a symbol of yer parents' love. It has a place in yer heart. The bed is only a reminder of the joy of physical joining. There is no remembrance of love attached." He turned and strode from the chamber.

She followed him. "I think you're wrong, Ross. I bet your great grandfather and the woman who owned that bed loved each other. No matter what you say, I can feel the love in that bed."

Nina Bangs

The talk of love bothered him, even though he'd never admit it to her. He felt the need to escape the cave, to walk beside the sea with no thoughts of seduction or his brothers' challenge.

"I would ride to the shore and walk there for a while. Ye must come wi' me." He would leave her sitting on a rock where he could see her; then he would let the joy of the sea take him, free him as it always freed him when he worried overmuch.

"Sounds like fun." Her smile was full of eager anticipation, and he pushed aside his immediate response to that smile.

"I can't remember what fun is for."

Peter's voice reminded Ian of Colin's when he was a wee lad and followed their father around begging for a sweet.

His father would laugh and give him what he whined for. Ian received very few sweets because he would never beg. His father had taught him young that the Pleasure Master never beseeched others for anything.

"Can we take Peter?"

" 'Tis amazing. Ye condemn me for trying to manipulate ye, but yon wee devil is manipulating ye, and ye dinna say a word." He didn't want to share his morning with Peter.

"Yon wee devil holds my ticket back to New York in his wee power."

Resentment touched him. She couldn't wait to escape him. But he swore that when she left she'd take with her a memory like no other.

"If we take Peter, Malin must go also. He willna

204

allow Peter to go wi' out him." That should discourage her.

"Great. We can pack something to eat, and it'll be like a family picnic." She was fairly bursting with excitement.

Bloody hell. "A passing strange family." His muttered insult had no effect on her.

"Will your horse carry all of us?" She frowned. "I've never ridden a horse before. The closest I've come was a merry-go-round horse when I was a kid. It made me sick, and Dad never took me on one again."

He should ask what a merry-go-round was, but something else interested him more, something that pulled at him even as it made him uncomfortable. "Ye speak fondly of yer parents."

She smiled at him. A soft, sad smile. "They're the best. Married thirty years and still in love. They gave me a wonderful childhood." She dropped her gaze. "I don't want to think of never seeing them again."

Would she feel such sadness at leaving *him?* He shook off the thought. Her sadness touched him, as did the tale of her parents. But he must not let sentiment affect him. He must only think of what he had to do to win the challenge. He needed no tales of love and happiness to distract him. "I will ready the horse."

As he walked from the cave, he gloried in the rare sunny day. The sea would be so blue they would have to shield their eyes against the brightness. *The same blue as Kathy's eyes.*

205

He reached his horse in a few angry strides. Curse the woman for sliding into his every thought.

When the horse was ready, he led the animal to the cave entrance.

Kathy emerged, blinking in the bright sunlight, with Peter and Malin behind her. Ian couldn't tear his gaze from the gold shine of her hair. It seemed that everything about her was bright and shining. She brought newness to everything she touched and danger to a man who must feel nothing for any particular woman.

"What do I do now?" She looked uncertain.

"I'll set ye behind the saddle, then hand Peter and Malin up to ye. 'Tis simple." His mood lightened in direct proportion to her look of horror.

"Behind the saddle? Why can't I sit on the saddle with you?" She eyed the horse's rump.

"We wouldna all fit. Ye'll be fine. I willna ask the horse for more than a walk."

She reached out to pat the horse on the nose, but Ian pushed her hand away just before the animal laid its ears back and snapped at her.

She gazed at the horse in bewilderment. "What is it about your animals? They both have attitudes."

Ian grinned. "The horse isna overly friendly. Ye're fortunate he but nipped at ye. There are several Mackays who suffered broken bones in the taking of him. But he is steady and true in battle."

"Does he have a name?" She eyed the horse's wall-eyed glare and stepped back.

"Nay. Naming him would make him a pet. Ye

canna grow soft over an animal ye ride into battle. Their lives may be verra short."

She gazed at him with an expression he couldn't read. "I bet you wish I didn't have a name. No name, no emotion."

He could tell her it was not her name that drew him, that made him wish no other woman would seek him out, that made him want to . . . "We must get started." Before she could voice another doubt, he lifted her onto the horse, then handed Peter and Malin up to her. Malin hissed his displeasure.

An hour later, Ian caught sight of the sea. Never had anything looked so welcome. He'd swear the trip had been the longest of his life. Malin had growled, Peter had never stopped talking, and because Kathy held them in front of her, Ian could not even enjoy the feel of her body pressed against his back.

He stopped well back from the shore, then helped Kathy dismount. She almost tumbled off, clasping Peter and Malin in her arms.

"You know, Ross, that was the pits. My bottom hurts, my legs hurt, and my sexy car with the balloon payment is looking pretty darn good about now."

He wouldn't bother to ask her what a car and balloon payment were because she would only explain in other words he didn't understand. There were moments, though, when he yearned to see her land with its many wonders.

He drew a deep breath of sea air. For now he wanted only to walk along the shore and think. He clasped her hand and walked toward the waiting sea. "I would walk alone for a while. Ye may sit on yon rock and wait. If ye willna sit, dinna wander far."

He waited for her inevitable complaint at his orders, but she only nodded. Mayhap she also wished to think. *Would she think of him?*

He left her rubbing her bottom as she gazed at the sea. Peter and Malin made no attempt to follow him.

He'd believed he'd be alone, but he was mistaken. No matter how he tried to think of other things or to think of nothing at all, his thoughts would not leave Kathy.

Why did he not make a stronger attempt to seduce her and be done with the foolish challenge? Why had he not finished it last night? His brothers wouldn't care if he took her by way of trickery so long as he joined with her. Why had he refused to do so?

Gazing at the sand, he paused. Reaching down, he picked up a shell that had caught his attention. Strange, but he'd never noticed the shells that lay on this beach before. Refusing to question the foolish action, he slipped the shell into the pouch he wore at his waist. Then he went in search of another.

Kathy gazed in the direction Ian had gone. She'd wanted to go with him, but everyone needed a moment's privacy once in a while. Besides, it was quiet and beautiful here. Even Peter hadn't interrupted the silence.

She had plenty to think about. As much as the idea made her want to throw herself on the sand and wail, she had to face the fact that she might never return to New York. If they didn't solve the puzzle that was Peter, she might be a permanent resident of Scotland.

Would her cell phone continue working? Would she at least be able to talk to Mom and Dad? What could she possibly tell them that they'd accept?

And what if you do find a way to go home? How will you feel saying goodbye to Ian forever? How will you accept knowing he's been dead for more than four hundred years? And why do you care?

As long as he tried to use his power to manipulate her, she'd resist. *He used his power last night, and you were melted cheese in his hands.* Okay, so much for resistance. But even if he succeeded in seducing her body, he'd never touch her heart. Her heart was immune to manipulative men.

All this introspection was giving her a headache, and what the hell did her heart have to do with anything, anyway? Suddenly angry at the world and Ian Ross in particular, she strode down the beach in the opposite direction from the way he'd taken. She'd never let another man dictate to her. She ignored the clatter of Peter tagging along behind her.

Deep in thoughts of what she'd tell Mr. Pleasure Master next time he cozied up to her, she rounded a curve in the beach and came face to face with five shaggy men mounted on five shaggy horses.

They didn't look friendly. She glanced behind her, but Peter hadn't kept up. Curse his short little legs. Where was a wee spawn of hell when you needed one?

"Hi. Great day for a walk on the beach. Looks like it might rain later, though." Okay, she'd exhausted her supply of meaningless chatter.

"Cease yer blather, woman. We look for Ian Ross. Where is he?" The leader glared at her and moved his horse closer.

He looked better far away. "Nobody on the beach but me and a few little friends. Ian Ross? Who's Ian Ross?" Maybe she should've changed her few little friends to hundreds of hulking berserkers. Hindsight didn't do much good.

"Dinna tell me lies, woman. I know he is here somewhere." His gaze slid over her. He smiled. A very ugly smile. "But if we dinna find Ross, we must make do wi' ye. Ye'll help soothe our anger over not capturing him."

Ohmigod! "Help!" Her screech echoed up and down the beach. She was surprised they didn't drop their weapons to clutch their ears. Shouting at taxis had strengthened her vocal cords.

She'd opened her mouth to scream again, when she noticed the leader's attention had slipped past her. The approaching clatter warned that Peter had arrived.

She watched the men's eyes widen in shock. Good. Now they'd make some babbling comments involving demons and devils, then gallop off bellowing in fear.

" 'Tis a devil's demon. Kill it!" Raising his sword,

the leader charged toward Peter. The rest followed him with slightly less enthusiasm.

She turned in time to see Malin leap from Peter. He obviously wasn't willing to lose one of his nine lives in a minor tussle.

Oh no! She had to save Peter, and she didn't even have her mousse with her today.

Peter, however, was never at a loss for words. His lights flashed defiantly. "The trouble with Scotland is that it is full of Scots."

"We are *not* in *Braveheart*, Peter," she muttered.

The leader jerked his horse to a sliding stop, but not in time to halt his momentum. He careened into Peter, knocking the toy over.

At the same time, with a mad howl of rage, Malin launched himself at the horse. Three legs didn't allow for any record-setting leaps, but he managed to dig his claws and teeth into the horse's leg.

Confused, the horse reared, then bucked. Its rider slid to the ground while Malin was flung into the air. The cat landed with a thud beside Kathy.

Through a haze of fury, she charged the fallen rider. "You hurt my cat and my friend. You're toast, bog-breath."

Dimly, she could hear Peter yammering, "The time traveling is just too dangerous. Better that I devote myself to study the other great mystery of the universe: women!"

As she flung herself onto the fallen rider, she heard the pounding of hoofbeats and a shout she recognized as Ian's. Thank God, the cavalry had arrived.

Kicking and screaming, she vented all her accumulated frustration on her hapless victim. She must have connected with a sensitive area because he rolled away from her cursing, and clutched the affected body part.

Glancing up, she saw Ian in the midst of the other men, slashing left and right with his sword while his horse struck with deadly front hooves and bit anything within reach. Now she understood the value of a horse with attitude.

While she gawked at Ian, her victim managed to crawl back onto his horse. In panicked disarray, the five men galloped away.

Ian flung himself from his horse's back and ran to her, gathering her into his warm embrace. "God's teeth, woman! I leave ye for but a moment, and ye find five Highlanders to battle. Ye're a menace to all Scotland."

Then he kissed her. A hard, savage kiss that took her breath and accelerated her heartbeat to a triumphant drumroll. His lips tasted of salt air and conquering male, a combination she'd never duplicate in New York.

He broke the kiss to pull her head against his chest, where she could feel the pounding of his own heart. "Ye've just met the Mackays. I dinna know how they knew where to find us."

Kathy turned to search for Malin and Peter. Malin was already on his feet, none the worse for wear. He limped toward a still-prone Peter.

Ian hurried over to Peter, with Kathy close behind. Peter's lights flashed weakly.

"And the last thing he said to me, 'Rock,' he said. 'Sometimes when the team is up against it and the breaks are beating the boys, tell them to go out there with all they've got and win just one for the Gipper.' "

Ian lifted Peter upright while Kathy touched a small mark on his shiny top. "Umm, Peter, there's nothing but a little dent here. You'll be okay."

She couldn't help it, she picked Peter up and hugged him. "You and Malin were very brave. Did you see how brave they were, Ian?" She could feel the moisture in her eyes as she looked at Ian.

She didn't recognize the emotion that shimmered briefly in his gaze, but it warmed her from the inside out.

"Ye were all verra brave. The Mackays willna stop running 'til they reach the safety of their keep. 'Tis my guess they willna tell any how they were beaten."

His lips lifted in the smile that turned Kathy's resistance to melted butter. Or was it cheese? Whatever, it was soft and mushy.

Ian inhaled sharply at what he saw in Kathy's eyes. She'd gazed at him with desire and with anger, but never with the soft gaze she gave him now. It was a look that could unman the strongest warrior.

To cover his uncertainty, he scooped Malin up and awkwardly petted him. Malin and he didn't exchange many outward gestures of affection.

Malin rewarded him with something rare and

precious. He purred. The sound was rough and rasping, but still a purr.

"Is Malin purring? I can't believe that cat is purring. What will happen if you pet your horse?"

"He'll bite me. 'Tis his reaction to all who come near him. Each time I ride him we must speak of all that concerns the day's journey. If he doesna agree, 'twill be a ride on the devil's own back."

Her laughter brightened the day and pushed aside his dark thoughts of why the Mackays had been waiting for him in this place.

"I must wash the blood from me; then we may eat what ye brought."

Her laughter disappeared. "You're hurt? Where're you hurt?"

"Nay. 'Tis Mackay blood I must wash from me ere its poison sickens me. I would wish Fiona and her father gone from the Highlands. Their evil plagues me." He recognized the bitterness in his voice, but he couldn't hide his feelings where the Mackays were concerned.

Malin stuggled to be free, so Ian set him on the beach, then grabbed his horse's reins. Leading the horse, he strode back toward where they'd been. Kathy, still holding Peter, hurried to keep up with him.

"Who are you, Ian Ross? One minute you're the Pleasure Master, the next you're the avenging Highland warrior."

He shifted his gaze to meet her stare. She would see what she must in his eyes, and mayhap understand. "They are the same. There isna a dividing line." He lowered his voice. "Ye must know that all joys of the body have their birth in pain."

She frowned up at him. "That's a little too deep for me at this time of the day."

He looked away, studying the coastline with its gentle waves washing onto the shore. He could enjoy the gentleness because he knew the force of the waves' anger when a winter storm blew in from the sea.

"I enjoy a woman's body more after a battle, one in which I've faced death. 'Tis the closeness of death, the chance that all might be ended by one sword thrust, that heightens the senses, makes every feeling more intense." He felt her withdrawal even though she didn't step away from him.

"That's a pretty dark view of life."

He met her gaze once more. "Think of the man ye left in New York, the one who couldna bring ye pleasure, the one who made ye feel less than a woman."

Her eyes opened wide, then grew veiled. "I *never* felt less than a woman. Where'd you get that idea?" Her voice was angry, defensive.

He softened his voice. "Do you think ye're the only woman to feel so? Even if ye *have* come from a future time, ye must know that feelings dinna change."

"Maybe not, but you've got your feelings all wrong this time, Ross. I'm perfectly secure in who I am." Her eyes dared him to disagree.

"Is that why ye wished for a subservient man? A woman who knows she is strong doesna need a weak man to tell her so." He smiled, a smile he knew promised things she didn't think she wanted. "Ye'll see that 'tis not a weak man ye need, but one who matches yer own strength and can bring ye the pleasure yer husband couldna."

This time, she was the one who looked away. Stopping for a moment, she set Peter down so Malin could find his usual resting place, then she continued walking. "You sure do have a one-track mind."

"Can ye say ye ne'er think of it, lass? The pain yer husband brought ye will make our joining all the more wondrous."

"There won't be a 'joining' between us." She stopped when she reached her sack, then knelt down to take out the food.

"Do ye think of it?" He smiled at her bent head, the smooth strands of gold tempting him to slide his fingers over it.

She didn't look up. "I think of lots of things."

"Do ye think of it?" Irritation crept into his voice. Would the woman nibble around the edges of the truth forever?

She sighed. Her answer, when it came, was so soft he almost missed it. "Yes, I think of it."

" 'Tis enough for now." His answer was as soft as hers.

He allowed the silence to stretch between them, allowed her to think about what she'd admitted . . . then he took off his plaid.

"What're you doing?" Her voice was startled, shrill.

She could see very well what he was doing. "I canna wash blood awa' wi' my clothing on. Did ye expect me to rush into the sea, then sit beside ye dripping water?"

He slipped off his footwear, then his shirt.

She held his gaze, but her checks grew rosy. "Why don't you just go to the edge of the water and splash some . . . ?" Her eyes narrowed. "Hey, where's the blood? I see a spot on your arm, and there's one on your leg. Hardly enough to warrant a full strip."

He grinned. "Aye, but 'tis a fine excuse to swim in the sea on a sunny summer day."

She shivered. "How can you do it? It might be sunny, but it's not warm enough to go in the water. It'll be like ice."

"Highlanders are used to the cold. It doesna bother us." He turned his back to her and strode toward the water. Even as the waves lapped at his ankles, then thighs, he could feel her gaze skimming his back, lingering on his buttocks.

He plunged into the waves to rid himself of her gaze before he turned around and took her on the rock where she was laying out their meal. The decision he'd made as they walked away from the Mackays felt right. Kathy of Hair was special. He couldn't deny that. And he would pleasure her in a place that was special. He didn't know where this place was, but he would know it when the time was right.

God's teeth, but the water was cold. He didn't linger over his washing. When he walked from the water, she was watching him. Her gaze raked the length of him, from shoulder to feet, pausing at his groin. He hardened in acknowledgment of her interest.

He made no attempt to hide himself. Let her see what she did to him. He reached her and she looked up at him. At his face this time.

"Umm, you must *really* enjoy the cold water."

"Mayhap ye would like to sample it yerself." Giving her no warning, he shook his head, spraying her with the water streaming from his hair.

She screeched and grabbed his leg. Caught off balance, he tumbled on top of her. Together, they rolled across the patch of grass until a large rock stopped them.

"Look what you've done. I'm soaking wet." She sat up, laughing.

Grinning, he propped himself up on one elbow. "Ye canna ride home wi' wet clothes. 'Tis unhealthy for one not used to it. Ye must take them off and spread them to dry in the sun."

"Right. So we'll both sit in our birthday suits eating our picnic lunch. Different, Ross. Really different."

His mental picture did nothing to ease his arousal, which had suffered little from his roll. " 'Tis a fine idea, but if ye dinna think so, ye may wrap yerself in my plaid."

He rose, then put on his shirt. He was still a little damp and it stuck to his body. He squeezed as much water as he could from his hair. 'Twould have to do.

When he finished, he turned to find that Kathy had slipped behind a rock. When she emerged, he saw she'd enfolded herself in his plaid from the knees up. Clutching the plaid's edges with one hand, she laid her clothes out on the grass with the other.

"Ye look bonny in my plaid."

"Yes, but how do I . . . ? Wait, I've got it." She reached for his belt and used it to keep the plaid closed. "There. I can use both hands to eat now."

Peter's lights flashed. "That's what separates us from the animals, our ability to accessorize."

"Well, look who's back in working order." Her relieved expression belied her laughing words. The toy's long silence had worried her.

She returned her attention to Ian, flicking her gaze over his shirt. Her smile widened. "You look pretty okay yourself. Let's eat."

He felt himself relaxing in the unusually warm sun, allowing his thoughts to wander. And because he had no plans for seduction in this place, he thought of the land Kathy called home.

If he were not Pleasure Master, he would not mind traveling to her country. He would enjoy meeting Coco and seeing all the marvels Kathy spoke of. Most of all, he would enjoy blackening the eyes of her ex-husband. The thought gave him satisfaction.

"Your hair's all tangled. Let me see if I can comb it out a little before it dries." She knelt behind him and smoothed her hand over his hair. "I threw my comb into the bag with our food. What can I say,

I've been away from work too long. My fingers are getting itchy."

He tensed in anticipation of his hair being yanked from his head as she tried to run the comb through the tangled strands. But she was gentle, as she rarely was with her words. She smoothed the tangles from his hair a little at a time, and he found his eyes drifting shut as he relaxed beneath her sure strokes.

He couldn't remember being so at ease with a woman before, couldn't remember a woman caring about making him feel good. He brought pleasure to women, but they felt no need to think of his satisfaction in return. Because he enjoyed women, he had given little thought to this before. The sex act brought his release, and it was enough. At least he'd thought it was enough. He wasn't sure now.

"There, all done."

He blinked away the pleasant lethargy.

"You know something, Ross?"

She bent close, and he knew the smell of warm wool, the sea, and the clean scent that was hers alone would always carry a happy memory.

"I might be wrong, but I think we just experienced a spontaneous moment of fun and joy." Her voice turned suspicious. "You weren't doing any manipulating, were you?"

Ian grinned. "I dinna know how to manipulate spontaneous moments, whate'er those might be." He glanced at the sky. "Methinks ye should dress so we can start back. I would reach home before dark."

Rising, she grabbed her clothes and disappeared behind the rock. Staring out at the sea, Ian had the feeling that something important had happened this day, something beyond the attack by the cursed Mackays.

He smiled. A moment of fun and joy? 'Twould seem so.

From the corner of his eye, Ian caught the flash of Peter's lights.

"Women weaken legs."

Ian nodded. "And other things as well."

Chapter Twelve

Kick her if she ever climbed on a horse again. Everything that could hurt, did. And between Malin's growls and Peter's yammering, she thought she'd scream. "We're close to the cave, Ian. Let me off here, and I'll walk the rest of the way."

She didn't have to see his face to know he was smiling. "Methinks my seduction would go for naught tonight." He pulled the horse to a stop, then dismounted and helped her down. Only his arms kept her upright.

Finally able to stand alone, she tottered a few steps toward the cave.

"I'll care for the horse before joining ye. Dinna go into the cave wi'out me. I dinna think the Mackays will have the heart to make more trouble this day, but 'tis always wise to be careful."

Kathy was too tired to do more than grunt at him. She didn't care if a thousand Mackays were waiting, she was going to lie down. Not only did her leg muscles ache, but her bottom promised her she'd never sit again. And the insides of her thighs felt like they were rubbed raw.

Mumbling curses on all horses with bony rumps, she was almost at the cave entrance before she saw the woman.

Kathy blinked as the woman rose and swayed toward her.

"I would speak with the Pleasure Master. Has he finished with you yet?"

Kathy narrowed her gaze. She didn't like the way the woman said "you." Raking the woman's expensive-looking gown with her best eat-dirt stare, Kathy transferred her attention to the woman's hair. She allowed herself a small smile of satisfaction. Piling all that red hair on top of her snooty head couldn't hide the gray or its none-too-clean condition.

Kathy put on her sweetest smile. "Why, honey, he's so finished with me I can hardly walk."

The woman looked puzzled, but obviously felt that questioning Kathy was beneath her. "I am Lady Carlisle, a widow." Her expression hinted she took a certain amount of pride in her widowed state. "My husband left me enough wealth so I may amuse myself where I wish. Even London whispers of the Pleasure Master's prowess. I would try his body to see whether he is as good as others say."

Kathy frowned. She *really* didn't like this

woman's attitude. The witch was relegating Ian to boy-toy status, a body to be sampled and judged on performance. Since Ian would probably send this woman packing anyway, Kathy decided to save him the trouble.

"I know how it is when you need a body, sugar, but I'm afraid you're plumb outta luck tonight. Ian just got back from a house call. He makes house calls, you know." She opened her eyes wide. "Had to visit a woman who hadn't had a man for fifty years. The poor dear was so weak with want she couldn't drag her tired tush out of her cottage." Kathy shook her head sorrowfully. "He was too much for her. Her old heart just gave out. Too much ecstasy." She brightened. "But she died happy. Ian *always* leaves women happy."

The woman backed up a step. "Your speech is strange, and I do not understand much of what you babble."

Neither do I. "I don't know about your chances of trying Ian's body tonight. He has twelve women booked ahead of you. Let me see, at one woman every half hour that should take him . . ." She paused to let the woman do the math in her head. "Nope, he won't be able to squeeze you in."

"But—"

"Hmm. Maybe tomorrow night." Kathy tried to look apologetic. "Oops, I forgot. He has a tour bus booked for tomorrow night. He has to stop agreeing to these cheap tourist packages."

"He will pleasure a *bus?*" The woman looked horrified. "What exactly *is* a bus?"

A familiar clatter and flashing of amber lights warned Kathy they weren't alone.

"What we've got here is failure to communicate."

The woman took one look at Peter, screamed, then ran for the trees. A few seconds later Kathy heard the sound of hooves pounding away from the cave.

Kathy looked down at Peter. "Gee, she sounded upset. Guess she's not used to waiting in line."

Kathy heard running footsteps a moment before Ian broke into view with his sword drawn. Puzzled, he stopped and glanced around. "I heard a woman's scream."

"That would be me." She smiled weakly. "I saw a big roach."

"A roach?"

"It had red hair."

"What is a roach?" He looked suspicious.

"Very ugly insect. Really hard to get rid of." Hey, if you were going to lie, may as well tell a whopper.

He still looked suspicious, but evidently decided to ask nothing more. "I will enter the cave first." Keeping his sword drawn, he cautiously walked down the tunnel.

Kathy followed him. She couldn't imagine living in a place where you had to enter your own home with a drawn weapon. But what if she never went home? She shuddered. Staying here *wasn't* an option. She'd find a way to get back to New York.

Why even now, Janelle Thomas was probably announcing that *no one* touched her hair except Kathy Bartlett. On a less positive note, her slimy ex was probably rubbing his hands in glee if he'd found out she was missing. After all, he'd have her money to spend if she didn't show up in court.

What about Ian? No problem. She just wouldn't let him get close to her. *Reality check.* He'd gotten pretty darn close already, and no matter how much she denied it, she'd miss him.

She closed her mind to further conjecture about life without Ian. After that ride on a glorified pogo stick to and from the beach, her brain still felt scrambled.

"I loooove you."

Kathy sighed. Yep, they were back safe and snug in their comfy cave. Okay, so she was being unfair because she hurt so much. The tapestries and rugs covering the stone floor and walls were beautiful. The pillows lent a decadent opulence to the room, and the fire was cozy. It was just so *foreign* to her.

She glanced at Ian. He'd put his sword down and stripped off his plaid. His shirt clung to his torso, and his strong thighs and legs glowed golden in the firelight. Decadent pretty much described him, too. He belonged on that bed hidden in the other room. *She wanted to see him stretched naked on it, his bared body framed by the writhing snakes and crimson hangings. A memory to warm even the coldest New York night.*

The ringing of her cell phone shut down further hot thoughts for cold nights. She shuffled to where she'd left it sitting on a stone ledge.

"Why did ye leave yer phone here?" Ian walked to a carved chest placed beside his bed.

"I thought maybe Neil might want to talk to Coco." She lowered her abused bottom onto a large pillow.

He turned from rooting through the chest. "Ye would help Neil win?"

She couldn't read his emotion from his voice or expression. No use worrying about it now. She pressed the talk button.

"Where've you been, Kathy? Neil called and said you'd gone off somewhere with his brother, old hunky-and-hopefully-horny Ian. Why didn't you take your phone?" Coco didn't sound overly upset. "Oh, and the date is January thirty-first."

"Ian and I went to the beach, and I didn't take the phone because I was afraid I'd drop it."

There was a meaningful pause. "How'd you get to the beach?"

"Horse."

"Sure." Coco chuckled. "Talk about living the fantasy."

"What would I have to do to make you believe me, Coco?"

Coco didn't answer for so long that Kathy almost thought the connection had been broken. "I asked Neil what year it was when he called today. He told me the same thing you did." Again there was silence, and when Coco did speak there was a note of desperation in her voice. "I can't believe it, Kathy. My whole career has been built on coming to decisions based on hard evidence. Your cell phone is still working. Believing that you could call me from 1542 is too much to swallow. Asking me to believe you've *traveled* back in time is asking too much. I'm scared for you, girlfriend, but there's not a damn thing I can do if you won't tell me the truth."

"Right. The truth." If the smartest person she knew wouldn't believe her, who would? *Someone who really trusts you.* "So how are you and Neil getting along?" Out of the corner of her eye, she could see that Ian had stopped to listen.

"I like him, Kathy."

The softness in Coco's voice surprised Kathy. Coco could be hard, cutting, and funny, but never soft.

"He makes me feel like a woman. He doesn't seem intimidated by what I am or what I say. He's funny, gallant, and sounds sexy as hell. And he's all protective male. I never thought I'd like that in a man." Coco hesitated. "He asked if I'd sleep with him. I think I'm going to say yes."

Oh, no! Ian would lose. *So why do you care?* She'd be partly to blame. She could have tried to be a little more seduceable. *Ian could have tried to seduce a little harder.*

"That's wonderful, Coco. Once you get past that big wart on Neil's nose, he's a great guy."

"Wart?"

"I bet surgery could cure his snoring problem. If not, they put out some super earplugs nowadays."

"Snoring?"

"His drooling won't bother you because you already have a big drooly dog, and you love him. So Neil sounds perfect for you." Kathy almost hated herself for what she was saying about Neil. *Almost.*

"I'll keep that in mind." Coco didn't sound convinced. "Stay in touch. Oh, and don't forget, your parents will be back in a few days. They'll probably buzz you."

Her parents. What in God's name could she tell them? She shut off the power. No way did she want anyone else calling her. She'd been lucky no one from work had called, and none of her friends . . . *Why haven't any of them called?*

Her heart pounded as she glanced at Peter. Could someone or something be allowing only chosen calls to reach her? Why couldn't she have been flung into the past the conventional way, by a bolt of lightning? A bolt of lightning was random, impersonal. The thought of some monstrous power controlling her, even deciding who spoke to her, scared the hell out of Kathy.

Calm down. That's ridiculous. There was no need to control who spoke to her because no one would believe her anyway.

"Monstrous power?" She glanced again at Peter. "Nah."

Peter's lights flashed happily. "How do you know that my dimwitted inexperience isn't merely a subtle form of manipulation, used to lower people's expectations, thereby enhancing my ability to effectively maneuver within any given situation?"

Kathy grinned. Would a malevolent power be able to make her smile?

Thoughts of Peter vanished at the exact moment she sensed Ian behind her. He'd moved silently; still she *knew* he stood close, felt his soft breathing, could almost hear his heart beat. Were all women so attuned to him? Did they feel the air shift and grow thick, so thick they had to breathe harder, faster?

"Why did ye tell Coco those things about Neil?" He ran his finger across the back of her neck, leaving a trail of goosebumps.

"Neil asked her to have sex with him, and she was thinking about agreeing. I didn't want Neil to win."

"Ye dinna wish me to seduce ye, so I canna win either." He kissed the back of her neck, leaving his lips pressed to her skin long enough for her to believe the brand would remain there always. "That means only Colin can win, and Colin wouldna make a verra good Pleasure Master."

"It's complicated. I want . . ." What did she want? "When you were playing a bandit I thought I would die if you didn't make love to me, but it wasn't real."

"I dinna make *love* wi' anyone, and I wouldna say ye're a fine one to judge what is real when ye believe that ye come from a future time."

She'd had just about enough of people not believing her. She turned to face him. "You're purposely refusing to believe what's right in front of your face. How else do you explain my phone, Peter, and all the other toys? And how did I get here?"

She gazed into eyes so silver she almost believed she could see her own dark demons mirrored in them.

"I believe ye came from a distant land by some strange magic."

She threw up her hands in frustration. "I don't get it. You believe in magic, but you don't believe in time travel."

Her anger seemed to amuse him, because his lips tilted up in a smile that made her lose her train of thought for a moment.

"Many believe in magic and witches who cast dark spells, but I dinna know any who believe in traveling through time."

"Okay, go ahead, don't believe me. See if I care." She sounded sulky, immature, and she was afraid she was about to humiliate herself by crying.

He drew her into his arms and held her tightly. Once again she felt as if she could melt into him, become part of his body.

"I didna mean to make ye angry." His breath warmed the side of her cheek. "I thank ye for trying to help me. Most wouldna choose to aid me because they believe the Pleasure Master needs no help."

Kathy didn't know what to say to that, so she just nodded. How could one man be so alone? She'd had a loving family and friends. His kind of aloneness was beyond her imagination.

"What would ye have from me, Kathy of Hair? I willna trick ye as I did when I used yer fantasy against ye, but I canna tarry overlong. I would have ye come to me freely so I may end this challenge. Ye willna regret joining wi' me." He paused, and she allowed the steady beat of his heart to lull her.

"After 'tis done, I will help ye return to yer land."

Tempting. So tempting. All she'd have to do was murmur a yes, and he'd make love to her. And she *would* enjoy it. She no longer had any doubts about that. She'd just lie back and . . .

Just relax and enjoy it. How many nights had her husband made that demand? And like a dutiful wife, she'd tried.

"Ian, I want . . . caring, some sort of connection, not just the joining of two bodies for a moment of physical pleasure." There it was. Simple . . . and impossible for Ian to grant. The Pleasure Master wasn't about caring and connections. Besides, Ian Ross's caring wouldn't do her any good back in New York.

She felt his sharp exhalation.

" 'Tis something I canna give ye, lass. Ye ask too much." He released her and returned to the chest. "Ready yerself for sleep, and then I'll rub salve between yer legs to ease yer pain."

"Rub salve *where?*"

He turned to grin at her. "Ye've been walking as though ye still ride the horse, so I would guess ye hurt mightily. Mary gave me a salve that takes away pain."

"I can rub the salve anyplace it's needed."

"I dinna doubt that, but I can make it more pleasurable." The challenge was in his eyes, hot and demanding. "Do ye fear what I'll make ye feel? Do ye fear ye willna be able to stop?"

"Fine. Put the salve wherever you want." Had those words come from her mouth? Was she crazy, walking into the heart of the fire without an asbestos suit? *You want it, Bartlett, so don't be such a wuss.* Maybe she'd just let it happen, forget all her jabbering about caring and connections.

She argued both sides of the case all the way to the pool, where she washed the smell of horse from her and changed into her nightgown, then argued all the way back.

Entering the chamber, she thought for a moment everyone had gone. Peter and Malin were nowhere in sight. Then she saw Ian. He'd come from the tunnel, and he had on nothing but a cloth, wrapped around his waist. His skin gleamed damply in the hearth's light.

"You went outside?" It was *cold* out there.

"Aye. There's a small spring by the cave entrance. I went there." His lips lifted in a smile. "There are times when the cold is needed."

Kathy didn't respond to his insinuation. She felt uncomfortable, *stalked.* "Look, I really don't think I need any salve. I'll just take a few of my Advil and—"

He frowned. "What are advil?" He sat on her furs, then patted a spot beside him.

"They're medicine that takes away pain." This was ridiculous. She could simply say no if he did anything she didn't want. Resolutely, she sat down beside him.

"Ye willna need these advil tonight." She saw the small container of salve he'd set beside him, watched as he opened it and scooped out a creamy mixture with his fingers. "Lie back, and I'll take yer pain away."

She'd bet he would. She blinked, her only admission that a battle raged in her. The forces of caution raised their banner, red with the words "Men and cars can never be trusted." On the opposite side, the forces of wild abandon took a slightly less rigid stand with a green banner that read, "Catch the wave and ride it."

The decision was taken out of her hands as Ian firmly pushed her back on the furs, then slid her nightgown to the top of her hips. *No-panties alert!* She instinctively reached to push it back down. "Now just wait a minute. I don't remember agreeing to—"

He placed his free hand over hers. "Shh. Ye blather too much. If ye dinna feel the salve helps yer pain, ye need only say so."

He sounded so reasonable, and what he said was true. Maybe he only intended to put the salve on her legs, then leave her alone. Right. And maybe the sun would be purple tomorrow.

But what harm could there be in enjoying his touch? If things started to get out of hand, she could just call a halt. She trusted him enough to know he wouldn't do anything she didn't want.

Not waiting for her final decision, he eased her legs apart and smoothed the salve along the insides of her thighs. She almost gasped at the cool touch of the cream, the hot touch of his fingers.

Then he rubbed in the salve. She bit her lip so she wouldn't make any sounds of pleasure. The salve turned to liquid heat beneath Ian's fingers, and as he kneaded her abused muscles, her pain receded, to be replaced by a totally different pain, in a totally different area.

She closed her eyes and gave herself over to the rhythm of his hands, didn't object when he slid his free hand under her nightgown and laid his palm flat on her stomach. The weight and warmth of his hand was comforting, felt *right*.

Kathy sensed him leaning farther over her, and she drew in her breath as he brushed his hand higher on her stomach until his fingers rested beneath her breast.

She felt air flow across her stomach, her breasts, and knew he'd pushed her nightgown even higher, but had no memory of raising her hips. It was bunched beneath her upper back, arching her back so her breasts were thrust upward, an offering he obviously couldn't resist.

He groaned low in his throat, then cupped her breast in his large hand, rubbing the pad of his callused thumb across her nipple.

She pushed against his thumb, every sensitized nerve-ending screaming for more. And when he replaced his thumb with his mouth, she knew there could be nothing more . . . until he flicked the nipple with his tongue, then slid the edge of his front teeth across the tip.

"*Yes.*" It was the only word she could think of, the only one that expressed what she felt.

A fleeting thought. Amazing that the magic he was creating with his lips, tongue, and teeth canceled out all other brain activity. Her whole sensory world narrowed to his touch.

He moved his hand to her other breast, rolled her nipple between his thumb and forefinger, then placed his whole hand over her breast, a subtle signal of possession she'd never thought she'd enjoy. Life would be perfect if he'd only do something about the heavy ache building between her legs. She clenched her thighs tightly, holding his hand hostage to her need.

When he raised his head, abandoning her breast, she found she could say one other word. "No."

Cool air fanned across her breast, still damp from his mouth. Warm air touched her nipple as he chuckled softly.

"Ye must understand I have but one mouth, and I would put it to better use." His husky murmur promised she'd enjoy any use to which he put his mouth.

He moved down, trailing hot kisses over her body. She should make it harder for him, she should. . . . Her body wasn't listening. Her legs spread wide, welcoming him, without her permission.

Moving between her legs, he put his hands beneath her buttocks and lifted her to meet his bent head, his hungry lips. At some point he'd rid himself of his covering, and his erection was smooth velvet stretched tight over veins that throbbed with the blood feeding his need.

She wanted to touch, *needed* to touch him. But the thought was lost the moment he put his mouth on her. The heat of his lips, the slide of his tongue across flesh already moist and ready for him brought her close to screaming.

She wanted. . . . She wanted. . . . Almost at the point where nothing would matter except the sensation of him thrusting into her, filling her, *completing* her, she had to let him know how much she needed to touch him.

"Ian, let me touch you." *Let me slide my fingers across your flesh, feel you move beneath my hand, share my desire.*

"Dinna fash yerself, lass." His husky murmur invited her to sink back into the sensation. "Let me pleasure ye. Ye need do nothing but take joy from it."

"Lie back and relax, Kathy. I know what'll turn you on. Let me do the work." Her husband's superior words and smile drifted through her mind. She stiffened.

Suddenly, Ian withdrew. Her pounding heart slowed, her breathing grew steady, the haze of sexual anticipation faded. Weakly, she pushed her nightgown down, then turned her head to look at him.

He stood, then wrapped the cloth around his waist again. His gaze was cool, detached. She shivered. How could he look as though he hadn't been a heartbeat away from thrusting into her? How could he turn cold so quickly?

At least she could still see the outline of his erection through the cloth. He wasn't *that* detached. "Why did you stop?"

"Ye said no." He raked his fingers through his tangled hair, his only sign of agitation.

"I didn't say anything."

"Ye did. I felt it." His glance was merely curious. "But I would know why ye changed yer mind."

"You wouldn't let me touch you. I needed to feel . . . involved." *Weak, Bartlett.* She fiddled with the tie on her nightgown, any excuse not to meet his gaze. "My husband wanted to do it all, too. He thought I should just lie back and enjoy it."

Ian looked puzzled. "From what ye've told me, yer husband didna give ye much to lie back and enjoy. He thought only of his pride, while I would give ye true pleasure."

"And win the challenge. Don't forget the challenge." Kathy was furious, angrier than she'd ever been with her husband, and that was a revelation since she'd only known Ian for a few days. "You know what, Ian Ross? You need to get in touch with your emotions. Until you do, I can't call you the Pleasure Master, because true pleasure for a woman includes *feelings.*"

"I havena found it so."

She tried to offer him a calm smile, but she was shaking inside. "How about if I call you the *Pleasant* Master, because that's all you'll ever be to me."

He narrowed his eyes, and in the dim light he looked like the dangerous stranger he really was. Shadows turned his face into harsh angles, and his hair falling across his bare shoulders completed the picture of primitive anger. "The *Pleasant* Master? Many would argue wi' ye, Kathy of Hair. Mayhap ye need to learn the real meaning of hunger for a man's body, a hunger that doesna care whether he loves or hates, whether he lets ye touch him or not."

"You can't do it, Ian. I'm not one of the women who come to you in the night, all soft and do-it-any-way-you-want compliant."

His smile was easy, confident, but his eyes were still cold. "Are ye challenging me, Kathy of Hair?"

She smiled back. "Consider yourself challenged." She shook her head in mock sorrow. "Looks like you're going to have challenges lined up all the way to town at the rate you're going."

He shrugged. "I enjoy *some* challenges." His gaze turned predatory. "Know this, Kathy. I willna touch ye wi' my body unless ye ask, but I *will* touch ye."

She didn't like the sound of that. "What do you . . ."

She was talking to air, because he'd turned and strode from the cave.

Carefully, she drew the furs up to her neck. Feeling safe, she considered her mixed feelings about Ian Ross, and everything surrounding him.

Why had she tried so hard to protect him from the Mackays today? Simple. If anything happened to Ian, she'd be at the mercy of people like the village priest. Her reaction had been self-serving and didn't have anything to do with feelings for Ian as a man.

Okay, then why had she called Peter her friend and Malin her cat? She'd been in an emotional frenzy and not responsible for ridiculous statements. There. All explained.

And she was truly safe from Ian, because if he couldn't touch her, then what could he do? She fell asleep with that satisfying thought.

Chapter Thirteen

The need to escape pushed at Ian. He strode from the cave, then stood drawing in deep breaths of the cold night air. But even here she followed him. Her laughter, her scent, the feel of her skin beneath his fingers. He suspected he'd take her memory into the very fires of Hell, if Father Gregory's prediction came true.

He needed to bed the lass, then send her on her way. After pleasuring her, he'd find she was like all others. Until then, he must fight this fascination she held for him. Since her arrival, he'd cared nothing for any who might seek him, had felt relief that none had desired to lie with him.

Ian lifted his gaze to the moon, half hidden by clouds. He must remember who he was, who he would always be.

"You use sex to express every emotion except love."

Ian looked down to find that Peter had followed him. For once Malin wasn't draped across the toy's top. "I dinna need love. I want only sexual pleasure. Why would I want a woman's heart?"

"Never underestimate the power of denial."

Ian smiled. "What are ye then, a wee matchmaker, that ye would plead the cause of love?"

"It's the truth. From a certain point of view."

"Ye waste yer time, Peter. I willna fall in love wi' Kathy. 'Twould mean the loss of who I am, and a man is nothing if he knows not who he is." He must learn to guard himself from growing too close to the lass. No woman had ever stirred his anger, nor any strong feeling other than physical satisfaction, until Kathy arrived. "I dinna understand my promise not to touch her. 'Twill make the challenge more difficult. 'Twas my pride speaking, and my pride doesna always speak wisely."

"She was a thief. You've got to believe me. She stole my heart and my cat."

Ian leveled a hard stare at Peter. "Ye amuse me, but I still believe ye're responsible for Kathy's journey from her own land." Something Kathy had said nudged at him. "Ye speak only lines from movies. Mayhap Kathy must think more on these lines." He turned back to the cave, considering what he'd just said. It made little sense, but then nothing about Peter made much sense.

As he moved down the tunnel, he could hear Peter clattering behind him. "Ye're a wee evil demon, to play wi' humans so." Ian could find no anger to put into his comment; against all reason, he liked Peter.

"Evil will always win, because good is dumb."

Something in Peter's tone gave Ian pause. This didn't sound like the mindless chatter he'd grown used to. Truth rang in Peter's voice, as though whatever controlled the toy was allowing him a glimpse into its soul. Ian's shudder had nothing to do with the chill air. He crossed himself.

When he entered the chamber, he forced his gaze from where Kathy lay beneath her furs, pushed aside thoughts of seducing her in that half-waking state when the will is weak and desire races unchecked.

Instead, he sat on his bed, then carefully took out the shells he'd collected that day. None had broken, and he decided to take them to Mad Mary. She would tell him how to make that which he wanted. Mayhap he would see how Colin fared.

Standing once more, he moved to blow out the candle.

"I loooove you."

God's teeth, but he'd throttle that cursed flower before all was done.

Ian rose early the next morning. He'd not rested easily, plagued as he was with visions of Kathy spread naked beneath him, reaching for him with words of need, of hunger for what he could offer.

Several times he'd almost risen and gone to her,

but his promise stayed him. 'Twas a fool's promise and one he already regretted.

But he *had* promised, and so he must begin drawing her to him without touching her. He allowed himself a moment of anticipation as he stared at the rising sun before returning to the cave after bathing. He enjoyed a challenge, and no woman had ever challenged him before.

He found her in the chamber with the Pleasure Master's bed. She'd lit one candle and stood staring at the panel that had no painting. She'd dressed, but her hair still hung damp from her bathing. His gaze followed the line of shoulder, back, and hip, stripping away the layers of clothing in his mind. It would be so easy to move up behind her, wrap his arms around her, and pull her to him. Instead, he moved close, so close he knew she felt him, sensed his power as all women sensed it.

"Doesn't it bother you that this bed was never finished?" She still spoke in the hushed voice she'd used before when near the bed. "Don't you think the woman who had this bed made would want it finished? Don't you think the *bed* would want it?"

" 'Tis only a bed. It isna human and canna feel." He knew not why, but he turned his head to gaze at Peter, who was happily chattering to a bored-looking Malin.

Kathy's gaze followed his. "It has a very old soul."

He wasn't sure whether she spoke of the bed or Peter. Maybe both. " 'Tis foolish."

She nodded and flushed. "I don't know where

that comment came from. Anyway, it's a wonderful bed. I'd love to . . ."

"Ye'd love to lie upon it wi' a man who'd do all the things painted upon it, fill ye as no other has filled ye?" He leaned close, letting his breath fan across her neck, inhaling an elusive scent that was rich with the promise of passion.

"Not really."

She stepped away from him, and he smiled. She would never be able to move far enough from him.

What if she really had traveled from a distant time? He could not follow her there. He pushed the thought from his mind. To believe in such a thing, he would have to reach beyond everything he'd experienced or been told in his life, everything he'd ever thought possible, and trust only her. That kind of trust came only with love, and he would never love.

She ran her fingers lightly across one of the paintings, then pulled her fingers back as though burned. Her laughter was nervous. "I'd disgrace this bed if I lay on it. After looking at these paintings, I'd never be able to rise to the occasion. Hot doesn't even begin to describe what your great grandfather did on this bed. He must've been quite a man."

"Aye, that he was." He watched as she blew out the candle and walked back to sit beside the hearth.

"Thanks for carrying and heating water for my bath." She hesitated. "And thanks for not staying to watch."

Women softened to a man who thought of their

comfort. That was his only reason for having the water ready when she rose. He had *not* considered how she would ache after riding his horse.

"I stood outside and pictured ye as ye bathed, yer smooth body sliding into the water, the water flowing around ye, wrapping ye in warm arms, touching ye wi' soft fingers. I saw myself touching ye as the water touched ye, my mouth warm and moist on yer breast, yer nipple. My hands sliding across yer stomach, between yer legs. Did ye open yer thighs to the warmth, Kathy? Imagine the warmth was my mouth, my body?"

"Stop it, Ian." She didn't meet his gaze.

"Ye willna have me touch ye wi' my fingers, so ye must bear the touch of my words."

She sighed and met his gaze. "I don't understand you, Ian Ross. Being the Pleasure Master is the most important thing in your life, and yet you passed up a chance to win the challenge."

" 'Twould not have been won fairly."

"Because you were using my fantasy against me?"

He nodded.

"You had other chances, but you didn't take advantage of those either. Why?" She wasn't sure where her questions were leading, but at least they gave her the chance to recover from the mental pictures he'd been painting. Pictures too graphic to ignore, too close to her own imaginings to be comfortable.

He moved close to her, using his heat, his scent, his body to overpower her. "There is a special time and place for every woman. 'Tis that time and place I wait for." He reached out and almost touched her. She held her breath, then let it out on a soft sigh of . . . What?

"Ye'll return to yer land, but each year at the time of our joining ye'll remember, no matter where ye are or who ye're with. Ye'll see the place, ye'll see *me,* and remember always." His hand skimmed the side of her face, and she felt the connection that needed no touch. "That will be my gift to ye, Kathy of Hair."

Her emotions threatened to overflow as surely as the tears filling her eyes. Desire, regret, sadness. How could he manipulate her feelings with just his words? She had to take back control. "What would you say if I told you to do it right now? That I'd just lie back and you could join with me. We could get this challenge thing over with and you'd win."

His eyes were shadowed. "That was yer ex-husband's way. 'Tis not the Pleasure Master's way."

She backed away from him, from the truth she hadn't realized was a truth. That *had* been her ex's attitude. *Do it my way, get it over with, and I win.*

He held her gaze then turned and walked to the tub. "I'll empty this, then we'll walk to the village. I need talk wi' Mad Mary and see how Colin fares."

He left her standing there, her thoughts in turmoil. She wanted him as she'd never wanted her husband, but she still refused to let him manipulate her. *She* wanted to choose the time and place.

Surprised, she realized her body, if not her mind, had accepted that there *would* be a time and place.

Refusing to debate the decision with her body, she checked the things in her backpack. Hairstylist to the end, she automatically took her supplies with her. Never knew when you'd have to perform an emergency cut and curl.

She fingered her butane curling iron, then glanced in Ian's direction. He wasn't paying any attention. Quickly she heated the curling iron and pulled out her mirror. In the first panic of traveling to this time, she hadn't worried about how she looked, but as her awareness of Ian grew, so did her desire to shed her prehistoric-hag-rising-from-primordial-swamp image.

Just a few unobtrusive curls here and there . . . Hmm. Were those roots starting to show? She peered more closely.

"What manner of thing do ye use on yer hair?"

Kathy jumped at Ian's question. She turned to find him standing behind her, staring suspiciously at the curling iron.

She sighed. There was something to be said for the run-like-hell reaction of most people to the things she'd brought with her. At least then she didn't have to give them a detailed explanation of how the gadgets worked. "This is a curling iron. It curls your hair to make it more attractive. See?" She demonstrated on her own hair.

He reached for the curling iron.

"Watch out, it's hot." She turned it off to let it cool.

Picking it up, he examined it. "I would know how this works."

She narrowed her gaze. "You will *not* take my curling iron apart."

He grinned and handed the curling iron back to her. "I saw ye searching through yer hair. Were ye looking for wee beasties?"

She stared at him blankly until realization hit. "Bugs? You think I was looking for bugs? Ugh. Yeck." Even the thought made her want to scratch.

She'd opened her mouth to fire another blast of denial, when she noticed his expression. He looked relaxed, open, teasing. Ian Ross was no longer the Pleasure Master. This was the same man who'd rolled with her on the beach yesterday. A man who was just enjoying himself. Instinctively, she knew Ian didn't have many happy moments, and she was fiercely glad she was responsible for a few of them.

"I was checking my roots." Ordinarily, even torture wouldn't wring that admission from her, but she wanted to keep that look on Ian's face a little longer.

"I dinna understand." He reached for one of the curls she'd just created, but stopped short of his goal.

Already, Kathy was rethinking the positive and negative aspects of Ian's no-touch vow. She'd *wanted* him to touch her hair. "Okay, here's the deal, Ross. This is *not* my natural color. But it's fine for this month. I've been thinking of going red in a few months, but I'm not sure. I don't know if I have a 'red' attitude. What do you think?"

She'd hoped to shock him, but she was doomed to disappointment.

"In yer land women change the color of their hair like a worn shawl? What is yer real color?"

Rich brown? Warm brown? Earthy brown? "Mousy brown." It had been a long time since she'd seen her natural color, but no matter how many exotic shades she put over it, she'd still felt mousy brown until . . . until she'd met Ian Ross.

" 'Tis an admirable color."

"It is?" She peered closely at him, looking for sarcasm. She found none.

"Aye. The color of a wee mouse is familiar, comfortable. Its hair is smooth, *soft.*" He lowered his voice to a husky murmur.

"So . . . you've petted a few mice in your time, huh?" *Touch my hair. Please touch my hair.*

"On a cold winter's night when Malin sleeps and none need me, there isna much else to do."

"Mice? In this cave?" She widened her eyes and glanced quickly around before she caught the teasing glint in Ian's gaze. "Well, no matter how familiar and comfortable a mouse is, I don't want to look like one." Even though she tried to avoid the thought, she had to admit Ian made her feel good about who she was. *Everything* he'd done had made her feel good.

"Hmm. Henna. Maybe Mad Mary knows about henna. I might go red sooner than I expected." She thought about red hair as she watched Ian finish emptying her bath water. And from red hair, her thoughts drifted to dark hair. Ian's hair, sliding across her bare flesh. Her fingers clutching the long strands as she urged him to put his mouth on her breasts, her stomach, the back of her knees. . . . The back of her *knees?* Admit it, the thought of Ian Ross's mouth on any part of her body was an earth-moving concept.

" 'Tis done. We'll walk to the village. The horse needs rest after yesterday's journey." He slanted her a teasing grin. "Mayhap someone's bottom also needs a rest."

Kathy started to glare at him, then opted for honesty. "You're right. *Nothing* could make me climb on that horse again." She glanced at Peter. "Should we leave him here?"

"I'm coming and Hell's coming with me." Peter stated his opinion as Malin jumped to his favorite resting place.

Ian shook his head. "I dinna have the courage to leave him here. We would be listening to his complaints all night when we returned."

Kathy nodded. Some fights you couldn't win. Peter was one of them. She followed Ian from the cave, and Peter clattered along behind her.

They'd almost reached Mad Mary's cottage when Ian turned to her, his gaze thoughtful. "Ye've said Peter speaks only in movie lines. Mayhap 'tis a certain line that will send ye back to New York."

"The concept's great, Ian, but there're millions of movie lines." It made sense, though. With his warped little sense of humor, Peter would love it. "How would I figure out the *right* line? And besides, what's the motive? Why am I even here?"

"It's the millennium; motives are incidental," Peter offered.

251

Ian shrugged. "I dinna know the answer, but 'tis a thing we may speak of later."

I don't want to talk to you. I want you wrapped naked around me on that fabulous bed while you tell me all the wicked things you'll do to me. Kathy couldn't believe she'd ever thought she was frigid.

Colin opened Mad Mary's door to them and distracted her from more thoughts of Ian.

Ian frowned and Colin grinned. Kathy noted it wasn't a "gotcha" grin, but more of a silly, happy grin. She wondered what was going on.

"I would speak wi' Mary about a matter." Ian's tone suggested that Colin didn't need to hang around and listen.

"Aye. She's sorting herbs by the hearth. I've helped her, and she's taught me much this morning." His comment left what she'd taught him open for conjecture. "Ye may talk to Mary while I gather more herbs from the garden."

"I'll go with you, Colin." Kathy hurried after him as he strode toward the small garden. "So how're things going?"

He stopped to lean over a plant and peer at its leaves. "Ye gave good advice. Mary takes joy in speaking of her plants." He plucked a few leaves, then straightened to look at her. "And I find I have a great interest in hearing her speak."

Something in his gaze made her ask, "Because of the challenge?"

His expression warmed. "Because of *Mary.*"

"Oh." This could be unexpected luck for Ian. "Have you played your bagpipes for her?"

"I told ye before I would only play for one I loved."

"And is there a chance you *might* play for Mary?"

His smile was uncertain. "I might, lass. I might."

Leaving her with that possibility to chew on, he strode back toward the cottage. Kathy followed him inside.

Ian was cramming some things into the pouch at his waist as Mary watched with an amused expression. Ian did *not* look amused. "Mary says ye've learned much about herbs. Have ye learned other things as well, Colin?"

Colin looked noncommittal. "I havena spent enough time wi' Mary to know all that I might."

"Hmmph." Ian's comment needed no translation. "If ye have no reason to stay, Kathy, I would start home."

"You go on, Ian. I want to ask Mary a quick question, then I'll catch up."

Ian nodded, then left the cottage and walked slowly down the path. Kathy smiled as she watched Peter toddling along behind him like a slightly weird shadow. Ian turned onto the path they'd come on, the one that skirted the village. Wise move. Peter would look strange even on a New York sidewalk, and that was saying a lot.

She turned back to Mary. "I have a quick question. Do you have anything that colors hair?"

Mary frowned. "I have something that would turn yer hair red, but it wouldna look as lovely as yer own hair."

"My *own* hair is brown."

253

Mary's eyes shone with excitement. " 'Tis amazing. What wondrous plant would give ye such a color?"

Kathy glanced down the path. Ian was still walking slowly. She had to hurry. "Uh, it's sixty milliliters of forty volume, twenty-five milliliters of eleven P, and five milliliters of blonding cream. Look, I've gotta run. I'll get back to you about the color."

She rushed from the cottage, leaving Mary with a befuddled look on her face.

Halfway along the path that Ian still walked, Kathy saw the child. He stood next to a large rock and was looking down at his badly scraped knee. The part of her that couldn't ignore a hurt child carried her to his side. "What happened, sweetheart?"

He looked up at her, and she could see he was fighting tears. "I fell off the rock. 'Tis a wee scrape." He offered his explanation with a trembling lip.

She knew he wouldn't want any soft sounds of sympathy. Soft wasn't an option in this time. *Except Ian's glance when he's in his Pleasure Master mode.*

Putting her backpack on the ground, she fumbled around for something that would distract him from his injury. She pulled out a small plastic police car. Quickly, she handed it to the child. Any minute Ian would turn around, and she'd have to listen to his lecture about not showing anyone her toys. But what could one small police car do? She doubted it would change the course of history.

Intrigued, the boy crouched down and rolled the

car along the ground. The wail of a piercing siren emerged from the car while its red and blue lights flashed brightly.

Damn. She hadn't known it would do that. Her worst fears were confirmed as she saw Ian striding toward her. He was frantically gesturing behind her. Things couldn't get any worse.

She glanced behind her. Yes, they could.

The priest was charging across the field toward her, his robes flapping in the breeze like giant bat wings. Behind him, many of the villagers, including Neil, hurried to see what was happening.

Father Gregory's appearance was a little too convenient; he must have been watching every move Ian and she made.

"Didna I tell ye the woman was a witch? She is trying to steal the soul of the child wi' her devil's toy."

Kathy winced. In a hog-calling contest, he'd win hands down for pure volume. Beside her, the boy clutched the police car to him.

Ian was running now, but the priest reached her first.

She gaped at him as he jerked the car from the child's hands, threw it to the ground, and stomped on it. The crack of broken plastic was loud in the sudden silence.

"There, I've destroyed the demon's plaything." The priest wore a triumphant expression.

Beside her, she heard the soft sobs the boy tried to muffle, and suddenly she was mad. Mad at everyone and everything that had to do with this time.

She narrowed her gaze and advanced on the sputtering priest. "You are such a jerk. When you die and knock at the pearly gates, God's going to kick your butt into Hell."

The priest huffed and puffed. "Ye canna speak so to a servant of God."

"You're no servant of God. Look at you. You're a disgrace to the priesthood."

"Dinna say more, lass." Ian's quiet advice cut through her fury.

Ian held his breath. If the priest chose to condemn Kathy, would the people support him? He hoped he could get Kathy safely away without finding out.

Ian looked down in time to see Peter's lights flashing. *No.* Not now.

"Do you have any control over how creepy you allow yourself to get?"

"We must destroy the woman and this . . . demon." Father Gregory glared at Peter as he reached out to grab Kathy's arm.

He never touched her. Ian stepped between them first. "Ye'll not take the woman. She is a stranger to the Highlands and under the protection of the Pleasure Master."

This was it then, the confrontation he'd known must come, but never suspected would begin over a woman. Still he would not let any man take Kathy from him, and the fierceness of his feelings surprised Ian. "Ye dinna speak for God, but for yerself. Ye want only to show yer power while ye hide behind the name of priest."

He ignored the collective gasp of the people who'd gathered.

The priest's eyes narrowed to evil slits. "Move aside, Ian, so I may take her, and God will forgive what ye've said about His servant."

Ian could feel Kathy trying to push past him, and he shoved her back behind him none too gently. Unfortunately, he couldn't handle Peter quite so easily.

"The last time I saw a mouth like that, it had a hook in it."

The priest transferred his anger to Peter. "I will throw that abomination into the sea."

Ian knew he must make his stand before Kathy found her voice or Peter thought of some new insult to fling. "Ye must kill me before I'll let ye take the woman or the toy. Are ye willing to risk so much, priest?"

The gasp now came from the woman behind him.

The priest's gaze grew speculative. He turned to the crowd. "Mayhap ye can now understand why I've condemned Ian Ross. He protects evil because he is a minion of the devil. Help me seize him and reap yer reward in Heaven."

Suddenly, Colin stood beside him. "If ye take my brother, ye must take me also. The Pleasure Master has done nothing but protect a helpless woman who has done no wrong."

From the struggles behind him, Ian doubted the helpless woman part.

Neil also stepped to his side. "Ye must deal wi' me as well. Ian is right to protect Kathy of Hair.

257

And mayhap ye should practice more meekness and worry less about the pleasures of the flesh." His gaze held contempt.

The crowd muttered and shifted restlessly, the people's uncertainty plain.

Jamie pushed to the front of the mob. "This woman is good. She gave my wife back to me after we lost our babe. I willna take part in harming her."

A murmur of assent flowed through the crowd.

Mary walked calmly to stand in front of the people and as one they stepped back. She raised her arms. "I see great misfortune visiting the Highlands if this woman is harmed."

The crowd waited to hear no more. They scattered, hurrying back to their homes, leaving the priest to stride fuming in their wake.

"I didna know ye saw so much, Mary." Ian drew in a deep relieved breath.

"I see much more than ye'll e'er know, Ian Ross." She smiled at Ian and a furious Kathy, who'd finally emerged from behind him.

"I appreciate what everyone did, but I won't let you put your life on the line for me." Kathy glared up at Ian. "I was perfectly capable of discussing the situation reasonably with—"

"Ye would've made a fine fire on a cold night for the good priest to warm his hands by."

"Oh." Her eyes widened at his blunt speech. "Well, since you put it that way . . ." She glanced around. "Thanks, everyone."

She turned to watch the retreating priest, and Ian

knew she was wishing herself safely back in her own land.

Before leading Mary back to her cottage, Colin turned to Ian. "Watch yer back, brother. The priest has lost power wi' the people, and he willna take it well."

Neil added his voice. "Aye. Take care. I'll see ye tomorrow. I must speak wi' Coco."

Ian watched Neil and Colin walk away . . . and realized that for the first time in his life his brothers had stood with him.

Something warm and new moved in him.

They had stood together as brothers.

Chapter Fourteen

Kathy lay beneath her covers that night watching
Ian through half-closed lids. He sat with his back
to her in front of the hearth, working on something
that had held his attention for hours. She'd drifted
off to sleep several times only to waken and find
him still there.

The flickering flames cast light and shadow
across the ancient rock walls, the jewel-colored tapestries, the doorway leading to the bed that seemed
to fill more and more of her thoughts.

And the man. It always came back to the man.
Ian Ross had shielded her with more than his body
today. Only now, hours after the fact, could she
appreciate what he'd been willing to give up for
her. His reputation, his *life*.

She watched the play of muscles across his

strong back, could see each time he fumbled with the small objects he was trying to work with. She smiled. The same hands that could slide across a woman's skin leaving a trail of fire and need weren't meant to do piecework.

"Yer sleep is troubled, lass?" He didn't turn around.

"I guess so." How did he sense her wakefulness when she hadn't made a sound? "Peter and my toys have blown any chance I had of being accepted, haven't thcy?"

"People dinna want to accept that which is strange to them. It has always been so. Is it different in yer land?"

"No, I guess it isn't." Except that she'd never been on the receiving end of intolerance. This was a heavy life-lesson kind of thing.

"Ye mustna give yer toys to others. 'Twill cause ye grief."

Kathy admired the curve of his spine as he bent over, trying to thread something. She didn't have the energy to look closer. "I know, but I couldn't stand seeing that kid cry."

"Would ye want yer own bairn, lass?" His voice gentled.

She pulled and pushed the idea around in her mind, examined it from every angle. "Yes. I'd like a baby." She'd never burned any brain cells thinking about motherhood before. Why now?

Maybe because today she'd had an up-close and personal view of life's frailty. Without Ian's intervention, she'd probably be dead. Not a good thing to be when you came from a family in which every-body lived into his or her eighties, and you'd sort of planned your future around that expectation. Was that why she was suddenly giving the moth-erhood thing some thought?

Okay, that was a small part of it. The major part? Ian Ross. Old PMS had never instilled any I-want-to-have-your-baby thoughts. He hadn't even been able to instill any I-want-to-have-sex-with-you thoughts.

But Ian Ross? Thoughts of having his baby made her feel all soft and mushy. Yech. She didn't like what he was doing to her.

Liar. You love what he's doing to you. So what was she going to do about her feelings? After her marriage, she'd sworn never to sleep with a wom-anizer again, but she'd also sworn never to back away from another challenge.

She wouldn't back away from this. She'd make love with Ian. Tomorrow. She'd ask him to touch her tomorrow. He'd work his magic, and she'd have an unforgettable memory to take home with her. *And if you never go home?* She'd still have her memory.

"What is yer real name, Kathy?"

"What?" Her *real* name? "You don't think Kathy of Hair is my real name?

His soft chuckle made her close her eyes so she could absorb the sound, store it away with her other memories.

"I believe yer name is Kathy because ye answer to it easily, but I dinna believe the Hair part. And

I dinna believe yer father is a king. A king would kill yer husband for treating ye so. The tale shouldna shame ye. Ye were frightened and said what ye must to save yerself. But I would know yer real name."

Kathy felt deflated. So much for her cleverness. "My name is Kathy Bartlett."

His fingers paused over their work. "Bartlett is an English name."

Not good. An English name in Scotland was not a good thing. "I'm not English. I'm American. We haven't been English for at least two hundred years. No English blood left in my veins, just good old American blood."

"There are English spies in the Highlands."

Oh boy. "Didn't you hear what I said? I . . . am . . . not . . . English."

"Aye. I heard ye, lass."

She couldn't tell from his tone whether he believed her or not. Fine. Something else to worry about.

But not even Ian Ross's suspicion that she might be an English spy could keep her awake. She supposed being mistaken for a witch and almost turned into burnt toast tired a body out. As sleep claimed her, she knew Ian was still working by the fire.

She could sense him near, feel him as surely as if he touched her. He knelt and placed something beside her.

Even without opening her eyes, she knew it was still dark. With a sleepy mutter meant to explain in detail why even chickens wouldn't get up this early, she pulled her covers up to her chin and turned over.

His soft laugh soothed her, made her feel safe.

"Sleep well, lass. I've made something to remind ye of yer home. Ye'll feel strong when ye wear it, as ye did wi' the one yer father gave ye."

She drifted back to sleep with the warm huskiness of his voice to fuel her dreams.

When she awoke again, it was to the usual sound of Peter's morning chatter. There was something different about it, though.

She opened her eyes just enough to see Peter hurrying toward the cave entrance spouting yet another movie quote.

"There's no reason to become alarmed, and we hope you'll enjoy the rest of your flight. By the way, is there anyone on board who knows how to fly a plane?"

Strange. His line didn't fit the calm morning, and Peter's comments *always* fit the situation. Maybe the Scottish humidity had short-circuited him. And where was Ian?

Now completely awake, she sat up . . . and saw it. Beside her lay a delicate necklace made of shells. Pale pink, with the pearl-glow of summer sunsets on cool ocean waves, it was a stark contrast to the dark emotions of the man who'd made it.

I've made something to remind ye of yer home. She picked the necklace up with fingers that shook. Unbidden, tears slid down her face as she examined the careful placement of each small shell, remembered his shoulders hunched over as he concentrated on what must have been a tedious task for hands used to wielding a sword.

For her. He'd made this to heal her heart, not to conquer her body. The only thing old PMS had ever given her was a video for the sexually adventurous so that he could "go where no man had gone before."

Standing, she reverently placed the necklace beside Suzy.

"I loooove you."

"I know, Suzy." Kathy blinked away tears that didn't want to stop. "I know."

She cried while she bathed and while she dressed, and continued crying as she made a cup of tea from the mysterious leaves Ian had been given. Only as she took her first sip did she realize her tears weren't for her life in New York, but for the man who'd cared enough to make a small shell necklace for a woman who'd been nothing but a pain in his behind.

He *deserved* to be Pleasure Master, and tonight she'd make sure he continued in that role. Still holding her tea, she walked into the other room; it seemed to draw her in a way she didn't understand. Lighting a lone candle, she stared at the bed.

Did its first owner haunt its crimson hangings, still rest on the silken cover, wait forever for a lover who'd never again touch her?

No matter what Ian said, Kathy believed the woman had loved his great grandfather.

Maybe she only waited for another man and

woman to make love on it, to touch each other as she'd touched her lover, so she could be released.

Kathy shook her head. What a bunch of nonsense. Scotland was making her as superstitious as everyone else here. She blew out the candle and wandered back to the main chamber. Where *was* Ian?

Footsteps echoed down the tunnel, but they weren't Ian's. Even in such a short time she'd learned to recognize so much about him.

Neil entered the chamber, and Kathy let her breath out in a whoosh of relief.

"Did you see Ian outside?" She looked behind Neil, but Peter hadn't followed him. Why was Peter still outside when there were people inside he could harass?

Neil shrugged. "Mayhap he takes care of his horse." He strode to Kathy's phone and hit the button that would connect him to Coco.

He smiled. Coco must have answered.

"I've thought on our joining all night, lass." He dropped to one of the cushions, obviously settling in for a long chat. "Ye said ye didna want a man who'd bore ye in bed, so I thought what might amuse ye. Do ye have a liking for cream and honey?"

Kathy did *not* want to hear this. Besides, Ian's absence worried her. After yesterday, she couldn't believe he'd leave her unguarded for such a long time. And why was Peter still outside? Come to think of it, Malin was nowhere to be seen either.

She hurried out of the cave and glanced around.

No Ian in sight. Next, she walked to where he kept his horse. The horse was there in a small corral, but she didn't see Ian. What the—?

Then she saw Peter and Malin. Malin sat by a small bush while Peter stood in the middle of a faint path worn through a small grove of trees.

She hurried over to them. "Why're you guys out here, and where is—"

"If ye search for Ian Ross, daughter of evil, ye willna find him here."

Kathy spun to face Father Gregory. Fear made her want to race to the safety of the cave, but she couldn't let him see her panic. She had to find out what had happened to Ian.

"Wow. Daughter of evil. You gave me my whole title. This must be important." Out of the corner of her eyes, she saw Peter hurrying toward the cave. Malin moved up to sit beside her.

"Ian Ross willna be here to protect ye, whore. I helped the Mackays take him, and he willna escape from them easily. He'll ne'er see ye again."

Kathy had never seen real evil, but she knew she was looking at it now. "The people didn't follow you yesterday. What makes you think they'll follow you now?"

There was a mad glint in the priest's gaze. "They are all weak. Vessels of Satan I'll kill ye now and no one will e'er know. They'll think ye returned to yer own land."

"I dinna think so, coward." Neil's voice shook with rage.

Kathy turned to see Neil striding toward the

priest while Peter toddled behind. She let out the breath she'd been holding and moved toward Neil.

"He helped the Mackays capture Ian. What'll we do?"

Neil didn't answer as he strode past her and reached the priest before he could flee. Neil swung his fist, and the priest fell without uttering a word.

Peter stood over the fallen man. "I do not envy you the headache you will have when you awake. But in the meantime, rest well, and dream of large women."

Neil turned to Kathy. "Ye'll not do a thing, lass. Stay in the cave where ye're safe. Ian would want it so. I'll take this craven back on my horse and gather the men to rescue Ian. The Mackays willna keep my brother."

Kathy watched Neil heave the priest over his shoulder like a sack of fertilizer, then stride toward the front of the cave, where he'd left his horse. She had a feeling the priest wouldn't even have a flock of pigeons left by the time Neil got through telling everyone what he'd done.

His brother. Ian hadn't said he'd rescue the Pleasure Master, he'd said he'd rescue his brother. Ian would want to know that, and she intended to tell him. Soon.

No way was she going to sit around feeling safe while Neil went all the way back to the village to rouse the rescue force. That would take a while, and God knows what the Mackays could be doing to Ian in the meantime.

Kathy didn't think of herself as a brave person,

The Pleasure Master

but it was amazing how fierce she felt where Ian was concerned. She had her own army, an army of toys that in its way could be more effective than a score of bellowing Highlanders. Fear was a powerful weapon.

Without giving herself time to consider the possible consequences, she ran into the cave and emptied her backpack of everything except her mousse and butane curling iron. The curling iron was the closest thing she had to a real weapon.

Then she stuffed as many toys as she could into the backpack, along with something to eat, and tied one last toy to her waist. Satisfied, she put on the backpack.

Finally, she picked up her shell necklace and carefully fastened it around her neck. *Ye'll feel strong when ye wear it, as ye did wi' the one yer father gave ye.*

She paused before Suzy Sunshine. "You hold the fort here." *In case I don't come back. In case you're the only thing left to remind Ian of me.*

"I loooove you."

Kathy smiled as she headed toward Ian's horse.

She stopped smiling the minute he came in sight. Now what? She'd found where Ian kept the saddle and stuff, but this would be like trying to saddle a tiger. Not a fun thought.

Okay, she'd be strong, determined. *Scared.*

"Look, horse. We can do this the hard way or the easy way. But if you don't let me ride you, I'm going to kick your Scottish butt."

The horse had pinned his ears back the moment

269

Kathy approached him, but at the sound of her voice, his ears pricked forward. Hmm. Obviously a male who liked an assertive woman.

A half-hour later, she'd managed to get the horse ready with only a stepped-on foot and nipped shoulder to show for the ordeal. Fair exchange as far as Kathy was concerned.

Leading the horse over to a large boulder where she'd put Peter and Malin, Kathy climbed to the top of the rock and slid onto the horse's back, then waited for the explosion. It didn't come. For some reason known only to the god-of-cantankerous-horses, Ian's horse had decided to humor her.

Sighing, she set Peter and Malin in front of her. She knew why she was taking Peter. If he didn't scare the Mackays to death, he'd talk them into an early grave. But Malin? No logical reason, except something in her knew Malin would want to be there for Ian.

If she could keep the horse to a walk, and if she could follow the faint trail, and if she didn't fall off, she might be able to help Ian. A lot of ifs.

Hours later, she finished munching on the bannock she'd brought with her as she stared down at a small abandoned cottage with at least ten Mackays sitting outside it. Thank heavens they'd decided to rest, because her abused bottom was reminding her why she'd said she'd never climb on Ian's horse again.

She didn't see Ian, so they must have him inside. The food sat like a lump of dough in her stomach as she decided on a course of action. Brave and fearless seemed easy when the danger was at a distance. Now? She was scared witless.

She'd have to make her move before they reached home. Ten Mackays were a lot better odds than the whole clan would be. This would probably be her best shot at rescuing Ian.

One of the Mackays took out his knife and began cleaning it. Kathy's imagination supplied the dried blood. She swallowed to rid her throat of the boulder lodged there.

Why the heck was she doing this? She'd known when she climbed on the horse, but she couldn't quite remember now. Oh, got it. A night on that incredible bed. And a night on the bed wouldn't be much fun without Ian, so of course she had to rescue him. Besides, she owed Ian. He was her protector, her . . . friend, and it was her duty to free him. There, all neat and tidy.

A plan. She needed a plan. Kathy forced her thoughts away from the truth that whispered around the corners in her mind.

How about a decoy? Something that would draw away the men stationed outside the cottage without alerting anyone inside. Something nonthreatening.

Lowering Peter and Malin onto a convenient tree stump, she slid from the horse's back and opened her backpack, then rooted around inside. Food. Those men must be as hungry as she'd been, and they hadn't stopped to eat. An easy meal might be tempting. Something fresh and yummy like . . . roast duck. With a flourish, she pulled out two toy ducks. "I hope you guys have loud quackers."

She didn't think too far ahead as she pushed the button at the bottom of each. If she thought too much ahead, she'd imagine fifty more Mackays inside the cottage, fifty more Mackays bursting through the door brandishing foot-long bloody knives in their fists. Nope, thinking ahead was bad.

At the first quack, she turned to lead the horse away, then stopped. She frowned. The quacking sort of had a rhythm, and sort of sounded like words. Kathy closed her eyes, concentrated, then groaned. *Please, God, no.* But God must be too busy tapping his feet to the rhythm, because when she opened her eyes the ducks were still rapping the ABC's. Snatching up the nearest duck, she turned it over and peered at the label. Rapper Quacker.

Great. Just great. Puff Daddy Duck. What more could go wrong?

Too late to do anything about it now. Peering through the bushes, she saw one of the men pointing. They all stood and started in her direction. If she was lucky, they wouldn't notice anything strange until they got close to the ducks.

Leading the horse, she avoided the approaching Mackays and headed toward the cabin. Peter and Malin tagged along behind. She stopped at the edge of the clearing and set up her line of defense. Carefully, she placed her toys along the return path of the men. Not too close to the cabin, because she didn't want to alert anyone inside, but close enough to discourage the Mackays from reaching the building. Thank heavens she'd had enough sense to bring the toys with motion sensors. Kathy grinned as she placed the Village Gorilla in the grass right beside the path. If she were a sixteenth-century Highlander and met a miniature gorilla happily singing "Macho Man" while he danced, she wouldn't stop running till she got to England.

She tied the horse to a tree near the cabin, then took her butane curling iron from her backpack and untied the Star Wars Lightsaber with the energy hum and glowing light beam from her waist. She glanced at the one toy left in the pack. Her ace in the hole. She hoped she didn't have to use it.

She crept to the cottage. Hmm. One didn't just charge through the door yelling and waving one's weapons unless one was a force of thirty. Since she was only one, she decided to first look through the square opening that served as a window in the crumbling cottage. A damp chill touched her, and she looked up to see mist moving in. Good. Cloaked in gray, she'd feel a little less visible.

Crouching, she slowly raised herself until she could see inside. And froze. She didn't think she'd ever move again, breathe again.

273

Chapter Fifteen

Ian stood naked, spread-eagled, his hands and feet bound to stakes that had been driven into the dirt floor and overhead beams.

He cared not that his body was spread, bared to whatever Fiona chose to do with it. Knowing Fiona, he doubted there would be any imagination involved. At one time, he could have called up a wee bit of interest in how she intended to devour him after all her years of being thwarted in her quest for his sexual services. Not now.

He felt only anger. And fear.

Anger that his thoughts of Kathy had made him careless. When he'd left the cave to check his horse, he'd been deep in argument with himself over her claim that she came from a future time. He could not believe it. He would rather believe in magic and witchcraft. At least those were things many thought possible. No way could she *prove* what she claimed. If he ever chose to believe her, he must abandon all he knew of his world and set himself adrift on a sea where only his faith in this woman anchored his soul. And if he chose to believe, then he must also accept that if she returned to her time, she would be lost to him forever. He chose not to believe.

Fear. Had Kathy discovered him gone? Had the priest harmed her? He flexed his muscles in a vain attempt to free his arms. If she was unharmed, had she gone for help? He closed his eyes at the thought that she might get none. If the Pleasure Master didn't return, then a new one would have to be chosen. Neil and Colin would be happily rid of him.

Ian's greatest fear? That Kathy would not wait for the men of his clan to free him. That she would set out on her own. He opened his eyes. That she would try to . . .

He narrowed his gaze on the window behind Fiona. Watched as blond curls rose above the ledge, followed almost immediately by a pair of wide blue eyes.

. . . rescue him. "God's teeth!"

"Aye. Ye ken there'll be no escape from me, Ian Ross. Ye're truly mine." Fiona drew her tongue across her lower lip.

Ian was reminded of a bitch in heat.

Fiona offered him a practiced pout. "Ye'll not be able to show me yer skills this first time, but I

275

couldna wait to see *all* that I've missed these many years."

"Ye should free me so I may give ye *all* ye've missed." The blue eyes peering at him over the window ledge narrowed.

Fiona's laughter offered a husky promise. "Not this time, Ian. I must take my pleasure from gazing on yer body, and"—her voice lowered to a hungry whisper—"touching ye where I wish. 'Tis a joy I've waited long for."

"And does yer joy include touching me wi' *that?*" He dropped his gaze to the whip she held by her side.

He lifted his gaze in time to see his blue-eyed watcher's attention shift to the whip. Her eyes immediately widened again.

Fiona shrugged. "I use it when riding. I would only use it on an animal that didna give me a pleasurable ride." Her smile suggested that the using of it on him might bring her added excitement.

Ian frowned. For all the beauty of her red hair and green eyes, Fiona Mackay had a dark heart. But Fiona was not his greatest problem.

He must find a way to keep Kathy from bursting through the cottage door to attempt his rescue. Where were the men who'd been outside? If Kathy remained out there, she'd have a chance to escape into the forest when they returned. He must keep her outside until the Ross men arrived to release him.

Even as he coldly planned what he must do, something warm and new moved in him. She'd cared enough to follow him. To arrive so quickly, she must have ridden his horse. Few would be so brave. Now he must keep Fiona from turning and seeing Kathy at the window. He must also hold Kathy's attention long enough to give the Ross men time to reach them. *If they were coming.*

"Let me guide ye, lass." He dropped his voice to a husky murmur filled with erotic promise; it was what Fiona would expect from the Pleasure Master.

"Guide me?" Fiona's gaze turned predatory, heated.

"Aye. Listen to my words even as ye touch me, and ye'll know an . . . orgasm such as ye've ne'er known before." The men had lit a small hearth fire, and even though Ian's back was to it he could feel its heat. Sweat dampened his bare body, and he felt a drop of moisture slide down his chest, over his stomach, until it reached his groin.

"Orgasm? What is an orgasm?" Fiona's gaze followed the path the drop had taken.

Her greedy stare should have excited him, but he felt only distaste.

" 'Tis an . . . explosion of pleasure." Ian looked past Fiona to where Kathy had raised herself higher, so he could now see her mouth.

For a moment, the corners of her lips curved into a small smile at his remembrance of her orgasm description.

Even as he watched her lips, he felt another drop of moisture slip down the side of his neck, bead on his nipple, then continue its journey over his stomach until it slid between his legs.

Kathy moistened her lips with the tip of her tongue, and Ian didn't need to look into her eyes to know what she was looking at. He could *feel* the touch of her gaze.

Desperately, he tried to focus on Fiona, to ignore the familiar stirring, the growing pressure. But it seemed he had no control where Kathy was concerned. His gaze returned to her, to the wet sheen of her slightly parted lips. He could imagine her warm breath between his open thighs, her soft lips touching—

"Ye grow hard thinking of what we'll do together, Ian," Fiona said. "I ken why women have whispered of ye. Ne'er have I seen a man so . . ." She seemed unable to think of a word worthy of his erection.

Ian's pitiful attempt to think of all things disgusting had no effect on his arousal, which seemed determined to live its own life. And it was responding to the warm flush in Kathy's cheeks, the growing heat of her gaze.

"I must have ye, Ian." Fiona's eagerness was like rolling naked in honey. No matter how sweet some might say the honey tasted, 'twas not comfortable when it was sticking to every part of one's body.

"But I want ye in the comfort of my own bed. I'll call my men, and we'll leave immediately. We should reach home by night."

Thank God for Fiona's unwillingness to mount him amid the dirt and dust of the cottage floor. And mount him she would. Fiona would always need to be most powerful. She would ride him as she rode the stallion she had tethered outside, and he had no doubt she'd use her whip if he didn't move strongly enough.

I'll call my men, and we'll leave immediately. No! He couldn't let Fiona turn around and see Kathy. Her men would capture Kathy, and Ian knew what her fate would be once Fiona realized who she was.

"Dinna be so quick to call yer men." *Think*. What should he say? He'd used words to weave sexual fantasies for so many, and the words had come easily. But knowing that Kathy's safety depended on his words somehow robbed him of his wits. "Let me give ye a taste of the pleasure ye'll have wi' me."

Fiona's smile was all things savage. "Show me yer power, Pleasure Master." She tapped her whip lightly against her thigh. "Dinna disappoint me."

A quick glance at Kathy assured Ian of her outrage, her readiness to hurry to his rescue. He rushed into speech. "Close yer eyes, Fiona, and listen to me well.

"Ye enjoy power. The power to bend people's bodies to yer will, even though their hearts, their minds deny ye. 'Twould ne'er please ye to have a man who didna fight ye. 'Tis the power to take yer pleasure from a man's body even as ye see the hate in his eyes that has always been yer desire. Ye've hidden it well from ycr father, for it isna seemly for a maiden to have such dark wishes." He watched Fiona carefully, as he'd watched so many women, looking into their souls and sensing their most hidden desires. Desires they often feared admitting even to themselves. *Why havena ye looked into Kathy's soul? What do ye fear?*

"Aye. 'Tis what I wish." Her eyes remained closed.

Ian watched Fiona swallow hard. He wouldn't look at Kathy, didn't want to see the revulsion in her eyes as he did what he'd always done so well.

"Imagine, Fiona." His voice lowered, roughened with no conscious thought. "Yer father has died, and there are no others to lead yer clan. *Ye're* the new laird of Clan Mackay. Ye may have anything ye want and none may say nay."

He couldn't stop himself. He glanced at Kathy. And wished he hadn't. Her face was wiped clean of all expression, but he saw the confusion, the dawning horror in her eyes. He looked away. He would do what he must to keep her safe.

"Ye're in the keep's dungeon, Fiona. Yer men have captured yer greatest enemy, one who has fought many battles wi' ye, one who hates ye above all others. Ye've ordered that he be stripped naked and chained spread wide for ye. Now ye will have yer revenge." He watched Fiona's breath quicken, her fingers clench around the butt of her whip. "Open yer eyes, Fiona. See yer enemy. Look into his eyes and see the hate."

Fiona opened her eyes and stared at him with a gaze already glazed with the picture he'd drawn in her mind.

"Know him, Fiona. Ye canna break him wi' torture. He'll die defying ye. But there is another way."

"Tell me." Her voice was choked with her need.

"Humble him wi' yer body, Fiona. Touch him, stroke him, until he moans wi' his lust for ye, knows that not even this part of himself can he keep from ye." Curiosity pulled at Ian. "And before ye begin, tell him what fate awaits him if he fails ye." He'd like to know whether he would suffer her whip if his fantasy didn't please her. Thoughts of her whip would spur him to greater effort.

"I would give his body to all the women to use until he died from the using." Her satisfied smile anticipated such an event. "And I'd watch."

" 'Tis a horrible end." *Ah, Fiona. Most men would storm yer keep to experience such a fearful fate*. He made sure he didn't show his amusement.

Remembering his own personal watcher, he glanced at the window. Kathy's gaze locked with his, and she offered him a tentative smile that didn't quite reach her worried eyes. He shared her smile in his mind and realized how much comfort the sharing gave him.

"Touch him wi' yer hands, yer mouth, until he grows so hard for ye he fears he'll die from the wanting." He stared into Fiona's eyes, allowing her to see all the hate and contempt he knew she'd expect from her greatest enemy. He didn't have to pretend overmuch.

Ian despised what he must do next. He lifted his gaze to Kathy once more, kept it fixed on her eyes, her mouth. Fiona would not accept his fantasy if he had no arousal, and to keep his erection he must create his own fantasy.

His own fantasy would be of Kathy, and in weaving it he must involve her, whether he wanted to or not. Once before, she'd almost yielded to him because of his power to create a make-believe world. That was not how he wanted it to be between them.

But he knew if he involved Kathy, she wouldn't rush into the cottage to face Fiona. She would be safer outside, and Kathy Bartlett's safety meant more to him than anything else.

"Tell me what ye feel, my enemy." Fiona moved close, then slid her fingers over his chest, his stomach, between his legs. Cupping him, she squeezed gently.

Ian shuddered.

He closed Fiona from his mind, looked only into Kathy's eyes, thought only of Kathy touching him.

"The scent of ye fills me—warm woman's flesh and cool morning mist. I want to hate it, but I canna. I can only think of my need to hold yer breasts bare in my palms, to bury my face between them, to be close to yer scent. But I canna reach ye. I can only accept what ye give me." *Heed me, Kathy*. He sensed Kathy's desire to look away, to break the web he wove, but he wouldn't let her, would make her understand that he spoke to *her*.

Fiona's lips touched the pulse in his neck, then seared a path to his nipple. But it wasn't Fiona's tongue that flicked the sensitive nub, then touched his chest, his stomach with light kisses that made him moan within his fantasy. It was Kathy's lips, trailing a heated line of erotic torture.

"Tell me what ye feel."

The whisper was every woman he'd ever

touched, every woman who'd ever touched him. No, that was wrong. It was *Kathy*.

"Yer lips touching my body excite me." His hips began the slow thrusting motion of mating as he sank deeper into his fantasy. With each thrust his erection scraped the cloth covering the breasts of the woman who now knelt in front of him. He was so hard, his flesh so sensitive, that he thought he would die if he couldn't soon slide his arousal over warm bare skin. Over *Kathy's* flesh. "Would that I could taste ye as ye taste me. I would kiss the soft skin low on yer stomach, listen to yer soft gasp, feel yer muscles clench wi' yer need, see yer legs part in readiness. I would move between yer thighs and kiss a path along the inner sides—slowly, gently." He stared into Kathy's eyes, saw his own hot intensity reflected back. "Then I would put my mouth on ye, slide my tongue over yer most sensitive part, hold ye as ye writhed."

"What do I taste of?" The voice was harsh, barely in control. He didn't recognize it, didn't care. His whole world was centered on Kathy.

"Yer skin is the taste of the sea on a warm summer's day." *Know that I speak of ye, Kathy.* "The warmth between yer thighs is the sweetness of . . . rich chocolate."

He watched the awareness grow in Kathy's gaze. The deep glow added to the heat and desire he already saw. Never before had he wanted a woman with such hunger. But he sensed with a detached despair that her desire was for the Pleasure Master, not for *him*.

"I dinna know what chocolate is. Tell me what ye would do next."

The harsh demand was accompanied by the slide of the whip handle between his legs. Back and forth, back and forth.

It was Kathy's fingers sliding between his legs, fondling him, clasping him. He could hear the rasp of his own breathing, felt as though his chest could no longer hold his pounding heart. "I'd bury myself deep inside ye, feel ye tighten around me, thrust again and again until I could hold back no longer, then I would spill my hot seed into . . ."

He could stand no more. "Free me, Kathy, so I may pleasure ye in all these ways."

The sudden stillness seeped into him. He blinked, suddenly aware of small sounds—ducks quacking, men shouting in the distance, Fiona's quiet hiss of anger.

"This was not for my pleasure, was it, Ian Ross? Ye werena thinking of me. Ye were thinking only of this Kathy. Ye bastard!"

The shock of Fiona's whip slashing across his lower stomach brought a shocked gasp from him. God's teeth! She'd barely missed his—

The crash as the door was flung open shook the cottage. Vengeance stood in the opening wielding a sword that glowed and hummed, along with the dreaded curling iron. Vengeance was *not* soft spoken.

"Bitch! You hurt him."

Ian could feel a trickle of blood sliding down his stomach, but he was as stunned as Fiona, unable to take his gaze from his small, fierce-eyed rescuer.

"I'm going to curl your toes and everything north, then I'll kick your behind all the way back to your sorry castle. You don't mess with a New York woman or her man." Kathy's eyes narrowed to vicious slits of righteous wrath. "If you start running now, you might work off some of that fat and maybe some man'll want you, but I don't think so."

Her gaze fixed on the glowing sword, Fiona shook with fear as she edged toward the door. But obviously one of Kathy's barbs called for a response. "I'm *not* fat."

"Hah!" Kathy continued to stalk her.

With a shriek of mingled fear and fury, Fiona stumbled from the cottage.

Behind her, Kathy could hear the terrified shouts of the Mackays mingled with the cheery sounds of her toy defenders. The Village Gorilla was in great voice as he belted out "Macho Man," and she hoped the Mackays appreciated his enthusiastic dancing. A terrified shriek sounded behind her. Well, maybe not.

"Are ye mad, woman? Save yerself before the Mackays find ye."

"Gee thanks, Kathy, for saving my bare buns from Ditsy-the-Dominatrix." But Kathy couldn't maintain her sarcasm for long as she gazed at the bleeding welt on his stomach. "God, Ian, I can't believe she hurt you." Sinking to her knees, Kathy ran her fingers tenderly over the wound. "I wish she hadn't run so I could pull every hair from her head."

"Ye're a wee gentle lass."

Kathy glanced up to catch his wry grin, but his grin faded as her gaze locked with his. The memory of his fantasy moved between them, left Kathy with questions she feared to ask. She drew in a deep calming breath. They'd talk about it later.

"We've got to get you out of here." A sudden rise in the noise level made Kathy turn to glance outside.

"The Rosses are here." His harsh exhalation said all that needed saying about his relief. "My clothing is in the corner. Find my knife and free me."

Kathy grabbed his clothes and knife; then quickly cut him loose. She stood in the doorway checking the progress of the battle while he dressed.

When Ian joined her, she looked up and grinned. "I think the Mackays are getting more than they bargained for."

Peter was busily patrolling the line of toys, urging them on with quotes from every military movie ever shot, while Malin clung to Fiona's skirt with tenacious claws.

Fiona's shrieks joined the din. "Someone get the bloody beastie off me. Look, I have scratches all over my hands."

No one seemed particularly interested in looking at her scratches or stopping the battle to pull Malin off her skirt. Hiking up her skirt, she did a clumsy jig, trying to shake the cat loose.

Kathy couldn't help it, she laughed. Loudly.

Fiona turned to glare at her. "Someone kill that

woman. Don't kill Ian Ross. I'll do that." Her shrieked orders got the attention of a few of her men, who moved to obey her.

Ian crouched with his knife in his hand, ready to defend Kathy. Frantically, Kathy reached into her backpack and pulled out her last weapon, her final line of defense—a remote-controlled model Apache attack helicopter. She'd done a little of this with her dad when she was young, and she hoped to heaven she remembered how to work the thing.

Taking a deep breath, she flipped the switch. "Showtime, baby."

The helicopter rose into the air with a satisfying whirr, then flew toward the advancing Mackays.

The helicopter was the final straw . . . for both sides. With bellows of terror, both Rosses and Mackays scattered in all directions. Fiona, who'd finally managed to shake Malin loose, followed her terrified clansmen into the forest.

Kathy glanced up at Ian, who was staring at the hovering helicopter with disbelieving eyes. "Hmm. I guess they're not quite ready for the helicopter concept."

He gazed down at her with confusion, but no fear. Once again, Kathy marveled at how different he was from everyone else she'd met in this time. He might not understand, but he didn't immediately think everything strange was the product of demons and devils. A man ahead of his time. *But not far enough ahead.*

"I would know how ye make this thing fly."

"You can take it apart when we get back to the

cave." Kathy guided the helicopter to earth, then started to repack the toys she'd brought while Ian went for his horse.

Ian seemed strangely quiet as they all piled onto the horse and started the long walk home. Just when Kathy had decided she couldn't take one more second of silence, Ian spoke.

"Why did ye say Fiona was fat when she isna fat?"

That's right, Ian. Pussyfoot around what that incredible fantasy did to both of us. "It's one of the arrows-to-the-heart insults every woman hates. I guess you'd have to be a woman to understand." Truth wouldn't be denied. "Actually, Fiona is beautiful." Ugh. She hated admitting things like that.

Peter's lights flashed. "Picture a girl who took a nose dive from the ugly tree and hit every branch on the way down."

Kathy laughed and hugged Peter. "*Saving Private Ryan.* Great, Peter. Thanks for the loyalty. I love you, too."

Ian frowned. "Ye love this toy?"

"He isn't a toy, you know." She thought for a moment. "He isn't always good, and I know he's responsible for my being here, but . . . he makes me laugh." Now that made a whole lot of sense.

"Aye."

They plodded along in silence again.

Finally, Ian drew in a deep breath.

Kathy closed her eyes. *Here it comes.*

"I'm sorry." His gruff apology seemed dragged from him.

"For what?" She wasn't going to make it easy for him.

"For forcing ye into my fantasy. I wouldna have done it if I could have thought of another way."

With Peter and Malin sitting in front of her, she couldn't hug Ian, so she drew her fingertip down the middle of his spine, then let her hand rest on the top of his hip. His muscles clenched.

"I enjoyed the fantasy, Ian." Wow, no kidding. She'd wanted to heave Fiona out the door, then explore every inch of Ian's wonderful body. *And what else did you want to explore, hmm?* "You couldn't *force* me into a fantasy I didn't want."

"I could. Think of yer bandit fantasy."

Now she was getting mad. "I was responding to *you.*"

"Ye were responding to the Pleasure Master."

She heard the stubborn note in his voice that indicated nothing she said would change his mind. Interesting. It was almost as though he thought of Ian Ross and the Pleasure Master as two different men. This was important stuff, but she'd think about it later. There was something else she wanted to know.

"Why did you need me in your fantasy?"

He shifted in the saddle, and Kathy had the feeling he didn't want to answer.

"Fiona wouldna believe me if my body didna show desire for her."

Kathy frowned. Body? Show desire? Oh! She smiled. "Uh, could you make that a little clearer?"

"God's teeth!" He hunched his shoulders and

Kathy's smile widened. "I could only grow hard wi' thoughts of ye. Is that clear enough for ye?"

"I make you hard?" What an . . . energizing thought.

"Ummph."

She'd take that as an affirmative. "Here, you hold Peter and Malin for a while." Not giving him a chance to argue, she made the exchange.

Then she slid forward until she was pressed against his back. Wrapping her arms around his waist, she rested her head between his shoulder blades. Her eyes started to drift shut, the warm male scent of him triggering heated memories of the cottage, his body.

Don't even think about it. This would not be a good thing to do. But she was thinking about it, and she was going to do it.

Hoping that Ian thought her hands were slipping because she was falling asleep, she slid her fingers low on his stomach, then paused.

She heard Ian's soft laugh. "I think I've given ye a weapon I shouldna have given ye. If ye want to test yer power, dinna be shy about it."

He placed his hand over hers then guided her fingers beneath his plaid to lie warm against his skin. Slowly, he slid her hand up the inside of his hard, smooth-muscled thigh. He removed his hand and she knew she'd have to take the final step.

Knowing her fingers shook, but unable to control them, she settled her hand over his sex.

And stopped thinking. She *always* thought. In-your-face one-liners when she was scared or upset.

Warm fuzzy thoughts for friends and family. Analytical thoughts mixed with the previous two when she was working, depending on whose hair she was doing. But she *always* thought. Now, her mind was like Mr. Winston's head—bald except for a few wispy strands around the edge.

Oh, but she could *feel*—emotions, Ian's hot male flesh filling her hand, growing hard, pushing against her palm. The emotions were new, raw. Too new to understand, too sensitive to examine in the strong light of reason. And so she concentrated on his arousal—the size of it, the strength. Imagined it deep inside of her, stretching her. Knowing that he would make her . . . happy.

Kathy didn't want him to make her happy. She didn't want to know joy in this place because she didn't belong here, didn't want to take any ghosts with her when she returned home. *Too late.* She closed her eyes completely and slid her fingers the length of his erection, marveled at its smoothness, traced a tentative line around—

He inhaled sharply a second before he pushed her hand from him. " 'Twould be upsetting to Peter and Malin if I dropped them on their wee heads, but if ye keep touching me so, I willna have a choice."

She didn't open her eyes as she settled her hand around his waist, then smiled. It felt like Madonna's "Material Girl" smile, equal parts of wicked anticipation and sensual promise. In all her New York life, she'd never known she could smile like that.

Soon, Ian Ross. Very soon.

"Ye might wish to stick something in yer ears, lass. I think Peter readies himself to speak on the matter." His muttered suggestion sounded resigned.

Kathy pictured Peter's amber lights flashing.

"To love is to suffer. To avoid suffering one must not love, but then one suffers from not loving. Therefore, to love is to suffer, not to love is to suffer. To be happy is to love, to be happy then is to suffer, but suffering makes one unhappy, therefore to be unhappy one must love or love to suffer or suffer from too much happiness. I hope you're getting this down. . . ."

"Love and Death?" She wasn't sure, but she knew there was only one way to escape Peter.

She slept.

Chapter Sixteen

There were dreams, and then there were *dreams.* And they didn't get much better than last night's.

Kathy lay with eyes closed, listening to Neil's voice as he gave Coco today's new and updated rundown of the "wondrous" things he would do to her when they met. Fat chance.

She frowned, trying to remember. No, wait. There hadn't been any dream, it had all been real. The last thing she recalled was her hand on Ian's . . . She opened her eyes and smiled. That memory was almost enough to keep her hot and bothered for the rest of her life.

Neil's voice stopped, and Kathy realized he must be finished with his call. She sat up. "Bring the phone over here, Neil. I have to talk to Coco."

As he handed her the phone, Ian emerged from

the tunnel, his hair still damp. She was a slug. He was up and had already bathed even after what he'd gone through yesterday. He had only a cloth wrapped around his waist, and she was able to see the angry red welt left by Fiona's lash. She wasn't into physical violence, but Fiona had better hope they never met in a dark alley or any other space large enough for Kathy to get in a good swing.

She put the phone to her ear without taking her gaze from Ian. "Coco?" Something flip-flopped inside her at the thought of what she was going to ask her friend. She didn't want to examine the feeling too closely.

"Hey, girlfriend. What's happening in Never Never Land?" The words were Coco's usual irreverence, but the tone held something different. Guilt?

"Have you done something you need to tell me about, Coco?"

There was a long silence.

"Okay." Coco's admission was a resigned sigh. "This thing is just too strange, so I called the cops in. They've been listening in to the last few calls Neil made. They're listening to this one. Are you going to hang up?"

Kathy thought about it, then quickly dismissed the thought. "I know you're doing what you think will keep me safe, but I'm really fine." She thought about yesterday. Okay, maybe not so fine. "Besides, it won't do any good."

"Tell me about it. Their trace came up with nothing, and I think they're all taking personal notes on

Neil's insights into a fulfilled sexual relationship. Talk about embarrassing."

A horrific idea occurred to Kathy. "They haven't contacted Mom and Dad have they?"

Coco's voice was low, calming. "Yeah, they had to, Kathy. I called your parents and tried to do some damage control, but you might want to call them yourself." There was a long pause. "I told the police the truth about your going to Scotland to spend time with your man, but that it wasn't like you to just up and leave all your responsibilities."

Great. Just great. At least Coco hadn't told them the part about her traveling back to 1542, but Coco wouldn't want them to think she was a wacko. "I haven't been kidnapped, and what I'm doing is my own business." That was for the cops; now for Coco. "Hey, would you look through as many movie quotes on the Net as you can? I'd like you to give me any that have to do with going home."

"And the point is?"

"Um, we're just playing a game." She tried to laugh lightly. "Find me *the* one and maybe I'll come home."

"Right." Coco's voice indicated she'd gotten the message.

Kathy knew she shouldn't ask this with the police listening, but she had to know. "What's the date, Coco?"

Coco laughed and almost made it sound convincing. "February eighth. You need to come up for air once in a while and pay attention to what's happening. You don't want to miss February fourteenth. If you don't show up, the police might even suspect your ex of foul play."

Tempting. "I'll be there." Her gaze found Peter, and she offered him her where's-my-compactor glare.

She hit End and looked around to see who was paying attention. Ian and Neil were across the room deep in argument over something. Good. Quickly, she punched in her parents' number. *Nothing.* Just dead air. She wasn't really surprised. She'd always believed someone or something was controlling the phone.

Maybe it was for the best. What could she possibly say to Mom and Dad that would calm their fears? Now she had a new reason to get back by the fourteenth. Every day she was away would increase her parents' worry, and Dad's heart wasn't the strongest. Depressed, she turned to put the phone away and gave a small start to find Peter beside her.

"I don't know why you're doing this, but it isn't funny anymore. If I don't go home, people will think I was kidnapped. Mom and Dad are too old for this." Could you appeal to the conscience of a metal hourglass?

Peter's lights flashed. "I once asked this literary agent what writing paid the best, and he said, 'ransom notes.' "

She sighed. "Not funny, Peter." She was too frustrated to even try to remember what movie the line came from. "Is there a purpose to this whole thing?"

"It doesn't matter if the guy is perfect, or the girl is perfect, as long as they are perfect for each other."

"Is that supposed to make sense? I mean, are you some kind of time-traveling matchmaker?" She laughed at the whimsy of the idea. "Why would I have to find a man in 1542 when there're millions of men in 2001?"

Kathy stood, grabbed her bath stuff, and then started toward the tunnel. She paused and looked back at Peter. "*Good Will Hunting*, right? How many quotes do you have stored in your little computer brain, huh?"

She continued walking before Peter could scan his hard drive for the perfect put-down.

Kathy washed quickly. The water wasn't freezing, but it wasn't warm enough for soaking. She hoped Neil was still around when she was finished.

Tonight. She would sleep with Ian tonight and make sure no one else would be Pleasure Master. But first she wanted to go to the village with Neil so she could visit Mary. There was something important she needed, and she didn't want to ask Ian.

Drying herself quickly, she hurried back in time to find Neil on his way out. He didn't look happy.

"Wait a minute and I'll go with you. I have some things I want to get from Mary." Kathy hoped Ian wouldn't insist on going with her. She had to do this alone.

"Dinna take long, lass. I must go home so I may think of new sexual enticements with which to tempt Coco."

Kathy hurriedly ran a comb through her damp hair. Hmm. Root alert. If she didn't return home soon, she was going to transform right before everyone's eyes. Sort of like a snowshoe rabbit—one minute bright and brilliant, the next brown and dull. No time for makeup. Ah, the joys of the natural look. Also known as Sleeping Beauty's evil twin, Sleeping Ugly. At least she'd blend in with all the other women. Let's hear it for blending.

"Phone sex is fine, Neil, but at some point it'll get a little . . . You know, not *enough*. Besides, someone has to hear Coco say she'll do the deed with you before you can win." Kathy glanced at Ian. He looked angry, and he wasn't paying any attention to either of them. This should be a topic of interest to him, and he hadn't said a thing when she mentioned going with Neil. Strange.

Neil looked unconcerned. "Our father will return soon. Coco may tell *him* that she agrees."

Right. She could just imagine old Dad holding a piece of plastic to his ear and calmly listening to Coco. Neil didn't have too firm a grip on reality.

"Come, lass." Neil started walking, and Kathy grabbed her backpack, then hurried to catch up with him.

She cast one last worried glance at Ian, who sat staring distractedly into the hearth flame, then followed Neil to his horse.

Ian listened to her footsteps echo down the tunnel until she was gone. The same way they would echo as she walked from his life. He had no doubt that would have to be soon because she was in danger here. He'd known that even before Neil said it. Neil and Mary would keep her safe today, but there would come a time . . .

What should he do? He must find a way to send Kathy home; then a part of him would die forever. Like Malin, he would still do what needed doing, but he'd always know he wasn't whole.

He stood, then paced before the fire.

"I loooove you."

Ian grinned. "Aye, so ye've told me often. Mayhap Kathy will leave ye wi' me when she goes." Would Suzy be his only memory?

He needed another. He needed to plunge deep inside Kathy, feel her body clench around him, holding him tight while spasms of pleasure shook her, so tight that even time couldn't tear her from him. And when she screamed a name, it would be his, not the Pleasure Master's.

Ian slumped before the fire again. 'Twas a sorry dream. He couldn't separate himself from who he was. This would be a grand joke to his father if he knew. Ian had berated his father for falling in love and abandoning his duty. Now he understood.

Love? Was that what he felt for Kathy? He didn't know. But no matter what he felt, he was the Pleasure Master, and as Neil had reminded him, he had a duty to fulfill. Neil had told him many women had need of his services. They'd waited long in the village for Kathy to be gone, but they'd wait no longer. He was alone today, so they would come. *Ye'll always be alone, Ian Ross.*

Peter's lights flashed beside him. "Nobody ever lies about being lonely."

"What's wrong with Ian?" Kathy asked, seated behind Neil on his horse.

"Humph."

"Okay, besides that, what's wrong with him?"

"Ian is still the Pleasure Master. He must remember this."

"And?"

Neil said nothing for a moment, and Kathy thought he would ignore her question.

"He has thought only of ye since ye came."

Kathy felt pleasure seep through her.

"But now he must think of others."

She wasn't quite sure what that meant, but it sort of stopped up the pleasure cracks.

"He isna happy to be reminded of his duty."

No kidding. She didn't think Ian's "duty" was too terrific either. Kathy didn't try to wheedle any more information from him. She hadn't liked what she'd heard so far, except the part about Ian thinking only of her.

It didn't matter what Ian did because she *was* going home. And she *was* sniffling at the thought of leaving him behind. Dammit, she would *not* get emotional about this. There, she'd stopped sniffling. Probably had a cold coming on. No wonder in this climate.

Relieved, she realized they'd arrived at Mary's. She slid from Neil's horse, thanked him, and walked to Mary's door.

When Mary opened the door and smiled at her, Kathy realized how much she missed female friendship. Go figure.

" 'Tis good to see ye, Kathy. Come in. Colin is here." She moved aside so Kathy could enter.

Colin sat at the table sorting through various herbs. He glanced up and grinned at Kathy. " 'Twas an amazing battle yesterday. I dinna think the Mackays will forget ye, Kathy of Hair." His smile disappeared. "Ye must be verra careful. The Mackays will rally others to their cause with tales of yer witchcraft. The Rosses also fear ye, and even Ian willna be able to keep ye safe. If he tries, he will be destroyed. Ye might want to soon begin yer journey to yer homeland."

Kathy sighed. If he had any good ideas for sending her home, she was open to suggestions. "I know, but I did what I had to do yesterday. I don't regret it." Not yet.

Mary pushed her onto a stool by the table. "I'll get ye something to drink. Then I have news for ye."

Kathy focused on Colin and tried for a casual tone. "So, how's the Pleasure Master quest going?"

Colin's grin returned, and he looked up at Mary. "Ye might tell her now, lass."

Mary put a cup of pale amber liquid in front of Kathy, then sat next to Colin. "Colin and I will be marrying."

Kathy gaped. She *never* gaped. "Why?"

Mary cast her an amused glance. "I tired of talking to my hens."

"Oh." Ask a stupid question, get a stupid answer.

Mary shook her head and smiled. "We love each other, Kathy." She slid Colin a shy smile. "He played his pipes for me."

Kathy grinned at Colin. "I thought you only played your pipes when you were going into battle."

"Or for one I love. And ye think this wasna a battle?"

Kathy's eyes widened at the implication. "That means you're out of the Pleasure Master competition."

"Aye. 'Tis amazing. I thought becoming Pleasure Master was the most important thing in my life. But I know now that nothing else is important when ye find the lass ye wish to spend the rest of yer life wi'." He cast Kathy a sly glance. "Ye might tell Ian that."

Well. This certainly made things easier. Colin was out of the running, and Neil certainly wouldn't win Coco before tonight. She was home free. "Mary, do you have any kinds of colors I can use to paint with?"

"Aye." Mary looked puzzled. "Ye're painting a picture?"

Kathy knew her smile was anticipatory. "A very special picture."

Colin watched Mary gather the paints and several brushes. "When ye're ready, I'll take ye back. Dinna travel anywhere wi'out Ian, Neil, or me." Colin glanced away. "Ian didna think we'd come for him yesterday, did he?"

Kathy blinked at the change of subject. "He

didn't mention it." But she remembered Ian's look of relief when the Rosses showed up, almost as though he hadn't expected them.

Colin looked uneasy. "Ian has ne'er thought Neil and I care for him. He has ne'er thought anyone cared for *him,* only for what joy he can bring as Pleasure Master. He was taught to think thus by our father."

"So why don't you tell him that you . . . care for him?"

"Men dinna speak to each other of such things."

She gave herself a mental head slap. "Right. It's a man thing. Then why are you telling me?"

Colin's voice grew gruff. "He needs know that he is more than just the Pleasure Master."

Kathy waited for Colin to enlarge on the topic, but Colin was obviously finished delving into Ian's psyche. She'd have to fill in the blanks.

A short time later, she sat atop Colin's horse with Mary's painting supplies safely stored in her backpack. Luckily, Colin didn't have much to say because she had too much to think about to hold up her end of a conversation.

Okay, she'd admit it. Her uncertainties were jigging and jogging all over her stomach. She'd known Ian for such a short time, and yet she'd known him forever. His dark sensuality, his delight in each of her toys, his curiosity about everything in her world, his patience and kindness no matter how she irritated him. Well, maybe not so patient. But she even liked his looming bad temper. Now *that* was scary.

How would she feel after tonight? If he could heat her to whimpering, panting desire without even touching her, what would happen when he touched her with serious intent? She'd ignite in a flash fire that would reduce her to a pile of smoking ashes, that's what. It would make Peter's job easier. All he'd have to do was blow her ashes back to New York.

That didn't change her mind about making love with Ian. She was determined that he'd be happy and secure as Pleasure Master after she went home. *Even if you wake every morning for the rest of your life with his scent, his taste, his memory filling you?*

Yes. It was her responsibility. *What if it weren't your responsibility?* Fine, so she'd do it anyway. Because she wanted Ian Ross with a teeth-gritting, fist-clenching, heart-pounding need that wouldn't even consider that he didn't want her, too.

What if he really doesn't want you? What if everything he's shown you has simply been what the Pleasure Master has shown countless other woman? What if you're just part of a cast of thousands?

I'd still want him. And wouldn't that give old PMS a hoot if he knew. Kathy-the-ice-queen gets her comeuppance from Ian. All-women-are-welcome Ross, the ultimate womanizer. Cosmic justice at its finest.

Then there was Colin's cryptic message. Of course Ian was more than the Pleasure Master. He was . . . Ian. *But does he know it?*

Relieved, she realized they were climbing the hill

to Ian's cave. No more opportunity for stress-headache thoughts.

" 'Tis about time."

Colin's muttered comment focused her attention on the cave entrance. Would Ian come out to meet . . . ?

"Ohmigod! There's a line of women waiting outside the cave." Kathy counted. Ten. *Ten?*

"Aye. The women have been waiting long for Ian, ever since ye came, in fact. Only Lady Carlisle took courage and visited him." Colin pulled his horse to a stop and helped Kathy off. " 'Tis strange. When she returned from here she was sorely upset. She told a tale of a woman who said that Ian couldna see her because there were twelve women before her. Lady Carlisle doesna wait for any man." He slid her a thoughtful glance. "Ye wouldna know who this *woman* could be?"

"Umm." Kathy could feel the heat rising to her face.

" 'Tis no matter." He nodded his head toward the women. "Neil said he would speak to Ian this morn. Ian will do his duty as Pleasure Master now."

Not if I can help it. Kathy didn't even question the rage, the *jealousy* that sent her stomping toward the waiting women. She heard Colin leave but kept walking. She'd think reasonable thoughts later about why she was so furious when she claimed she wanted to make Ian's job as Pleasure Master secure. This was what he did, for heaven's sake. So why was she so mad?

Ten! Fine. So he could do what he did after she

was gone. Just so she didn't have to know about it.

Gone. Something about the word emptied her, made her feel hollow. *Lonely.*

She reached the woman at the end of the line before she had time to think about never seeing Ian again. Good thing. She could feel tears welling, and in a few minutes she would have been blinking madly.

"This is the end of the line, huh?" She offered the woman a sympathetic smile. "Must be important for you to stand out here this long. Looks like it might rain." The sky was bright blue with fluffy white clouds. "Maybe I can save you some time. Tell me your problem, and I'll see if I can help. I've had lots of experience with men." Kathy cast a cautious glance at that blue sky. Any minute now . . . Was it possible to dodge a lightning bolt?

The woman sighed. "I dinna wish to wait so long, but I must ask the Pleasure Master"—she hesitated and cast Kathy a shy glance—"how to make my husband take more time wi' our loving." She shifted her gaze to the ground. "I love my husband and know that he would wish me to enjoy our joining, but as soon as we climb into our bed, he's ready. 'Tis not long enough to blink."

"Hmm." Kathy tried for a thoughtful look. "Got it. Clothes. Lots of clothes."

The woman stared blankly.

"First of all, you need to tell your husband the problem, not the Pleasure Master. Suggest that you both wear lots of clothes to bed. Then explain how much joy it would give you to take his clothes off him. Slowly. As you take each piece from him you can touch his body. You know, kissing . . . and other things." No way was Kathy getting more specific. "This will make you kind of . . . receptive. When you're finished with him, ask him to do the same for you. Bet it livens up your love life a whole bunch."

The woman considered Kathy's words, then smiled. "Aye, it might work. I'll try." She stepped out of line. "I didna wish to spend hours here. Maeve is first, and she will spend much time wi' the Pleasure Master."

"She will, will she?" Kathy narrowed her gaze on Maeve. "How do you know the Pleasure Master isn't already busy with someone?" *Please* let him be alone.

"The cat isna sitting at the entrance."

"Cat?"

"Aye. The Pleasure Master puts his cat without when he has a woman within. The cat is jealous, ye ken."

"Right. Jealous." Kathy never thought she'd empathize with a cat, but . . .

"The cat willna move from the entrance until there are no more women, and the Pleasure Master allows him within again." The woman frowned. " 'Tis strange. He has no woman wi' him, but he hasna come out to invite any in."

"Sounds okay to me," Kathy murmured as she moved to the next woman in line. "So, what's your problem?"

The woman turned to her. "Ye gave the lass good

advice. Mayhap ye can help me. She speaks true about Maeve. None of us will see the Pleasure Master this day once she gets him."

Kathy drew her lips into a tight line. She *really* didn't like this Maeve. "Maybe I can help old Maeve shorten her visit with the Pleasure Master." First she'd get rid of these other women. "But let's see what we can do about your problem."

" 'Tis the opposite of the lass ye just helped. My husband is old, ye ken. He must work long before he gains release. *Verra* long. A body grows weary waiting for it to happen."

"Got it. You need to speed things up." Thank heavens she'd read all those magazines when she was trying to find the key to the great orgasm. Unfortunately, she'd have to give body-specific directions here. Leaning close, she told all.

When she'd finished, the woman's face was bright red, and Kathy could feel the heat flushing her own face. She probably had a neon-red glow. "That should do it, but in case it doesn't, you'll need to spend your waiting time in a meaningful way." She reached into her backpack. "Here's a bottle of Dark Passion nail polish. Put on two coats and let both coats dry. Your man should be done by then."

The woman looked a little dazed as she left, holding the nail polish. Kathy smiled. Now on to the rest of the line.

A half hour later she'd worked her way up to the dreaded Maeve. She'd kept one eye on the woman while she doled out advice just in case the line began to move. In which case she would have taken emergency action.

Maeve gave her no time to make her pitch. "Ye willna get rid of me so easily." Her gaze defied Kathy to try. "When the Pleasure Master comes forth, *I* will have his body first."

There would be no body-having while Kathy Bartlett was on-site. "Hey, don't get your panties in a bunch."

"Panties?"

"Never mind." Kathy sighed. "You can wait for the Pleasure Master until you take root for all I care." She slid a considering glance over Maeve. "Of course, it's a shame you can't go to him looking a little more . . . desirable."

"I dinna ken what ye mean."

"Okay, let's look at the big picture. All those other women just wanted to talk to the Pleasure Master. You want some body contact. Right?" "

Maeve slanted her a sly smile. "Aye."

"Well, you look like hell, girlfriend. If you want the Pleasure Master to show some up-close-and-personal interest in you, you'd better do something about . . . your hair."

Maeve frowned. "What is wrong wi' my hair?"

"Split ends, sister. Your hair looks like your family tree, ends branching out in every direction. Why don't you let me do a little snipping and shaping? Hey, a man appreciates good hair on a woman." *Stall.* While she was snipping and shaping, maybe she could think of some way to get rid of Maeve without the embarrassment of a down-and-dirty

hair-pulling fest. Kathy always did her best thinking when she was creating great hair.

"Mayhap ye're right."

"Sure I am." Reaching into her backpack, Kathy
pulled out the basic hair supplies she always carried
with her.

A few minutes later, she was into the flow. She
knew hair. It gave her a calming sense of certainty.

"I dinna understand why ye're cutting my hair
when ye could be lying wi' the Pleasure Master."
Maeve's voice was slyly suggestive. "Mayhap he
doesna want ye. 'Twould be truly hard to live wi'
him and not sample his body."

*Never mess with a hair stylist who has scissors
in her hand.* Kathy grabbed a large chunk of lank
hair from the back of Maeve's head. She readied
her scissors. She gritted her teeth and tried to ignore the hairstylist's code: Never be the cause of a
bad hair day.

A sudden flash of amber lights announced Peter's
presence and desire to join in the conversation. "I
can assure you that my personal tragedy will not
interfere with my ability to do good hair."

Maeve screeched and jumped. Kathy's hand
slipped. And the huge chunk of Maeve's hair fell to
the ground. Maeve turned to stare at it in horror.

Kathy stared, too. "Gee, I guess that takes care
of those nasty old split ends."

Maeve shifted her horrified gaze to Peter, who
was sidling closer, then back to her shorn locks.
With one more expressive shriek, she fled.

Kathy pulled a small plastic bottle from her pack.

"Sure you don't want to take this conditioner sample with you?" she shouted after Maeve's fast disappearing figure.

Kathy turned to Peter. "Guess not. And here I was counting on a great tip from her. Win some, lose some."

She drew in a deep breath. Now for the tough stuff. She had a date with a man and a bed.

Chapter Seventeen

Ian stood with his back to the cave entrance, staring into the fire. All was quiet without. Had the women gone? Would they return to their villages to spread the tale that the Pleasure Master would see no one? And why didn't he care more?

The lethargy, the unwillingness to perform his duty whispered that it didn't matter. None of it mattered.

He noted without interest the sound of footsteps coming toward him from the tunnel. One of the women must have worked up the courage to enter his lair. She would be rewarded by being sent away.

The footsteps paused behind him. Silence.

Ian exhaled sharply. He'd always hated lies, excuses meant to escape that which was unpleasant. All the same, he lied. "I canna help ye or any of the others today. I am not well. I have a . . . headache."

"I think that's my line, Ross."

He felt Kathy's amusement touch him with playful fingers that ignited a joy out of all proportion to her words. He turned.

"They're gone, Ian." Her gaze was soft, tentative.

He moved closer, reached out to slide his fingers through her hair. When he was old and bent he'd still hold the memory of her scent—elusive and tempting with the promise of a world he'd never know.

She offered him a cautious smile. "Hope you don't mind my handing out advice to those women. I just used a little common sense. No personal experience, you understand, but I've read a lot. Sorry, but I couldn't help Maeve. She sort of left before I could get a handle on her problem. And somebody stop my babbling mouth."

He stopped her babbling mouth. Lowering his head, he covered her lips with his. He forced his hands to remain at his sides no matter how badly he longed to wrap his arms around her, hold her captive to his need. He wanted nothing other than her desire to keep her with him—neither physical restraint nor the power of the Pleasure Master.

With a quiet moan, she slid her fingers across his stomach, then put her arms around him.

He felt a surge of triumph that lasted but a moment. Was she choosing *him* or the remembered joy she knew the Pleasure Master could bring?

Ian tried to drive away his doubt with the pressure of her body, the glide of her tongue across his lips, then the building excitement as he explored her mouth, his tongue tasting hers, her heat matching his.

When she molded her palms to his buttocks and pulled him more tightly against her, he groaned into her mouth and enfolded her with arms that shook. Lifting her off her feet, he thrust between her thighs, and was rewarded when she wrapped her legs around his hips, then pressed down on his arousal. He could have her now. He could shove aside the layers of cloth separating them and plunge deep into her body. And even as he eased the desire that seemed to have been building from the first moment he saw her, he'd give her pleasure that would wipe away the memory of all she'd suffered at her husband's hands.

Pleasure. Just as the cloth separated them, so did the title of Pleasure Master. Ian had a need he didn't fully understand to know that Kathy made love only to Ian Ross, not the Pleasure Master. When had that ever mattered? And were they even two different men?

Beyond the taste, the scent, the feel of her, and beyond his heart-pounding need to bury himself in her body, he knew that for the first time in his life it was important that a woman make love to Ian Ross, the man, and not the legend.

He stepped away from her, creating a space filled with unanswered questions and unfulfilled desires. Kathy gazed at him across the space.

"I want you, Ian. I know women say that to you on a daily basis, but it's a new line for me. I've never said it to another man." She took a step into the space he'd created.

"And which man are ye saying it to now, lass?"

"Did I miss something? I only see one man here."

Ian watched her clench her fists, her nails digging into her palms. Kathy wasn't as calm as she pretended. He wanted to uncurl her fingers, smooth away the nail marks in her skin with his tongue, and tell her how much he wanted her. Tell her the lack wasn't in her, it was in him.

"And is that one man the Pleasure Master?"

Her gaze narrowed. "That man is Ian Ross. The man who took in a very strange woman, even though she said she was from another time. The man who held her when she cried for her world. The man who put up with a bunch of odd toys and protected her from his own people. The man who *cared* for her." She offered him a wry smile. "Even when he found out she wasn't Kathy, Princess of Hair."

The sound of her phone stopped his reply.

Never letting her gaze wander from his face, she lifted the phone from where it rested beside Suzy.

Intent on his own thoughts, he paid little attention to what Kathy was saying. She was speaking to Coco, and he watched as she pulled a strange writing implement and a piece of paper from her purse.

As she wrote down whatever information Coco was giving her, Ian thought about what would happen once Kathy ended her call. He'd always prided himself on being a reasonable man, but his growing determination that Kathy would *not* make love to the Pleasure Master made no sense. The Pleasure Master was his whole life, who he was. Why would he think that making love with this woman was more important?

The truth smote him with no warning. He no longer wished to bed faceless women, those many who'd need him until he could offer them nothing more. He no longer wanted to be alone, and the Pleasure Master would always need to be alone. He'd never recognized his loneliness until Kathy.

He didn't think. He reacted. "I would speak wi' Coco."

Kathy cast him a puzzled glance, then handed the phone to him.

"Coco, this is Ian. I would hear from yer own lips whether ye would join wi' Neil were he wi' ye at this moment."

He listened to Coco's reply, refusing to heed the ancient voices of past Pleasure Masters whispering that he was throwing all away. Refusing to question why he was doing so. Refusing to ask what he would do for the rest of his life. The rest of his life once Kathy had gone.

He swallowed hard, closing his eyes against Coco's answer. 'Twas done. The words had been spoken, and he could never go back to what he'd been. There was but one thing necessary to complete it. "Would ye say those same words to Kathy?"

Kathy backed away from him, her eyes wide.

"No. I won't listen. I won't let you do this to yourself."

"I dinna do this to myself. I do this *for* myself. Since the moment my father wrested me from my mother's arms, I have lived for the pleasure of others. I willna say I didna enjoy it, but I dinna enjoy it now. I havena enjoyed it since ye came to me." He dropped his voice to a harsh whisper. "I willna e'er enjoy it again."

"I . . . I don't understand." But the dawning glow in her eyes said she did understand.

"Speak to Coco, Kathy." He shoved the phone at her.

Hesitantly, she took it from him. "Coco?"

Coco must have heard what they'd said, because Kathy listened silently, then put the phone away without one more word.

When she finally turned to him, tears flooded her eyes. "Well, Ian Ross, you got your wish. Neil is the new Pleasure Master." The tears now slid unchecked down her face. "Why, Ian? Just tell me why?"

He closed the distance between them in one stride, but he didn't try to touch her. She must understand, or what he'd done would have no meaning. "Every woman who e'er came to me knew me as Pleasure Master, expected to feel what others had told them they would feel wi' me. I have often wondered whether they gained satisfaction from me because they *expected* it would be so, thought no one could resist me and so they didna try." Ian exhaled sharply. He confused even himself. "I dinna think they even saw *me,* only the man who was Pleasure Master. Any man bearing the name would have done as well."

Kathy's gaze grew fierce. "That's not true. I always saw *you.*"

He finally touched her. Carefully, he brushed a strand of hair from her face, allowed his fingers to linger, then dropped his hand to his side again. "Are ye sure?" He knew his smile was bitter. " 'Twas not Ian Ross ye almost joined wi' on the night the bandit chief captured ye. And 'twas not Ian Ross, but a helpless enemy ye hungered after as ye watched me in the cottage wi' Fiona." He voiced his deepest doubt. " 'Twas the fantasy ye desired, ne'er the one who created it. Since I reached twelve years of age, it has always been the fantasy women hungered after."

Kathy couldn't stop her tears, no matter how madly she blinked. "That's not true. The fantasies always worked because *you* were the fantasy man. How can I make you see that?"

She saw the answer in his gaze and experienced a moment of fierce anticipation. As crazy as it sounded, Kathy knew she'd crossed the time barrier to find the one man who could tear down the wall she'd built around her heart.

"When darkness falls, I'll wait for ye. And there will be no Pleasure Master between us."

She drew in a deep breath. "There won't be any fantasies either, Ian. You'll never again be able to claim I made love to a fantasy."

He nodded. "No fantasies."

There was only one thing left. "I want us to make love on the Pleasure Master's bed. It was made for love, Ian, and no lovers have lain on it for almost a hundred years."

She watched his lips curve in a faint smile and shivered at the thought of those lips on her body.

"Ye make it sound like a living thing."

She glanced toward the room where the bed and its memories waited. "Maybe it is."

His gaze followed hers. "Mayhap ye're right. The bed didna call to my grandfather or father. It didna call to me." He drew in a deep breath. "It calls to me now because I'll lie upon it wi' ye." He smiled. " 'Twould seem the bed chooses carefully those who usc it."

I'll bed the lass I love on it. The words he'd spoken when she'd first seen the bed hung between them. Did he remember?

He started to turn away, then paused. "I would protect ye from having a bairn."

I would not. "All taken care of. I have something for birth prevention." Pills she'd stopped taking after breaking up with old PMS because she *knew* she'd never want to get close to another man. Pills that at this very moment rested happily in her medicine cabinet. She wouldn't pass up any chance that she might take a part of Ian home with her.

" 'Tis amazing. The people of yer land have thought of all things."

All things except how to bring home the most wonderful man I've ever known. "My *time*, Ian.

319

When are you going to admit that I've come from a future time?"

He didn't speak, but she saw his answer in his gaze.

"You still don't believe me, do you? You'd give up being Pleasure Master before you'd give your trust." The revelation shocked her.

He nodded, his glance touching hers with regret. "I canna give that which I dinna have to give. Mayhap 'tis because I've watched so many believe the fantasies I've created and known the fantasies werena real." His gaze turned hard. "Mayhap 'tis because I've known the lies people tell themselves and others." He shrugged, then smiled. "To trust another would be to put the last piece of myself into their hands. And I dinna understand why ye find it so strange that I'm loath to do such. Didna yer husband betray yer trust?"

He was right. What had happened to her women-who-trust-men-are-too-stupid-to-live attitude? It was gone. She would trust Ian Ross with her life, *and her love.* No, she wouldn't go there. Kathy shifted her thoughts quickly away from possibilities that would hurt like hell if, no *when,* she returned to New York. Alone. Because she'd be selfish to ask Ian to abandon the world he knew, especially since he didn't love her.

So why don't you stay? She could never live here, would never do that to her parents. And the way people reacted to her, she would always be a danger to Ian. No, *nothing* could make her stay.

She sighed. "You're right."

He didn't look particularly happy with his victory as he turned and left the cave. Kathy wandered over to where Suzy guarded her shell necklace. When she went home, the necklace was one memory she wouldn't leave behind. She had a feeling it would haunt her every day for the rest of her life.

"I loooove you."

Kathy smiled. "Easy for you to say, Suzy."

By dim candlelight, Kathy studied the movie quotes Coco had given her that afternoon. Only three. Coco had sifted through the most likely ones and come up with what she thought were the most powerful. The neglected corner of her mind that housed her remaining honesty admitted she wished that Coco had given her hundreds. That way she could take a long, long time to go through all of them. *But time is the one thing you don't have much of.*

Carefully, Kathy placed the quotes beside her shell necklace and Suzy. Neat and tidy. The necklace to give her courage, a quote to send her home, and Suzy to offer her a loving goodbye.

But not tonight. Tonight Ian waited for her.

She smoothed unsteady fingers over her skirt. Tonight would be a night of honesty, so she had put on her New York clothes. Ian might want to deny she came from the future, but tonight she'd face him as herself, as a woman of the twenty-first century.

Of course, while she faced him as a bold woman of the future, she wished her underwear wasn't thumbing its nose at the "bold" concept. She longed to whip off her skirt and blouse and reveal deliciously daring bits of Victoria's Secret masterpieces. Unfortunately, after old PMS had done his thing, she'd traded in her skimpy red lace for white cotton. Not the statement she wanted to make tonight. White cotton would be a yawn for Ian after dealing with women who didn't know the meaning of underwear.

Fine. So she'd cope. Drawing a deep breath, she checked to make sure Peter was in his down mode, then walked toward the entrance with what she hoped would look like serene confidence.

She remained serene and confident until she reached the doorway. Three candles set in different parts of the room cast a dim glow, their flickering flames creating a sensual dance of light and dark on the rough stone walls, leaving the bed and the man who lay on it in a circle of shadowed silence.

Her heart pounded in the silence, and she thought each beat must be imitating the uncertain rhythm of the flames' dance, echoing off the ageless stone, shouting her panic.

She took a step forward and stopped. And breathed. She didn't seem able to breathe and move at the same time.

The bed creaked as Ian pushed himself to a sitting position and propped his shoulders against the headboard. To Kathy's ears, the creak seemed like a sigh of relief. Finally, the bed would know love again.

"Come to me."

His husky command brought her full circle. It

felt like a lifetime ago that he'd said those same words to her. Had it really only been . . . ? She didn't remember and she didn't care. Time had no power in this room, on this night. Kathy didn't fear that anyone or anything would send her home tonight. They wouldn't dare. She wouldn't allow it.

She wondered at her courage, and knew who was responsible. She'd dare the devil himself for Ian Ross. Of course, she sort of hoped the devil wasn't tuned in to her defiance. He probably had worse things to do.

While she was occupied daring the devil, her feet took her closer to Ian.

For the first time, she saw him clearly. Maybe the devil wasn't busy tonight. Maybe he was watching her with gleaming silver eyes as he lounged against a headboard decorated with paintings that celebrated lust, passion, and past erotic joys. She swallowed hard.

He leaned his head against the bed and slanted her a wicked grin. "Ye dinna seem overly bold tonight, lass."

No kidding. "I thought I'd try for maidenly tonight."

His gaze slid the length of her, stripping her right down to her white cotton panties. "I like ye well as a bold woman. Dinna change."

Okay, she could do bold. Eventually. Right now she'd work on semi-bold. She didn't slide her gaze over him. She studied him in hummingbird fashion—hover, savor, move on. Spot checks were all her heart could stand right now.

The golden gleam of the bed and the scarlet shimmer of the silk proved a dramatic contrast to the darkness of the man. Not a cold light-absorbing darkness, but a warm darkness that radiated all that was sexual. A darkness that drew her, promised her total fulfillment in the heat of his body, the touch of his hands, his lips.

No matter what name he called himself, Kathy knew he would always be the Pleasure Master for her.

Kathy reached the foot of the bed and grasped the bedpost to steady her nervous progress. The rest of her might still be engaged in mental hand-wringing over the uncertainty of what would happen next, but at least her gaze had found some courage.

She'd seen his muscled chest before, his flat stomach, strong thighs and legs. She'd even seen his impressive erection. But tonight he looked different. Except for the scarlet silk he'd draped across his hips, he was the same man she'd seen in the cottage with Fiona. Then what . . . ?

The bed. It welcomed the true Pleasure Master, wrapped him in rightness, proclaimed him able to search a woman's heart, smooth away love's cuts and abrasions, and give it back to her whole again. His power had never been just his ability to touch a woman's body in the right places, but to touch her soul.

Kathy sighed. Heavy stuff for what was supposed to be a night of fun. No, fun would never be a strong enough word for what she suspected she'd experience with Ian.

"Ye'll need to move yer hand from the post if ye expect to use it for a more worthy cause than keeping ye upright." His voice was soft, teasing, *inviting.*

Challenged, she released her any-port-in-a-storm lifeline and stepped to his side. "And what would you consider a more worthy cause, Ian Ross?"

"There are many, lass." He leaned forward and patted the bed beside him.

Gingerly, she sat down, almost afraid the passion played out on this bed by the man and woman pictured on its panels would reach out and claim her before she was ready. *Who're you kidding, Bartlett? You've been ready since the first moment you saw Ian Ross.*

"Ye may use yer hands to remove yer clothing." He tilted his head, thinking. "But I dinna believe so. I would remove yer clothing myself."

"Talking about clothes . . ." She glanced pointedly at the silken slash across his hips. "Why bother when I've seen everything?"

His smile was all things sensual and secret. "Ye've seen nothing, lass. And ye've yet to learn that 'tis the anticipation that makes the lovemaking memorable."

She returned his smile in kind. "Oh, I've been anticipating for a long time, Ian."

"Still, ye're a wee bit nervous."

She wasn't prepared when he sat up, spread his legs, and pulled her back to rest against his chest. The silk was gone.

"Uh, a little." His body heat seeped through her

blouse, warming her, quieting the warning voices all too ready to point out that she'd *never* had an orgasm with any man, so why should this be any different? Sure, she'd worked herself into a frenzy during Ian's fantasies, but this wasn't a fantasy.

"Ye worry overmuch about things that may ne'er happen." His breath fanned the back of her neck a moment before his lips touched her skin. Goose bumps trailed from the point of contact and traveled south.

"That's what I'm afraid of." She dropped her head forward to give him easier access.

"Ah, ye fear ye willna know an orgasm wi' me." Wrapping his arms around her, he carefully undid each button on her blouse, then slipped the garment off.

"Sort of." She smiled as he fumbled with the front clasp of her bra and breathed soft puffs of annoyance that heated the side of her neck.

"Ye will, ye ken." He murmured his triumph as the bra fell away from her. "Yer land may have many wondrous things, but it also creates much that is useless."

"You mean the clasp?" The cool air moving over her nipples hardened them and served as a reality check. This was really happening.

"I mean the cloth." His hand cupped her breast while he rubbed the pad of his thumb across her nipple.

She shivered at the sensitivity that spread like sparks from a bare wire to every part of her body.

"Are ye chilled?" His lips touched her shoulder

while he drew a finger the length of her spine.

"No." *Never with you.*

She felt the glide of his hair as he lowered his head to study the zipper on her skirt. Her imagination supplied other places his hair could touch, and she drew in her breath.

He carefully pulled down the zipper, then pulled it back up. After several up and down forays, Kathy grew impatient.

"Hello? Have I lost you to a zipper?" Darn. She must sound like every greedy woman who'd ever lain with him.

His soft chuckle reassured her. " 'Tis a long night, lass, and the waiting willna hurt ye. These metal teeth are wondrous things."

"Right." She wondered whether he knew how close she was to pouncing and having her way with him. "Wondrous things."

He lowered the zipper once more and this time he didn't pull it back up. "But there are other wondrous things." His whisper enticed even as his hands slid the skirt down over her hips. "A woman's body holds more fascination than all the wonders ye could e'er imagine."

Kathy's whole body felt flushed even as she shifted her hips so he could push her skirt down. The skirt fell to the floor and she kicked it away while Ian now discovered the wonders of elastic. He pulled the elastic out, then let it snap back.

" 'Tis amazing, but I dinna have any more patience left to admire such as this. 'Twould have been more tempting if there were less cloth *here*."

He bent down, pulled the elastic away from her body, then slid his tongue across the top of her buttocks. "And *here*." He slipped his fingers under the waistband, circled her waist, then splayed his hand between her legs.

Always accommodating, Kathy spread her thighs wider and breathed deeply, trying to slow her galloping heart rate.

"I would have chosen a different color also." With one finger, he easily found the spot guaranteed to end any fears Kathy might have of not enjoying complete fulfillment with him. "White isna a warm color, and ye're a warm and exciting woman. Ye deserve better."

Kathy didn't agree. She felt she was getting more than she deserved, and if Ian Ross stopped what he was doing with his finger she'd scream.

She stared blankly at the floor and wondered how her panties had gotten there. Maybe she should say something to prove she could still speak.

Nothing meaningful came to mind.

"Mayhap 'tis time to prove to the old ones ye believe still dwell here that we are worthy of their bed."

Kathy mourned the loss of his finger as he knelt, lifted her from her sitting position, then effortlessly laid her on the scarlet silk.

It seemed she looked up a long way to his face. With the flickering candle glow behind him, he became a shadow man, an image in black and gray. She could just as well be looking up at his great grandfather, the first Pleasure Master. She shivered and felt the bed shift under her, almost imagined it enfolding her, holding her captive so it would never again be alone.

" 'Tis not yer death ye go to, lass." His soft chuckle teased her.

She exhaled on a relieved sigh. This was her Ian. *Hers?* When had she started thinking in terms of possessive pronouns?

Kathy felt Ian's sudden start of surprise.

"Ye have a wee crown here." He traced with his finger the small tattoo hidden high on the inside of her thigh, and Kathy knew she'd always be able to close her eyes and remember this moment, trace the tattoo with her fingers and remember the feel of him doing the same.

"It's a tiara. I got it because I always wanted to be someone's princess. It's a tattoo, and it'll never wash off. I guess this is the closest I'll ever get to the princess thing."

"Ye'll always be my princess, lass." Easing down on his side, he lay propped up on his elbow, his gaze touching her. Everywhere. She felt each touch of his eyes like a dot branded into her flesh, and she didn't doubt when he was finished he'd connect the dots in a searing pattern she'd carry to eternity and beyond.

"This night I'll give ye all the joy ye've ne'er had, the joy that even a princess could not command." He leaned over her, his hair trailing a dark cloud of promise across her bare stomach.

She gasped, then exhaled sharply as he touched each nipple with the tip of his tongue.

"All those who came before, who passed on the secrets of pleasure, are with us tonight." His breath drifted hot between her breasts, and she clutched the silk with clenched hands to keep from pulling his mouth to her nipples.

"No offense, but I'd rather it just be me, you, and the bed tonight." It seemed even spiraling sexual excitement couldn't shut down her smart mouth.

His sudden laugh surprised her. "Aye, ye're right." His voice softened. "This night is for your joy only."

He slowly traced the shape of her lips with his finger, then followed the same path with his tongue, and Kathy opened her lips—impatient for him, greedy in a way she'd never imagined she'd be.

When he took her mouth, it was a true taking, a foretaste of what was to come. His lips moved over hers, hot, demanding. His tongue tangled with hers, his taste forever after a part of her memory, one she knew would always knot her stomach with need, hunger.

She clutched his hair in her fists, holding his mouth to hers, holding his *realness* so that no demented time demon could snatch him away.

He slid his leg across hers, his arousal hard against her thigh, proof that he was no longer the detached dispenser of pleasure.

Lifting his head, he gazed down at her with eyes that shone molten silver in the candlelight. With his long hair tangled, untamed around his face and shoulders, his lips still damp from her mouth, he was elemental male—powerful, dangerous.

But she was equal to him. The fire, the burning need for one man that had inspired a nameless woman from the past to create this bed, these paintings, was now *her* need. She recognized it in the spasms that clenched her thighs, the wet readiness she already felt.

She gazed at him and licked her lips. Lips that felt swollen from his kiss, that still tasted of him. She memorized the way his chest looked and stored it away for cold winter nights in her future—the light sheen of sweat that delineated every taut muscle, the dark shadow of his nipples, the path of dampened hair that was her own personal Yellow Brick Road.

He smiled at her, and his teeth flashed white in the dimness. "I havena invited my great grandfather to join us, but ye may enjoy all the knowledge he brought back wi' him." He paused to nip her earlobe, then trail his tongue the length of her neck. "He was the first, and he would expect me to honor him tonight."

The truth. She had no idea where the thought came from, she just *knew*. "No."

She sensed his stillness, his surprise. "What?"

"Your great grandfather *wasn't* the first. The woman was the first. *The Pleasure Mistress.* She taught your great grandfather everything. This bed is a *woman's* bed, and she'd want a woman to give the man she lo-. . . cared for pleasure on it." Did she only imagine the light shimmer of laughter that echoed in the night?

331

The stillness surrounding Ian was a living, breathing thing. "I dinna understand."

In her need to make him understand, she slid her hand down his stomach, felt him lift his hip away from her leg in an instinctive move to free his erection to her touch, then heard his sharp gasp as she ran her fingernail the length of his arousal.

"I want to pleasure *you,* Ian. I never wanted to do that with any man before. Heaven knows, all I wanted my husband to do was get it over with. And he did. Quickly."

"Ye want to pleasure *me?*"

She heard the disbelief in his voice.

"Yes." She wrapped her fingers around his flesh and squeezed gently, felt his shudder. "I want to taste every inch of your body." Her voice was husky with her need.

She glanced up to see the flash of shock in his gaze, then the glow of something that turned her warm and liquid. Everywhere.

"No one has *e'er* cared about my pleasure."

His voice held a wonder that brought unwelcome tears to her eyes. Determinedly, she blinked them away.

"I'm glad I'm the first." Her unshed tears softened her voice. "Lie back and enjoy it, Ian." She chuckled. "God, I sound like my ex."

His lips curved in a half smile, but there was nothing halfway about the heat of his gaze. "I'll lie back, and I dinna doubt I'll enjoy what ye do, but ye canna keep me from taking part." His half smile widened into a wicked grin. "I've waited too long for this moment, Kathy."

"Hmm." She watched as he relaxed back against the headboard, his hands braced behind his head. His relaxed attitude didn't fool her. If she looked past the anticipatory gleam in his eyes, she'd find the soul of a hunter.

Kneeling, she gazed down the sleek, smooth-muscled length of him and couldn't conceive of a time before him or after him.

She longed to start with his hair, rake her fingers through the silken mass, lose her hair stylist's heart to the seduction of the dark strands sliding across her skin. But she'd save that for last. Okay, almost last.

Closing her eyes, she skimmed her hands over his legs, his thighs. Pausing, she tightened her fingers on his upper thighs, felt the muscles bunch, and memorized the feel. Many years later, she would close her eyes and recall the texture of him. Not just skin and muscle, but the hot surge of his blood, the hard pounding of his heart. She would know him from the inside out.

Opening her eyes, she bypassed her eventual destination. Barely. Lowering her head, she trailed hot kisses across his abdomen, then slid the tip of her tongue into his navel. His stomach clenched and she heard his sharp exhalation.

"Ye dinna have much shyness about ye, lass." He didn't sound displeased by the observation.

"Umm. Not when you're such a delicious man." She tried to collect her scattered thoughts. "You make me feel free, Ian. I can do what I want. I don't have to live up to someone else's expectations."

All gone. She didn't have one more logical thought left.

Moving upward, she traced the breadth of his chest, circled each nipple with her finger, gloried in his faint groan. She put her mouth on his nipples in turn, slid her tongue across each one, memorized the hard puckering of his flesh against her tongue.

She knew he'd abandoned his hands-behind-his-head position when she felt his fingers slide through her hair, tighten, then urge her upward.

Always obliging, Kathy slid her tongue along the side of his neck, pausing to enjoy the hot pulse that carried his life-force.

His lips touched her ear, his teeth nibbled at her lobe. The sensation took some of her breath away. Enough to keep her from pointing out that he was breaking her unspoken rule of noninterference.

"Mayhap ye didna notice, but ye're going in the wrong direction. Since yer eyes were closed, ye may have missed it in the dark."

His voice held a husky, breathless quality that matched her own.

"I'm taking the scenic tour. I'll save the Highland's legend for last. When it's time, I'll pull over and read the historical marker."

His laughter sounded pained. "Ye speak in riddles, but I would know what yer historical marker says."

She eased down beside him, and whispered in his ear. "It says that in the year 1542 . . ." Deliberately, she walked two fingers down his chest, his stomach, then paused. "On this very spot . . ." Her fingers scaled his erection, stood proud atop the summit. "The universe tilted, and the stars fell."

He jerked, his groan obviously a testament to her storytelling ability. Unfortunately, his arched hips tumbled her from her exalted perch. Okay, so she'd just find another place of interest.

Gently, she cupped him, wanting to do something more, something she'd never wanted to do with her husband. Sliding down until her head was even with his hips, she leaned over him.

"And the world was never the same again." Still cupping him in her palm, she kissed the flesh she cradled, touched her lips to him and trailed an abstract pattern with the tip of her tongue.

He shuddered but said nothing, his breath now harsh rasping gasps, and she felt in his silence the coming explosion.

With every sense alive to the wonder of this moment, she tasted his arousal. Her tongue skimmed the length of his hot, smooth flesh. His scent filled her, the primitive scent of aroused male. Her pounding heart played a counterpoint to her body's hunger, the clenching emptiness that demanded filling.

She had to have more of him. Parting her lips, she took him into her mouth, enveloped him in moist heat and urgent need. Slid her lips up and down over his flesh in an instinctive motion as old as man and woman. *Feel it, Ian. Feel all I want from you, all I can never have.*

335

"God's teeth, woman." His strangled growl broke her concentration.

She lifted her head away from him to glance at his face. His dark roiling gaze told her he felt it all too well.

With seemingly no effort, he pulled her beneath him and knelt towering above her. " 'Tis no use, Kathy. Ye've ruined me for all other women. 'Twas my pride that I could pleasure a woman longer than any other man wi' out taking my own satisfaction." He leaned over her and touched his lips to her forehead.

She almost groaned her despair. *No. Touch me everywhere. Now.*

"But I find that I canna do that wi' ye."

And when he touched her, it was with fire and light. His mouth took hers with heat and a savage possession while his hands skimmed her, leaving a trail of raw want over every inch of her bare flesh.

He kissed a searing path to her breasts, and she lifted them in anticipation. When his lips closed over her nipple, she moaned and raked her fingers through his hair, then dug her nails into his taut shoulder muscles and held on. His tongue and teeth teased each nipple, and at that point she ceased to think, stopped cataloging the things he did to her body, only *felt*.

She writhed against his mouth, against his hands, which she recognized only as ribbons of sizzling pleasure that touched her in places she'd never thought would bring pleasure. Spreading her legs, she arched her hips while breathing wordless entreaties for something more, when she knew *more* would shatter her into a million shards of razor-sharp, screaming . . . She didn't know, couldn't complete the thought.

The scrape of his body against her skin as he moved lower was the pleasure-pain of anticipation against bare nerve endings. And when he cupped her buttocks in his hands and lifted her to meet his mouth, she wrapped her legs around him and held her breath against his first touch.

He put his mouth on her.

She cried out. She couldn't help it. It was a cry of fulfilled fantasies even though Ian would deny the fantasy. It was his tongue probing and sliding across the nub that was so sensitive she felt the spasms beginning, spasms that would gather speed and send her careening helplessly into a free-fall with no sky, no earth.

Not yet. She fought the pressure, the need to let go, even as his tongue entered her, gliding in and out with a rhythm mimicked by the clenching of her body. *Empty. Still so empty.* An emptiness of the heart, the soul. And only *he* could fill the void. With his body, with his *love.*

At some point she realized his mouth was gone, replaced by his hard flesh, and she murmured soundless words of pleading, her body opening to him—wet, wanting.

"Take me home wi' ye, Kathy, in the only way ye can. In yer memory. As ye leap from yer machine and fall through the sky, yer heart pounding wi' the wonder of it, remember this moment. 'Tis all I ask."

337

The pressure increased as he slid into her, his words stored away to take out later and analyze. But now . . .

Now, she could wait no longer. Grasping his buttocks, she wrapped her legs more tightly around him and urged him deeper.

With a final thrust he buried himself in her and she cried out her satisfaction. When his motion began, the strong rising and plunging rhythm, she finally let go, felt the size of him filling her, stretching her, *completing* her.

They climbed the mountain together, his heartbeat, his harsh breaths her own. And when they reached the summit, she ceased to breathe, and in the silence felt the shifting of all she'd ever known, ever believed, to make room for the one truth: She loved Ian Ross as she'd never love another man.

The avalanche was an explosion of white light and careening motion, catapulting them down the other side, gathering speed and intensity. Kathy heard cries she knew were hers joined by Ian's shout of triumph, but she felt outside herself, hoarding these moments, trying to stretch them, make them last forever.

But nothing lasts forever. She knew that as she lay beside Ian minutes later, listening to her own breathing fill the silence. She didn't speak any words of love because no matter what they'd just shared, centuries still stretched between them, keeping them apart as surely as a wall of steel. And still some pitiful part of her hoped he'd knock down that wall.

Silence.

She stared at the candles that were sputtering and dying. "Coco gave me three quotes today that might send me home."

"Aye. Ye'll be anxious to leave then?" His voice was empty, disembodied.

Stop me. Tell me you never want me to leave. "I guess so."

Eventually, as she watched the three candles flicker out, leaving her in darkness as empty as her hopes for the future, she realized he'd never say the words. Like the candles, her three quotes would quench the only light in her life.

But she'd make love with him again. Before she left, she'd feel that total completeness one more time. She swore it.

And from the darkness beyond the room, Burt Lancaster's voice reached her.

"We just don't recognize the most significant moment of our lives while they're happening. Back then I thought, 'Well, there'll be other days . . .' I didn't realize that that was the only day."

Chapter Eighteen

Ian swept his damp hair away from his face and shivered. He must be truly daft to climb from his bed and the warmth of Kathy's side to bathe in the burn. 'Twas as cold as the devil's heart this morning, and the mist lay heavy on the hills. It reminded him much of the day Kathy came to him.

But 'twas Kathy's leaving that worried him now. Why had he not confessed his love last night? Mayhap because he'd had no practice. He'd never spoken of love to anyone in his whole life. If he'd told his mother, he'd forgotten, and after she'd allowed his father to take him, he'd much doubted her love for him.

Kathy was right. His trust of others was weak. But his trust in himself was weaker.

If he told Kathy he loved her, and she returned

his love, he'd be tempted to go with her when she returned to her . . . land. This he could not do. She would have no use for a Highlander who understood nothing of her ways, and he knew her distaste for men who had been with many women. She'd enjoyed joining with him, but she would not want him as husband, and he would accept nothing less after last night. 'Twas better to say nothing; in time the hurt would go away. *And if ye believe that ye're a fool, Ian Ross.*

As he strode into his living area, he could hear Kathy humming. Her voice led him to the Pleasure Master's bed. Surprised, he halted in the doorway.

Kathy sat cross-legged on the bed with several small pots beside her. Carefully, she was painting a scene to fill the empty space. Moving closer, he peered at what she'd done so far.

His quiet hiss of astonishment caught her attention. She glanced at him and grinned. "Hey, I painted a mean picture in high school. You know, that empty space always bothered me, but now I know it was waiting for our picture. What we did last night was a memory of a lifetime. It belongs here." Her smile turned satisfied. "And there's no more space. We'll be the last."

Recovering from his shock, Ian returned her smile. "Aye, ye've done the right thing. But ye've left something out."

Puzzled, she studied the picture. "Like what?"

"All who see the picture must know ye. I look very much like my great grandfather, so none will mistake me. But none will recognize ye. I would have ye add something that will tell all that Kathy Bartlett is a special woman."

"Okay, I'm open to suggestions."

He moved close. "Paint the wee crown here"—he touched the bare inner thigh of the woman in the painting and noted Kathy's thighs clenching even through her skirt—"so all may know ye're a princess."

She returned her gaze to her work, and he couldn't see her expression.

"Thank you, Ian Ross."

He didn't need to see her face. He could hear the tears in her voice.

He wondered.

"It's done. What do you think, Ian?" Kathy moved away from the bed to stand beside him in the doorway.

"Ye've taken a long time to finish, but 'tis wondrous."

He reached for her hand and rubbed his thumb over her palm to remove a small spot of color, then clasped her hand in his. He squeezed gently. " 'Tis almost night, and I didna like the time ye took from me to finish the painting, but 'twill serve as a memory when—" He couldn't say it, couldn't bring into the open his fear of what he'd feel when she left.

She leaned into him, wrapping her free arm around his waist, burying her face against his chest. He could feel her breath even through his clothing, hot against his skin like a blazing caress.

"I guess I shouldn't have filled up the whole

space on the bed, because now I won't have any room to paint other scenes . . . of other times."

The sound of running footsteps swung Ian around. Without thinking, he pushed Kathy behind him. His taking by the Mackays had made him more cautious.

She moved from behind him as Neil and his father rushed into view.

This was it then. He could sense the trouble they brought with them and knew that only danger would cause them to hurry so.

Neil spoke to Ian, but his gaze was focused on Kathy. "The Mackays are coming and some from our clan have joined them. I saw our Maeve with Fiona. 'Twas only because Father came home and wished to meet Kathy that we were on our way here. They've drunk overmuch, probably to give them courage, and are shouting that they will take the witch. Ye must send Kathy home."

Kathy's gaze locked with Ian's, and he saw the denial, the refusal to accept what Neil said.

His heart shouted its agony at what he must do next. For Kathy. "Ye must return to where we first met and say the quotes Coco gave ye. Take Peter and the toys ye brought. They may put the fear of the devil into the Mackays. I'll remain here to meet them. Fiona's need to capture me may give ye extra time."

"No!"

Kathy's cry reached into his soul and ripped it from his body. Though the rest of his life might be meaningless, he must find the strength to send her away.

But even if it condemned him to the fires Father Gregory swore awaited him, he could not let Kathy go without her knowing one thing. This only would he do for himself. "Ye canna gainsay me in this, lass. I would know that ye returned safely to yer own . . . time."

He saw the exact moment she understood what he promised her—his trust, his *love*. Now and beyond the reach of time.

Wonder glistened in her eyes, followed closely by a challenging tilt of her head. God's teeth, he'd forgotten she was not of a soft and submissive nature.

"Forget it. I'm not leaving. I love you, Ian Ross, and I'm staying right here with you. I'll reason with Fiona, but if that doesn't work I'll do some serious physical damage." The determined glint in her eyes dared him to refuse her.

"Ye canna stay, Kathy. Ye must go to court to defend yerself against old PMS. Ye must return to yer parents, to yer . . . coffee."

Clenching her hands into fists by her sides, she defied him. "I don't give a tinker's curse about my ex-husband. My parents will accept my decision, and I don't know how I'll survive without coffee, but dammit you're worth caffeine withdrawal. Take that, Ian Ross."

Dinna make me do this. "Can I say nothing to change yer mind?"

"Nothing."

He breathed out a harsh breath of inevitability.

"Neil, take Kathy to the place we met. Take all her things wi' her."

Neil nodded, picked up Kathy's purse, backpack, and bag of toys, then wrapped his free arm firmly around her waist. " 'Tis for yer own good, lass." His gruffness betrayed his regret.

She seemed suddenly to realize that Neil really intended to drag her away. Twisting and kicking, she fought him. "Don't do this, Ian. I didn't travel back more than four hundred years to find you, only to lose you like this. Please, let me stay." Tears shimmered in her eyes, slid down her face.

Ian knew what those tears cost her. She'd let him see her tears only a few times, but he'd always remember these she cried now at her leaving. It was fitting. He wished he could find release in tears, but he found that he was truly a creature of his time. Men of the Highlands didn't cry.

Narrowing his gaze, he focused on where Malin lay atop Peter. In one stride, he reached Malin, scooped him up, and placed him in the crook of Neil's arm. " 'Tis sorry I am to be burdening ye so, Neil, but I would know that Malin is safe. The Mackays have drunk too much and would take great joy in destroying anything belonging to me."

Neil nodded and began dragging Kathy toward the tunnel.

"Wait!" The thunderous command came from Ian's father, who'd stood forgotten while Ian's world collapsed around him. "My son didna introduce us, but I am Duncan, Ian's father." He moved to stand in front of Kathy, who'd grown still at his approach.

"I would thank ye for giving my son that which I failed to give him." He reached out to place his hand gently on her shoulder. "Ye gave him yer love, and for that I'll always remember ye. Go now."

Kathy shifted her gaze back to Ian. She no longer fought Neil's grasp. "Ian, I swore I'd never ask this of you, never be this selfish, but I guess love makes people greedy and selfish." Her weak attempt at a smile made him swallow hard. "Come home with me. We can watch movies in the dark and eat popcorn, dive from an airplane . . . make love forever. I can even get you legal papers. People will do anything for good hair."

The temptation. He might miss the Highlands and the people he'd known all his life, but the missing was nothing compared to the tearing pain of losing Kathy. "Go and be safe, Kathy Bartlett. Know that I will think of ye every day of my life."

"My necklace. I won't leave without my necklace." Her voice was small and for the first time, she sounded defeated.

Wordlessly, he picked up the shell necklace from beside the hearth and walked to her. He slipped it over her head, felt for the last time the slide of her hair against his fingers, the warmth of her skin. Calling on every bit of courage passed down from his great grandfather, he turned from her.

Behind him, Peter's amber lights blinked frantically. "I was born when you kissed me. I died when you left. I lived a few weeks while you loved me."

"I don't think Humphrey Bogart's going to help, Peter." Kathy's voice was a small sob of despair.

"Go wi' her, ye wee troublemaker, and see her safely home." *And I thank ye for bringing her to me so that I could know love in my life.*

She gazed at him one last time. "Take the leap, Ian. It's like when I jump from a plane. In that moment, I trust the parachute will open to catch me. I'll always be there to catch you."

He listened as her footsteps echoed down the tunnel, fading with each second, leaving him alone forever. Peter determinedly trundled after her.

And when he thought her finally gone, her call carried faintly to him. "Come home with me, Ian. I'll wait for you."

Home. He glanced around his cave. It would never be home again.

"Come. We will meet the Mackays before they reach here. They willna touch the Pleasure Master wi' me beside ye." His father started toward the tunnel.

Something was building in Ian, something explosive and defiant. " 'Tis a title I no longer claim nor want. Neil is the new Pleasure Master." He paced before the hearth with growing resolve.

"I loooove you."

The voice was faint. Startled, Ian glanced toward the sound. Kathy had forgotten Suzy. And even though he didn't understand exactly how Suzy worked, he understood that she was dying. But she'd lived long enough to say the words he'd found so hard to say his whole life, the words he hadn't

347

said to Kathy, the words he suddenly knew he *had* to say.

He turned to face his father. "I'm leaving. I find I canna let her go home wi'out me. 'Tis sorry I am for what I said to ye when ye married. I understand now, and . . ." *Say the words that need saying, Ross.* "I . . . love ye, Father."

Something in his father's face softened. "As do I, son. I should've told ye when ye were a wee laddie, but I didna think it right to show such emotion. My Meg taught me how wrong I was. I dinna understand much about yer Kathy, but I ken she loves ye, and 'tis a gift ye shouldna turn from." He grasped his son's shoulders and pulled him into a hard embrace, then released him. "Go wi' God, son."

Ian nodded, unable to find words, knowing all that was important had been said. Turning, he strode away from the man who'd made him the Pleasure Master.

Running from the cave, he didn't even glance back. That part of his life was over. For a moment, he thought of getting his horse, but it would take too much time, and he could hear the drunken yells of the Mackays in the distance. *Dinna let Kathy leave me. Please.* He didn't know whom he was begging—a wee metal demon, or a God who must be having a great laugh at his expense.

He was gasping by the time he reached the hill, but he drew in a deep, steadying breath as he looked up, fearful of what he'd see. Kathy was barely visible through the thickening mist. With a last burst of energy, he raced up the hill and pulled her into his embrace.

"You came. You came." Her words whispered through him just as her tears dampened his shirt, her heat seeped into his soul, her love lit up his heart.

"I love ye, Kathy of Hair, and I wish to fly in yer sky machine wi' ye. Then we will fall from the sky together." He buried his face in her hair as he murmured the words.

"We'll never fall, Ian Ross. You'll always take me higher." She raised her face to him.

And he knew the love shining in her gaze would be a bridge from a life that now seemed as gray as the mist creeping up the hill to a brightly colored future. A future with the only woman he could ever love.

"She wouldna say the words, Ian. She said she wouldna say them until ye came." Neil clapped Ian on the shoulder. " 'Tis lucky ye arrived when ye did. I can hear the Mackays."

"Aye. Ye're right." With one arm still around Kathy, he gazed at Neil. "Ye'll be the Pleasure Master now, and I know ye'll do a fine job. 'Tis sorry I am that I didna know ye better, didna treat ye as my brother, but the blame is mine. Tell Colin . . ." Damn, the words still would not come easily, but he would practice often with Kathy. "Tell Colin that I'll always think of ye both wi' love."

Neil said nothing, only tightened his grip on Ian's shoulder. It was enough for Ian.

"Kathy, ye must tell Coco I'm sorry we willna

join. 'Twould have been a wondrous thing for her to remember." Neil's voice held laughter and regret.

"I don't think you'll want to hear what she says to that." Kathy's laughter was shaky. "Oh, and take care of the bed, Neil. The bed should always belong to the Pleasure Master."

The shouts of the Mackays grew closer, and Ian knew they must hurry. "Neil, all that was mine is now yers. Hand Malin to me. I wouldna leave him behind."

"He's gone, Ian." Neil's voice was anxious. "He jumped from my arms and headed back to you. We canna search for him now. Ye must leave before the Mackays arrive."

Kathy saw the expression on Ian's face, knew what he'd say because she would have said the same thing.

"I canna leave him behind. He is too old and slow to escape the Mackays." He turned to start down the hill.

Neil grabbed him, and they struggled.

"I must find him, Neil. He wouldna abandon me."

Panic pushed all rational thought from Kathy's head. She stared down the hill into the thickening mist, then froze. Ian and Neil grew still beside her.

The Mackays appeared out of the shifting grayness like phantoms in a nightmare. But this was no dream, and she couldn't wake up when it got to the bad part.

A short distance behind the Mackays, unnoticed,

Malin struggled up the hill, determined to reach the master he'd lived for, and now seemed fated to die for.

Nothing. Kathy knew there was nothing they could do to save Malin. She felt Ian's despair, his helplessness.

Sudden motion shifted their attention to Peter. Lights flashing, Peter started down the hill. "If I'm not back in five minutes . . . just wait longer!"

Tears clogged Kathy's laughter. "I never thought I'd be glad to hear Jim Carrey's voice."

Ian said nothing, just stood with clenched fists staring down the hill as Peter toddled toward his old friend.

The Mackays stopped, then parted to let Peter through. They milled around in confusion, but they didn't run. Their shouts continued to sound uncertain as Malin scrambled atop Peter, but still they didn't run.

Kathy feared Peter might not make it. The Mackays had lost some of their terror of the toy, and probably Fiona had threatened them with a fate worse than Peter if they ran.

Kathy held her breath as Peter started the long trek up the hill, while the Mackays continued to argue and shout.

Then she heard it. Out of the mist drifted the haunting cry of a bagpipe. It gathered strength and volume as the piper launched into a powerful, lilting tune.

" 'Tis Colin." Ian's voice held wonder. "I've heard him but two times before as we went into battle, but I know 'tis he." His voice softened. " 'Tis a song for a warrior. A song of goodbye."

Kathy wrapped her arms around Ian's waist and hugged him tightly. "Colin told me he'd only play for someone he loved."

She felt Ian's shudder, the shattering of all the bonds that had separated him from his emotions, from others. " 'Tis holding the Mackays' attention. Mayhap Peter can reach us."

Urging the small toy on in her mind, she watched tensely as Peter moved faster than she'd ever seen him move. When he finally reached them, Ian scooped Malin up and Kathy lifted Peter into her arms.

As if a spell had been broken, the Mackays surged up the long hill.

Kathy stared at Peter face to face. Okay, face to whatever. She'd never been quite sure where his face was. "You've blown your cover, Peter. You'll never again make me believe you're an evil demon." She tapped his metal side. "There's a heart in there."

Suddenly, she felt it. Immense power, intelligence, and a wicked humor that almost made her drop him. There were no blinking lights now, no movie quotes, but she knew that she was meeting the *real* Peter for the first time, and the meeting left her shaking.

"God's teeth, lass, say yer quotes now. If they dinna work, we may still flee into the hills." Ian's frantic order jerked Kathy's attention back to the horde of Mackays halfway up the hill.

She drew in a deep breath of courage. What if she was wrong? What if the quotes didn't send them home? Great. Just what she needed. Doubts.

Ignoring her panic, she once again wrapped her free arm around Ian's waist and offered her first quote. "How do you find your way back in the dark? Just head for that big star straight on. The highway's under it, and it'll take us right home."

Peter didn't care.

Fine. Just fine. So *The Misfits* wasn't his thing. Her panic was getting harder to ignore. Quote two. "Then close your eyes and tap your heels together three times. And think to yourself, 'There's no place like home.' " Peter couldn't ignore *The Wizard of Oz*. It was un-American.

Nothing.

Her panic was close to the surface now, bubbling just below her frustration. "Damn it! What are you? Some kind of Rumpelstiltskin? Guess the quote in three tries or become Scottish crispy chicken?"

No flashing lights. No sarcastic line.

The Mackays were so close now she imagined she could feel their hot breath. Ian reached for his sword.

Okay, she'd saved the best for last. She tightened her grip on Ian, listened to the clatter as he dropped his sword to clasp her, prayed to whatever god was listening. *Now!* It had to be now.

"I'll think about it tomorrow. Tara! Home. I'll go home, and I'll think of some way to get him back! After all, tomorrow is another day!"

She almost didn't believe it when the whirling colors began. As Neil and the Mackays started to fade, Ian stayed strong beside her. "Thank you," she whispered.

Her awareness began to slip, but she knew there was one last thing. . . . "You gave me Ian. What can I give to you?"

Her vision had become a long tunnel wrapped in brilliant colors. At its center was Peter's flashing amber lights.

"Hey, my pleasure, Kathy. I like a woman who believes in compensation. How about naming your first kid after me?"

Peter had called her by name. He'd slid off his mask of movie quotes, letting her reach him for the first, and probably the last, time.

"My first kid?" The very thought warmed her.

"Yeah. Look, you're gonna have a bunch, so one measly name's no big deal. Whatta ya say?"

His voice. She almost giggled. Power like his should be wrapped in the deep tones of a James Earl Jones, not a New York cabby. Go figure. "What's your name?"

"Ganymede."

"That's . . . some name." She couldn't name her child Ganymede. "It's a little long though."

"Sure, sure. That's what they all say. Last two who thought Ganymede wasn't a great name're squatting on some lily pad hawking beer."

"Oh."

"Okay, so they're not sitting on a lily pad, but name your kid after me and it'll make me *really* happy. You'll be glad if you make me really happy."

She didn't have time to think about anything more as the whirling colors took her. Her last sense was of Ian's hand firmly wrapped around hers. She was going home . . . with her very own Pleasure Master and a lifetime of love.

Epilogue

There are only a few pleasures left to a reformed cosmic troublemaker like me—a fine bottle of wine, a superb dining experience, and a butt-kicking trip into the past to do some in-yo'-face matchmaking. And I did it all, baby.

Was I good, or what? Kathy and Ian didn't have a chance. Did you see Kathy's face when I zapped her with the opposite of what she wanted? Okay, so I'd already decided that Ian was gonna be her man, but when she asked for warm, convenient, and subservient it made everything . . . better, more satisfying.

And those three quotes at the end? I would've sent her home even if they'd been from her Aunt Claudia, but what can I say, I'm a sucker for dramatic moments.

Any regrets? Yeah, I didn't get to use one of my favorite quotes. Remember when Kathy made that Rumpelstiltskin crack? She was all frantic, trying to hurry my butt along. I was ready to hit her with Billy Crystal from *The Princess Bride*: "You rush a miracle man, you get rotten miracles." It would've been great. But I saw all those Mackays truckin' up that hill and . . . Hey, I was a little worried. So sue me.

Anyway, I haven't had that much fun since I wiped out all those dinosaurs with that meteor. Talk about your pinball wizard. . . . But I digress.

It was almost like the bad old days. I got to talk some trash, mix it up in a few fights, and scare the crap out of the general populace.

Of course, it was for a good cause. Everything has to be *good* now. You know something, I've been good and I've been bad. Bad is better.

This was okay, though. Those movie quotes were a challenge, and I like something that stirs the old creative juices. Next time I think I'll try a different form. Something that doesn't limit my mobility and my mouth. I got a lot of places to go and a lot of things to say.

Hmm. Wonder what's happening with Kathy and her Pleasure Master. I'll just hit the time-travel remote and surf into the future a couple of years.

Well, looks like old Ian has found his niche. Has a radio talk show, handing out advice of a romantic nature. The ratings look great, and wait till they get a look at him on cable.

Now here's something to warm the heart of an

old demon. Kathy named her first son Mede. Can you believe it? She gave him half my name. Hey, half is better than I usually get.

I'll have to send them something special to celebrate my namesake.

Hmm. Saw an old bed in a private collection last week. Gilded with great paintings. I especially liked the one with the blond woman who had a little tiara on . . . Yeah, I think I'll send the bed to Kathy and Ian. Seem like the kind of people to appreciate an antique like that.

You know, all this introspection makes me hungry for a Big Mac and some fries. Whatta ya say, babe?

"I loooove you."

"Here's looking at you, kid."

An Original Sin

Nina Bangs

Fortune MacDonald listens to women's fantasies on a daily basis as she takes their orders for customized men. In a time when the male species is extinct, she is a valued man-maker. So when she awakes to find herself sharing a bed with the most lifelike, virile man she has ever laid eyes or hands on, she lets her gaze inventory his assets. From his long dark hair, to his knife-edged cheekbones, to his broad shoulders, to his jutting—well, all in the name of research, right?—it doesn't take an expert any time at all to realize that he is the genuine article, a bona fide man. And when Leith Campbell takes her in his arms, she knows real passion for the first time . . . but has she found true love?

___52324-8 $5.99 US/$6.99 CAN

Seduction By CHOCOLATE

Nina Bangs, ♥ Lisa Cach, Thea Devine, ♥ Penelope Neri

Sweet Anticipation . . . More alluring than Aphrodite, more irresistible than Romeo, the power of this sensuous seductress is renowned. It teases the senses, tempting even the most staid; it inspires wantonness, demanding surrender. Whether savored or devoured, one languishes under its tantalizing spell. To sample it is to crave it. To taste it is to yearn for it. Habit-forming, mouth-watering, sinfully decadent, what promises to sate the hungers of the flesh more? Four couples whet their appetites to discover that seduction by chocolate feeds a growing desire and leads to only one conclusion: Nothing is more delectable than love.

___4667-9 $5.50 US/$6.50 CAN

Viking!

CONNIE MASON

The first time he sees her she is clad in nothing but moonlight and mist, and from that moment, Thorne the Relentless knows he is bewitched by the maiden bathing in the forest pool. How else to explain the torrid dreams, the fierce longing that keeps his warrior's body in a constant state of arousal? Perhaps Fiona is speaking the truth when she claims it is not sorcery that binds him to her, but the powerful yearning of his viking heart.

____4402-1 $5.99 US/$6.99 CAN

Mine To Take

DARA JOY

He is full-blooded and untamable. A uniquely beautiful
creature who can make himself irresistible to women. With
his glittering green and gold eyes, silken hair, and purring
voice, the stunning captive chained to the wall is exactly
what Jenise needs. And he is hers to take . . . or so she believes.
___4446-3 $5.99 US/$6.99 CAN

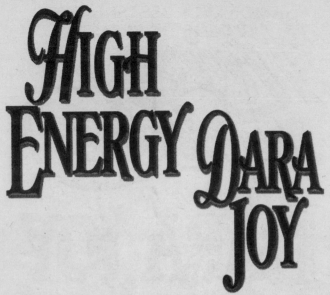

HIGH ENERGY DARA JOY

Zanita Masterson knows nothing about physics, until a reporting job leads her to Tyberius Evans. The rogue scientist is six feet of piercing blue eyes, rock-hard muscles and maverick ideas—with his own masterful equation for sizzling ecstasy and high energy.

___4438-2 $4.99 US/$5.99 CAN

Dorchester Publishing Co., Inc.
P.O. Box 6640
Wayne, PA 19087-8640

Please add $1.75 for shipping and handling for the first book and $.50 for each book thereafter. NY, NYC, and PA residents, please add appropriate sales tax. No cash, stamps, or C.O.D.s. All orders shipped within 6 weeks via postal service book rate. Canadian orders require $2.00 extra postage and must be paid in U.S. dollars through a U.S. banking facility.

Name_____
Address_____
City_____State_____Zip_____
I have enclosed $_____ in payment for the checked book(s).
Payment <u>must</u> accompany all orders. ❑ Please send a free catalog.
CHECK OUT OUR WEBSITE! www.dorchesterpub.com

Rejar

DARA JOY

Lord Byron thinks he's a scream, the fashionable matrons titter behind their fans at a glimpse of his hard form, and nobody knows where he came from. His startling eyes—one gold, one blue—promise a wicked passion, and his voice almost seems to purr. There is only one thing a woman thinks of when looking at a man like that. *Sex.* And there is only one woman he seems to want. *Lilac.* In her wildest dreams she never guesses that bringing a stray cat into her home will soon have her stroking the most wanted man in 1811 London....

_52178-4 $5.99 US/$6.99 CAN